LOVE CAME
LAUGHING BY

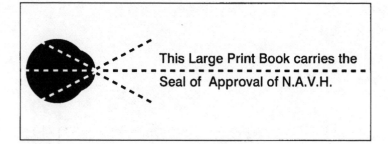

This Large Print Book carries the
Seal of Approval of N.A.V.H.

LOVE CAME LAUGHING BY

EMILIE LORING

Thorndike Press • Waterville, Maine

Copyright © 1949, by Emilie Loring

The lines from Eugene Field's "The Sugar-Plum Tree" are used by permission from Charles Scribner's Sons.

All rights reserved.

Published in 2003 by arrangement with
Little, Brown and Company, Inc.

Thorndike Press® Large Print Candlelight Series.

The tree indicium is a trademark of Thorndike Press.

The text of this Large Print edition is unabridged.
Other aspects of the book may vary from the original edition.

Set in 16 pt. Plantin by PerfecType.

Printed in the United States on permanent paper.

Library of Congress Cataloging-in-Publication Data

Loring, Emilie Baker.
    Love came laughing by / Emilie Loring.
      p. cm.
    ISBN 0-7862-5226-X (lg. print : hc : alk. paper)
    1. Diplomatic couriers — Fiction. 2. Washington (D.C.)
— Fiction. 3. Legislators — Fiction. 4. Large type books.
I. Title.
PS3523.O645L67 2003
  813'.52—dc21   2003041338

Across the gateway of my heart
I wrote "No Thoroughfare,"
But love came laughing by, and cried:
"I enter everywhere."

From "No Thoroughfare" by Herbert Shipman
by permission of Mrs. Julie Fremont
and Appleton-Century-Crofts, Inc.

I

Her foot was on the lowest step of the Pullman when she saw him striding toward the train. Instantly she abandoned her intention to buy a novel at the newsstand, turned, charged up the steps narrowly escaping collision with the colored man in dark blue who had started down.

"Porter," she whispered, "Porter, when you are asked if you have seen me, say *No.*" She tucked into his hand the bill she had had ready for a hasty purchase.

"But, who is you, Miss?" His eyes rolled like black marbles in milky pools. "How's I goin' to know who you is behind them dark specs? I'se—"

She darted past him, slipped into the compartment at the end of the car, closed the door softly behind her, and with a ragged sigh of relief backed against it. Her breath caught. Her heart stopped, broke into quickstep. The room she had thought empty had an occupant.

The man in gray who was bending over an open briefcase on a table at the window already littered with official-looking papers straightened and glared at her. A surge of red deepened the brown of his stern face.

"What's this? A plant?" he demanded.

"No. *No.* Please let me stay here until—"

"No, sah. I ain't seen no young lady in green with short, wavy black hair." The porter's high voice on the other side of the door interrupted her impassioned plea. The man's cool, suspicious eyes rested on the side of her head exposed by the cocky tilt of the suède moss-green beret the shade of her wool suit. Good heavens, can he see through—

"Has you looked in the other cars, sah?"

"Yes. She's not there. I am sure I saw her running up the steps just outside. Why are you standing in front of that door like a cop on guard?" Words and diction were American but the voice was slightly tinged with Latin.

"I ain't no cop." The porter's denial was low but loud enough for the girl to hear. "The gent inside's a big shot goin' to Washin'ton. He told me as how he was travelin' by train instead of flyin' so's he'd have

8

a chance to work on his papers. Had me set up a table."

"Just the same, I intend to make sure she isn't in that room — I — I — have an important message for her."

The girl shook her head violently in answer to the question in the eyes of the man regarding her. He crossed the compartment in one stride. She clutched his arm.

"Please, please, he hasn't, he *hasn't*." Her lips formed the words. He pushed her behind the door with his free hand before he opened it.

"What goes? What goes?" he demanded. "I told you, Porter, I was *not* to be disturbed."

"I knows you did, sah, but this gent'man's lookin' for a lady."

"*Lady!* You checked on my ticket. Single, wasn't it? Now stop this infernal rowing and get back on your job." He closed the door. The sharp click of the lock sent icy curlicues wriggling along her veins.

"If you've looked through all the cars, sah, you'd better stand on the platform an' watch, she may come hurryin' up at the last second — lots of ladies do that, or, she may've run through the car an' out th'other end. We're leavin' in about two minutes."

"Porter! Porter!" A masculine yell shut off the reply.

"I'se got to go, sah. Better get off quick. Thank you, sah, thank you — "

The porter's voice diminished in the distance. Hand over her pounding heart, eyes behind the dark glasses on the face of the man whose mouth registered a cynical smile, she waited till a shouted "All aboard" set the wheels of the train clacking.

"Thank you," she whispered. "Thanks a thousand—"

"Take off those goggles."

Bossy, must have been at least a major, she decided as she noted the ribbon in the buttonhole of his lapel — though I wouldn't put that snapped order past a second lieutenant. She removed the spectacles and swung them nervously from the fingers of her left hand.

"Now you look like a human being. What's it all about?"

"I — I can't tell you, you'll just have to trust me."

"Trust you? That's the joke for the day. Come across quick with the truth. You were sent here by Russ Ruggles, weren't you? Who is scheduled to burst in here and mess up my life?"

"No one." Her eyes were deeply, darkly

blue with horror. "Is that the sort of person I appear to be? My presence in this compartment has nothing to do with you, *nothing*. I—"

"Coast's clear, Miss." The sibilant whisper penetrated the door. "Mister Man was standin' on the platform when we pulled out."

"How did the porter know I was here?" she whispered.

"Those chaps have what is known as extrasensory perception."

"He rates another five." Tension relaxed with a suddenness that left her limp. "If I might sit down for a minute, relief has unstuck my knees." He swept other papers into a corner of the seat.

"Here you are. A faint is the next act on your program, I take it."

"It is *not*." His skepticism tightened her muscles. "I won't sit down and I never fainted in my life. I don't know of whom or of what you are scared, but—"

"I'm not scared of anything — that isn't true. I am afraid of a mix-up that will curb my usefulness to my state. When I open that door I'm willing to bet the candidate I licked will be grinning at me. It would be up his alley to plan something like this."

"It isn't up my alley to connive at it. Have

11

you forgotten that the man outside said he had an important message for me?"

"He could have been part of the show."

"He could have been but he wasn't." Her eyes were brilliant with anger. "Just so you won't begin to gnaw your fingernails from nervousness — I owe you something for not turning me out — I flew from a certain city in South America which had burst into political turmoil. When we deplaned, the man I was dodging a few minutes ago was twisting the end of a dinky little mustache as he watched the passengers come down the ramp. He tried to speak to me. I eluded him. I saw him again in the lobby of the hotel in which I spent the night, still twisting. I made a before-breakfast getaway. The doorman who told the taxi driver where to take me must have passed on the information as to my destination. When I saw my pursuer striding toward the train I had an attack of jitters and bolted in here. It's a long story, but that's the way it is."

"Why is he following you?"

"I suppose it could be — admiration?"

"Cut it." His exasperation at her flippant suggestion set a smile tugging at her lips. "You must be doing something crooked or you wouldn't suspect you are being shadowed. Perhaps you are smuggling perfume?"

12

"I am *not* smuggling. Now that the coast is clear I won't trespass longer on your heart-warming hospitality. If you are afraid of what may confront you when you open the door I could stay." She had made the absurd suggestion as teasing reprisal for his suspicion of her; it didn't shake his calm.

"Out you go. Exit, Miss, or is it Mrs.?"

"Mrs. John Smith," she supplied smoothly.

"Even the alias is old stuff. Quite safe. The Veterans' Index includes twelve thousand John Smiths. I expected something more original from you." He opened the door. "It has been a pleasure — Mrs. Smith." He bowed formally before it clicked behind her.

The sarcasm in the last sentence lingered in her mind as she swayed along the aisle between the green velvet chairs. A few passengers were finishing curtailed morning sleep. Many doubtless had gone to the car ahead for breakfast. Now that the excitement of the last half hour was over she could do with a little nourishment.

Luckily the porter had parked herself, her dark blue overnight case and camel's-hair topcoat before she started for the news-stand. She twirled the chair beside them to face the window. Seated, she tucked the spectacles into the pocket of her jacket, carefully deposited the green suède beret in her lap, drew off beige gloves, and rested her head against the white tidy on the chair back. Heavenly to relax. She had been tense since the moment Steve had groaned,

"Gosh! It's a revolution!"

Suppose she had told the man in the compartment the truth? A "big shot," the porter had said. Not an old big shot, early thirties, very early, and extremely good-looking, with poise that suggested responsibilities. Eyes closed she visualized him. Tall, straight as a general, a thin general, dark hair with a tendency to wave sternly repressed. Eyes might be gray, which anger had fired to brilliant black — eyes to trust, she had seen too many untrusty ones in the last two years not to know the difference; nose perfectly modeled, nice mouth, a hint of iron in the jaw, determined chin, well-cut clothes, glowing garnet tie, maddening that she couldn't remember for which decoration the ribbon in his coat lapel was a symbol.

Suppose she had told him the truth, described the horrors of her last night in a city being wrecked by a bloody outbreak after the news of the assassination of a candidate for high office had been broadcast, of the mob that raided the shops of loot to be sold on street corners?

In imagination she relived the hours from the moment she and Steve had stepped from the plush nightclub where he had been entertaining her at a farewell dinner into a howling, shouting populace. She could hear his voice:

"Gosh, it's a revolution, they are a dime a dozen down here." Suddenly the city was plunged into Stygian darkness. "Must have bombed the central power plant. Watch your step, Wendy. Thanks be, your father couldn't leave his patients to see you off, he's too valuable to take a chance in this bust-up."

They had reached her hotel without casualty to themselves though they had stepped over several groaning or motionless victims. Just inside the door he had whispered:

"Wait for me in the lounge as if you were too nervous to go to your room. I may have to send a message by you." He was away before she could answer. At two in the morning, his white dinner suit soiled and torn, black tie under left ear, silver-blond hair rough, he had returned, carrying, of all things, a florist's square box.

"Golly, it was a knockdown fight to get here," he had puffed, "but I couldn't let you go without a corsage, lovely. Open the box, as soon as you get to your room. Don't think I'm giving you up. I'm coming after you."

He had planted a hasty kiss in the region of her right ear and then, as if realizing that she was going, caught her in his arms. "Happy landings," he whispered. Was it a prophecy or only a hope, she had wondered as he dashed for the exit. There had been a hint of mystery in "Open the box as soon as you get to your room."

'Tis an ill wind that blows nobody good, she had thought as she sped along the corridor. She had dreaded this last evening with Steve after she had found that her father would be unable to dine with them, but the revolution had spared her the painful necessity of again telling him she wouldn't marry him.

In her room she snipped the cord about the box. Inside was a battered spray of white nun orchids, under them were three sheets of paper, the top one was a scrawled note.

We are forbidden by the party in power to send out news by mail, messenger or radio. This report must reach the State Department. *It's Dynamite.* You're bound for Washington. I'm counting on you to land it there. Planes here grounded. At 5 A.M. U. S. Embassy car will be at hotel to take you to the airfield of a city at peace. The driver will hand you an automatic. Keep it. Don't be afraid to use it. Watch your step. S.A. guys are cagey. You may be trailed. If you get into a jam destroy papers. Sorry to load this on you but my boss says it must go through, it's our one chance of getting out important stuff. Deliver to person addressed on top sheet. All my love.

The memory of "You may be trailed, the driver will give you an automatic. Don't be afraid to use it" gave her the shivers now as it had when she read the scribbled words, was followed, now as then, by a sense of breath-snatching peril, the same mounting excitement. She must make good for Steve. He had been a stanch friend to her father and herself during the past six months. She wouldn't marry him, but she could repay him for his devotion by getting this "dynamite" through.

How to carry the papers so that no one would suspect she had them was the $64 question. In her money belt? No, too bulky. Under the lining of her beret? During the war a girl she knew had sneaked her own money out of an Axis country that way. Worth trying. Suppose it blew off? It was up to her to make sure it didn't. She had mem-

17

orized the name of the high-up to whom the message was to be delivered, then had ripped, fitted, resewed till the lining was back to normal with the papers smoothly tacked under it.

She remembered her tense breathlessness as ready to go she waited for what seemed a century listening to the shouting and shots in the street, and she thought of the profuse apologies for "unpleasant conditions" of the hotel manager and his many Latin bows when he came to announce the arrival of the embassy automobile.

She recalled the strangled sensation in her throat where her heart had parked with motor racing as the car sped swiftly through the early morning dusk, the pearl-handled automatic the driver had delivered in the pocket of her topcoat. A squat revolver lay on the seat between the silent man at the wheel and herself. The chatter of machine guns, the sound of rifles and small arms grew fainter behind them, died away. Not until the plane climbed over the mountains had the taut muscles of fingers and toes relaxed.

Now they had tightened again. Had the man who had followed her to the train been tipped off that she was carrying important papers? Had a person in the turbulent city radioed him to trail her? She had decided against flying to Washington, figuring that whoever was watching her would take it for granted she would travel the quickest way. As it was, she would reach the city in the early afternoon in time to deliver Steve's papers before the department closed.

If the man in the compartment hadn't suspected her of being a double-crosser she might have asked his help to reach the State Department. He had said, "I am afraid of a mix-up that will curb my usefulness to my state," which declaration plus his stern face and steady eyes had given her the feeling that he would be a safe port in any storm.

Suppose she told him that she was returning after two years with her father, who was the leading pediatrist in a South American city; that Steve Graham, a loyal friend, was a U. S. Embassy attaché in the same place; that her mother — no, she couldn't tell him that, the memory still hurt unbearably.

"I am going to the car ahead for breakfast; there will be a seat for you at my table," the low voice bombed her train of thought to splinters.

She whirled the chair. A tall man in gray, hat at a rakish angle, was stepping into the corridor, the "big shot on his way to Washin'ton." There had been a no-appeal

19

strain in "There will be a seat for you at my table." Should she go? Why not? At twenty-four with three years of college and war work on the side, two as daughter-hostess for a distinguished man, a girl should have acquired a working knowledge of human nature. Could be that the gnawing of hunger was influencing her decision, but she would go.

The mirror of her compact was not too discouraging. She crushed on the green beret with the glistening ornament and concealed dynamite, discarded the idea of donning the "goggles" and slung her navy blue bag from her shoulder.

For a split second she sat motionless. Was it a trap? Steve had warned, "Watch your step, these S.A. guys are cagey." But the man who had wanted her to join him — her mistake, *commanded* was the word — was regular, Steve's word for a person he liked, she would wager her pearls. Why get jittery?

"Big Shot, here I come," she announced under her breath and rose.

II

He anticipated the dusky headwaiter and drew out a chair at the table opposite the one in which he had been sitting.

"I didn't dare order for you," he explained after they were seated. He passed the travel-worn menu to her. "Tell the boy what you want."

She was scanning the printed list while thinking that his matter-of-fact voice sounded as if they had been traveling together for years.

"Yes, Madam?" The waiter's red-mouthed knowing grin connoted that he had been too long on his job to be deceived, he recognized newly marrieds when he saw them, yes, *sah*. His fatuous smile brought color to her face.

"Sliced orange, bacon, coffee and one muffin," she ordered in a voice she hoped expressed bored indifference.

"Yes, Ma'am. Sliced orange comin' up.

I'se got your order, sir."

Sunlight poured in across the aisle. She turned from the glare of white tablecloths and concentrated on the panorama outside the window, rosy with autumn reds, fields checkered by stone walls, hills glowing russet gold under a cloudless, bright blue sky.

"There is an amazing lot of color on trees and in fallen leaves for the first week in November," she observed to break a silence which seemed to hum like telegraph wires with suppressed thoughts.

"This year the foliage was late in turning, its beauty has lingered."

The waiter arrived and arranged the breakfast dishes.

"Anything more, sir?" he inquired in the deferential voice due a man in the honeymoon state, a potential reckless tipper.

"That's all."

With an understanding, "Yes, sah," he faded from the immediate present.

"I delayed having breakfast until this car was practically empty, that we might have a chance to talk." The man across the table leaned slightly forward. "Time for a showdown. What's it all about?"

"Then you have decided that I am not a glamour girl set on your trail by an enemy who has determined to ruin your life?"

22

"Decision reserved." His sudden smile lighted his gray eyes and revealed a close-up of perfect teeth. "I'll start the Information Please quiz. I am Vance Tyler, Van to my friends, a pain in the neck to my political opponents, being returned for a second term in Congress as a representative, the lone survivor of the deluge of my party."

" 'Tippecanoe and Tyler too.' Are you a branch of that presidential tree?"

"We'll let it go as a twig. I see you know your American history."

"Than which there is none more thrilling and colorful. From which state were you sent to Washington?"

"I'm from the great Northwest."

"I guessed that, Westerners respect their r's. You seem young to have accepted the responsibility of lawmaking." The longer she kept him on the subject of himself, the longer she could stave off talking about herself. Curious, she felt an insane urge to sob out her perplexities on his shoulder, figuratively speaking. The urge was compelling. If she didn't watch out she'd be telling the story of her life.

"Not so young in spirit," his voice brought her resistance out of its tailspin. "My first term was in the way of appreciation of a war service in '45. The second, I hope, was

23

awarded because I made good on the job."

"Are you a lawyer by profession?"

"Are you looking for one, Mrs. John Smith? Was that a service for divorce you were dodging?"

She lowered her lashes quickly to hide the surprise in her eyes and arranged a design of crumbs on the white cloth with meticulous care as if to hide embarrassment.

"It was not. I'm — crazy about my John." Laughter tugged at her lips, it was to be hoped he would interpret it as emotion. His eyes were on her ringless left hand. A perceptive person, undoubtedly. Time to tune in on another station — and quick. "What was your job before politics, I assume you had one?"

"I was a soldier for five years, preceding that I took a degree in law as preparation for politics, after which I worked as an oil man and rancher to get an idea of the problems of the owners. Smoke?"

She shook her head.

"I'm a rugged individualist, I neither smoke nor drink." That information might offset the fact that she was breakfasting with a man she had never seen before she burst into his compartment.

He dropped the silver case into his pocket.

"It's your turn. How about it? Do I get an

explanation, *a true one,* of your dash into my bailiwick?"

"Give me a few minutes in which to collect my material — your stand-and-deliver voice threw my mind into a spin. My reason for that dash involves another person. Who is Russ Ruggles? Why are you afraid of him? Was the quarrel about a woman?"

"I'm not afraid of *him.* We battled for my seat in Congress. He is a newspaperman, top-rating, he let loose a blast on the amount of money I spent on the campaign; as previously indicated my family owned a few oil wells — 'gluttons of privilege' — you've heard that one recently."

He had sidestepped her question: "Was the quarrel about a woman?"

"Did you spend more than is allowable?"

"I did *not.* Page the State Committee for confirmation. Ruggles came up the hard way, made good in newspaper work, took a flyer in oil which rocketed him into high-bracket money, picked up the politics germ. He's of the 'I'll die but I'll get him' school, had a big following out to discredit me. Still has, I have been advised."

"But you won?"

"I won. Your turn. Give."

His stern reminder set little chills vibrating along her nerves. She would hate to be a

25

woman set on his trail by an opponent he had licked.

"Do I get the information?"

"You insist upon putting me to the torch, don't you? I have already told you that my reason for dodging a certain person had ramifications that involved another. I can't explain, but I am ready to raise my right hand and swear that when I bolted into the compartment I didn't know that a man named Vance Tyler was in the world. You must believe me, you do, don't you?"

"The blue of your eyes turns amethyst when you are in earnest, doesn't it?"

"Which evasion means that you don't. Play fair. I believed what you told me. Perhaps I was too easy, perhaps you are not Vance Tyler, perhaps you are the defeated candidate or a confidence man or a *wolf*." His laugh was low, rich, a laugh to love.

"Wrong wave length, Red Ridinghood. I don't eat little girls with short, wavy dark hair, I like 'em blonde. As you are in doubt—" he offered an envelope with canceled stamp for her inspection.

The Honorable Vance Tyler
House of Representatives
Washington, D. C.

The address was in a flowing hand, looked as if it might be the chirography of a blonde.

"I don't care for the satirical smile on your lovely mouth, of course I could have picked a pocket to secure it," he suggested as if he had interpreted her silence as doubt of his right to the exhibit.

"I believe the evidence. From your wife, perhaps?"

"Could be." He returned the envelope to the inside pocket of his gray coat.

"That would explain your terror when I burst into the compartment."

"It might, but it doesn't. I have told you the reason. Now that we are again on the subject of terror — we've completed the cycle — why were you frightened white because you were being — thought you were being trailed?"

"You make it sound as if you suspected I was eluding the FBI. I wasn't. I had reason not to want the man whom I thought was following me to know where I was going."

"Let me get this straight. You flew from a country in South America, which had blown its top in revolution. What were you doing there? Don't answer if you fear it will incriminate you. After all, I have no right to cross-examine you."

"I don't like that word 'incriminate.' I

have been keeping house for my father who is a distinguished pediatrist there."

"Your mother is not living?" His sympathetic voice sent a wave of color to her hair, set tears in her eyes. "I'm sorry. I have hurt you."

"No. I can't be hurt anymore about her, she is Mrs. Joshua Crandon. I'm a wishbone child."

"What kind of a child is that?"

"Three years ago Mother divorced Father to marry someone else. Because of his prominence in his profession the affair had coast-to-coast coverage. I love them both. Each tugs at my heart, each pulls me his way and her way, isn't that what happens to a wishbone?"

"Your father won?"

"He needed me most. He gave up his home practice and accepted an assignment as head of a hospital in South America. Six months ago an old neighbor was sent as attaché to our embassy in the same city. Father likes him. Now they are together, I'm off to a new world. I'm going to Mother. She and her husband lived in California and Europe after their marriage, last spring they settled in Washington. Why am I boring you with this emotional story of my life? Answer, I don't know."

"You are not boring me, I'm intensely interested. I hope the new world will prove a gay and happy hunting ground. About this 'old neighbor'? Old in years or chronologically? Your John, I take it?"

"No comment."

"I'm glad to see the sparkle of laughter back in your eyes. I figure the following sums up your situation, stop me if I'm wrong. You fled from a city ablaze with revolution; in that same city, a friend — interrogation point — is attached to a U. S. Embassy. You suspect you were followed after leaving the plane; discounting your beauty and charm, I can think of only one reason for your evident terror. You are carrying a message. If I can help you when we reach Washington, Mrs. John Smith—"

"I'm *not* married. I told my seat companion in the plane that was my name so I wouldn't be connected with Steve Graham. As I was coming down the ramp she called from behind me. 'Good-bye and good luck, Mrs. Smith.' She—"

A sound drew her eyes to the dark-haired, noticeably handsome man abreast of the table. He was staring at her companion who was leaning forward intent on what she was saying. His black come-hither eyes, wicked eyes, met hers and lighted with recognition,

29

his mouth twisted in a triumphant grin. Her heart zoomed. Dropped. How could he know her unless he had been tipped off by an accomplice? Another cagey S.A. on her trail? She must deliver Steve's dynamite. This man hadn't seen her deplane, hadn't heard her called Mrs. John Smith. She could fool him.

"Van, darling," she cooed. "A week has passed since our wedding in New York. Isn't it time we wired our great news to the family?"

Sharp suspicion succeeded amazement in Tyler's eyes. Color darkened his face. The man in the aisle rested his left hand on the table, his right held his hat. His voice held a note of triumph.

"I recognized you, Miss—"

Van Tyler was on his feet. His face went white. Suspense stopped her breath. He suspected that she was carrying secret papers. Would he betray her to this spy who had declared he recognized her?

"Where the dickens did you drop from, Ruggles?" his voice was hoarse. "Move on. Can't you see I'm in conference?"

"Sure, sure, I can see as well as hear. You've always showed A-1 taste in femmes, Van." He bowed impressively to the girl. "I'll see *you* again."

"Ruggles! You said *Ruggles?* Is he—" the next word of her shocked whisper stuck in her throat, her troubled eyes sought his. "Why don't you answer? Because you are sure now that I'm his accomplice. I saw it in your face. I'm not! I'm *not!* His eyes were so gloating, his smile so triumphant I was sure he was a spy. He is, isn't he? He said he recognized me. I made up that corny story about a wedding in New York so he would know I was not on that plane yesterday — I was panicked for fear he would discover that I carried — the man was right who said, 'Fright works without benefit of brain.'"

"Stop and get your breath or you will be sobbing in a minute. That guy can't be on your trail, and I don't think you are his accomplice. Is he the man who has been shadowing you?"

"No, but you heard him say he recognized me, would see me again in a horrid I've-got-you-now voice. Perhaps my picture was wired to him."

"Could be. I don't get it. I'm his dish."

"I'm his dish."

The words churned round and round in her mind to the rhythmic clacks of the wheels of the train. With her crazy announcement she had played into the hands

31

of Van Tyler's enemy. Could she undo the harm? She must.

"When I rushed into the compartment you accused me of having been sent there to mess up your life by the man who just spoke to us. Now I've done it. Suppose he repeats that silly stuff I improvised to your wife? Give me her address and I'll see her and explain."

"Forget her, that isn't as important as finding out why he is on your trail, if he is, which I still can't believe. Seeing you with me will be enough to set him digging up what he can about you. He can do your secret mission infinite harm, if, as I suspect, you are on a secret mission. I've guessed why you are afraid of being followed. A guess isn't good enough. I want to help you. Tell me the truth and quick."

She told him.

III

Two lines cut deep between his eyes as he listened. He leaned toward her across the table as she whispered the last words of her story which concerned the delivery of the "dynamite."

"I can't believe that Russ Ruggles is following you. Of course there's a chance he had been tipped off by an S.A. reporter pal that your story was front-page news. You mustn't take those papers to the State Department."

"But I must. I won't fail Steve."

"Crazy about him, aren't you? I'll deliver the stuff. Trust me?"

Dare she? If he were as dependable as her instinct insisted, the important message would be safer with him than with herself. She nodded.

"Okay, where are they?"

With her right hand she drew the moss-green beret a little lower over her right ear. His eyes flashed understanding.

"I get you. I'd better not speak to you again while on the train. When we reach Washington pick up a redcap to carry your bag—"

"I won't need him. I expressed my wardrobe case from the airfield. The overnight case isn't heavy. I can carry it with my coat."

"That will help. What became of the automatic the driver delivered? You can't carry that in your topcoat pocket in Washington without a license."

"I put it in the wardrobe case before I left South America."

"Good. I'll keep you in sight in Union Station. When you hail a taxi I'll step up and ask the cabby if he will take a second passenger — because of crowded conditions it's being done — make a slight protest and then relent. Tell him to leave you at the Mayflower. When you get out of the cab manage to drop the beret in it. You'll have time there for lunch. After that wait in the lobby for a message from me. Does your mother expect you at a certain hour?"

"No, I wired her that I would be with her today, no time specified."

"That's a break. Now, the name of the

person to whom the message is to be delivered?"

"When you take the papers from the beret you'll find it on the top sheet with Steve's name. Do you think you can put it across?"

"I'll make a terrific stab at it. Return to your seat and trust me. It may take hours to contact the man we want, don't get the jitters. If I do not appear at the taxi door—"

"Good heavens, I hadn't thought of that."

"Nothing in the possibility to whiten your face. If I am held up carry on yourself. Tell the cabby you have time for a bit of sightseeing, mention the White House, Lincoln Memorial, National Gallery, just the outside, of course, and as an afterthought the building where the Department of State is housed. You'll know what to do when you get there."

"What — what will you do about your political enemy? Suppose he continues to follow me?" She swallowed a sob of excitement.

"Why should he follow you? I don't get it. I'll cover the possibility, though. When the train pulls in at Union Station the porter will hand him a message to phone his boss at once, special order. That will take time. We'll make our getaway."

"Do you think he overheard what I said about — about—"

"Our marriage? Sure, he heard. He's at the present moment digesting the juicy tidbit, deciding the best use to make of it — my mistake, the worst."

"Why didn't you come right out with a denial, tell me you didn't care for my silly joke, or—"

"Your statement shattered my thinking machine for the moment."

"Can't I do something to help? I might send a note to him by the porter—"

"*No.*" He rose and drew out her chair. "Return to your seat and do as I have told you."

"Yes, sir." She looked up and laughed. "Yes, *sir.* Thanks for breakfast. I feel as if I had bitten the hand that fed me. Am I presuming when I assume I was invited?"

"It was an invitation, Mrs.—"

"I am *not* Mrs. John Smith."

"That's right. You are Mrs. Van—"

"Good morning!"

The laughter in his eyes set her cheeks on fire. They still burned when she resumed her seat in the chair car. Had she started serious trouble when she had claimed Van Tyler for a husband? She had done it in a frenzied attempt to mislead a man whom she suspected was on her trail and who wasn't. Why be so sure of that? Ruggles had admitted he had recognized her.

She had told Van her father's name, Steve's, her mother's, not her own. That was a minor matter in this crisis, and it was a crisis with possible tragic ramifications. Her heart pounded, her pulses raced, her nerves tingled from excitement. Each time a person passed her chair her breath caught in her throat until she was sure it wasn't Ruggles. She hadn't closed her eyes last night. If she didn't relax she would be worn to a gibbering frazzle by the time the train reached Washington, which wouldn't be for several hours.

Beret in her lap, fingers clutching it, head against the back of the chair, she watched the colorful gliding panorama outside the window. She mustn't allow herself to go to sleep, just to relax would rest—

"We'll be gettin' into Washin'ton in five minutes, Miss."

"Washington," she murmured sleepily, and stared up with dazed unbelief at the dark face with its gleaming eyes and teeth. "Washington?" she repeated incredulously.

"Yes, Miss," the porter's grin widened. "You'se been sleepin' all the way since breakfast. I guess the big shot in the compartment was worried 'bout you, he come past several times, an' told me to watch you wan't disturbed, an' then he had me put up a table across the aisle an' worked there till a few minutes ago. You'd better be getting on your hat, Miss."

Her hat! Her hat with the precious papers! Were they safe? Wide awake she flexed the cramped fingers which clutched the moss-green beret, gently pinched the top. They were there, glory be. Had Van Tyler changed to a seat across the aisle to watch that?

On the platform of Union Station, overnight case in hand, camel's-hair topcoat over her left arm, she shook her head at a redcap and joined the crowd hurrying toward the exit. Was Van Tyler behind her? She resisted an almost irresistible urge to turn. One possible catastrophe was off her mind, the man Ruggles whom she suspected had been alerted to follow her would be sidetracked by an order to telephone his boss.

A lone taxi was in sight when the passengers who had preceded her had driven away. She hailed the driver. He swung open the door.

"Where to, Miss?"

"To—"

"Cabby, I must get to the State Department. You are my only hope." Her knees threatened to buckle in relief as Van Tyler spoke behind her. She turned. Hat in hand, he smiled engagingly. "Madam, may I share the taxi? I have an important date with a government official. If I am late it will be 'off with his head.'" She regarded him as if in appraisal.

"Having been raised in the 'my country first' tradition, I'll say 'yes,' but, I don't like the idea. Leave me at the Mayflower first, driver."

"Yes, Miss. Step in. I don't like this doublin' up, neither, but, Lord love us, you're lucky to get any transportation today. I'll keep my eye peeled in case there's any trouble behind there, Miss."

"Cheerio, cabby, there won't be any, you may keep your eyes on the road ahead," Van Tyler assured as he followed her into the cab.

It slid into Pennsylvania Avenue. She glimpsed the dome of the Capitol and leaned forward.

"What's happened, driver? Why the crowds? Why the littered streets?"

"Don't you read the papers nor listen to the radio, Miss?" The man tempered the scorn in his voice. "The newly elected

39

candidate for President come back to the White House today an' I'll bet eight hundred thousand folks turned out to welcome him carryin' banners an' yellin' their heads off." In his excitement he turned to face her.

"I heard twenty-nine collapsed and were lugged off by Red Cross or hospital aides. Folks hung from the bars of the Treasury's windows. They like a fighter, and hell, did li'l ol' Harry fight, he slugged it out alone, too."

"I do read the papers, driver, but I had so much else on my mind that I forgot what day—"

"Glad I've arrived in time to see even the tail end of the party." Had Van Tyler interrupted for fear of what she might disclose? "I'll be darned if those tall, inverted V's arched over the Avenue aren't fire-department ladders. That 'Welcome Home, Mr. President' banner is colossal."

"This ain't anything. You should have seen the folks rush toward the candidate's auto as the motorcade come out of Union Station — he was perched up back with the new vice beside him an' the Missus and Margaret and the vice's daughter in front, them ladies sure looked pleased. After the boss had shook hands with near a hundred, he held up his clasped hands an' shouted:

" 'I'm shaking hands with all of you now.'

"The crowd yelled its heads off, someone called, 'Hi, Harry,' an' they let him go on. When they come to Post Square he spotted the big banner:

WELCOME HOME FROM
THE CROW-EATERS

an' he an' the vice just waved and laffed. He ain't one to bear malice, I bet. It sure was one great day, the kind that'll never be forgotten. You said the Mayflower, Miss?"

After that no word was spoken as she and Van Tyler sat side by side. She kept her eyes on the world outside the cab. Government buildings, marble white. Flags flying. The long green mall from the Monument to the grandeur of the Lincoln Memorial. Reflecting Pool, blue as the clear turquoise sky above it. Heroes in bronze on bronze steeds. Gesticulating groups. 1600 Pennsylvania Avenue done up in splints for repairs. Colorful shop windows. Fabulous furs. Ravishing frocks. Stimulating. Exciting. The atmosphere set her a-tingle.

"What a wonderful city!" Enthusiasm submerged caution.

"Your first visit?" the man beside her inquired as if it didn't matter to him if it were or were not.

"The first since I was a small girl."

"Are you planning to stay long?" His voice had warmed slightly. "If you are—"

"Mayflower, Miss." The driver interrupted curtly, pulled up to the curb and swung open the door. She drew a change purse from the side pocket of her coat.

"Allow me," the man beside her protested. "It was such an accommodation to share the cab." He picked up her overnight case and stepped out. "Watch your head," he warned, but not before she had managed to shake off her beret onto the floor behind her. She ignored his outstretched hand, his gay, "Have fun."

"Thanks, thanks," she mumbled and dashed after the gold-braided doorman who was handing her overnight case to a boy. Better get inside before the friendly driver noticed she was hatless and came running after her with the beret. Resourceful as Van Tyler had proved he might be unable to meet that crisis.

Inside the revolving door her heart threatened to choke her with its anvil beat as she looked out. Why didn't the taxi start? Had the driver found her beret? Was he insisting on returning it? It was off, thank heaven. Steve's important papers were on their way.

Now what? She might have to wait hours.

She would engage a room, change her blouse and freshen her makeup — that would rest her — then lunch.

She registered as Mrs. John Smith, New York City, with an uneasy feeling that there might be a penalty for using an assumed name. Later in a deep chair in the palm-sprinkled lobby where she could be seen from the entrance she watched the glass revolving door till her head threatened to whirl with it. The hands of the large gilt clock on the wall checked with those of the watch on her wrist. They *had* moved since she had looked at them before. Time *wasn't* standing still. Somewhere near an orchestra was playing "Lady of Spain, I Adore You."

Waiting wouldn't be so nerve-racking if recurring waves of doubt didn't sweep over her mind and set chilly inchworms looping up her spine, her thoughts tripped on to the accompaniment of castanets. Had she been criminally negligent to entrust Steve's important papers to a man she had seen for the first time this morning — was it only this morning — it seemed as if aeons had passed. Four o'clock! Glory be, it couldn't have taken him all this time to contact the high-up. She'd better begin to plan what she would do if he didn't come at all.

"Mrs. John Smith?"

She looked up at the round face and spectacled eyes of a boy in maroon livery, curbed the impulse to grab the green beret he held.

"My hat! Thank goodness. Where did you find it?"

"A gentleman came to the desk, pointed you out, said it was yours, he found it in a cab you left in a hurry."

"Where is he? I would like to thank him."

"Gone, I guess. He said he'd hang round till he saw you take the hat, then he'd light out." He grinned. "Maybe he was afraid you'd fall on his neck. Thank you, Miss."

Why hadn't he waited? Perhaps he feared that in gratitude she might call him "Van, darling" again. He needn't worry. Cautiously she pinched the crown of the moss-green beret. No papers there. The lining had been neatly pinned in place. Steve's message had been delivered.

IV

It was almost dusk when she stood before the wide, glass-paneled door of her mother's Virginia home, Red Terraces, in a colonial neighborhood just beyond the Washington line. Battered as she felt, she had had sufficient awareness left to appreciate the beauty of the old places she passed, the charm of stately white-pillared houses and box-bordered gardens. In response to her ring a gray-haired man in plum-colored livery lavishly sprinkled with silver buttons, with nose like an eagle's beak, opened the door. Her mother had achieved one of the ambitions of her life, a butler.

"Miss Adair?"

"Yes. Mrs. Crandon is expecting me."

"She is. Come in, Miss. I'm Propper." He took her bag and coat.

Propper by name, and proper by nature,

she disciplined the smile that accompanied her flippant thought.

In the broad hall with its black and white tessellated floor, its Persian rugs, a maid in plum-colored silk frock emerged from the background, a snowy French poodle kept pace beside her.

"Show Miss Adair to her room, Blossom," he commanded with a touch of imperial majesty. "Madam is out, Miss. She will return soon as she is entertaining at cocktails at seven. The day has been warm, they will be served on the veranda."

The house doesn't seem real, in spite of its evident age it is Hollywoodish in feeling, that would be Mother's touch, she thought.

She followed the maid and the dog up the lovely winding staircase and entered a large room with two floor-length windows. Hangings matched the ivory walls, bed and chairs were covered with shell-pink brocade, with wing chair and chaise longue done in avocado green. The furniture was satiny applewood. A violet envelope was prominently displayed on a desk lavishly supplied with pink stationery and shimmering silver appointments. The maid threw open the door of a dressing room that glittered with chromium and glass.

"The trunk and the wardrobe case you expressed from South America came today. They are in here, Miss. Give me the keys and I will unpack them."

"At what time is the cocktail party?"

"At seven. Madam said to tell you, you are going on to dinner and then to an embassy reception, to dress for them."

"I will have time to get out the clothes I want to wear. You may finish tomorrow."

"Just as you say, Miss. Madam told me I was to wait on you. Anything you want, ring. I'm Blossom, Miss."

"Thank you, Blossom. If Mrs. Crandon inquires for me tell her I will be in the living room at seven."

"It's the drawing room, Miss."

It would be in her mother's house. She picked up the note.

"Shall I leave Angeline here for company?"

Wendy glanced at the balcony visible outside the long windows, around the room, no third person in sight.

"Angeline?" she repeated.

"It's the pooch, Miss. You needn't be afraid of her. She's that pampered and friendly she'd be a pushover for a burglar."

"Let her stay. I adore dogs. It will give us a chance to get acquainted. That's all for the present, Blossom." She closed the door behind the maid who gave indications that there was more, a whole lot more she would like to say. She stood motionless looking about the room softly lighted by silver-columned lamps with shell-pink shades. Everything in it spelled wealth with a capital W. The pile of the ivory-toned rug under her feet was inches thick. Memory flashed a close-up of her father's present home, austere in its simplicity, warm with hospitality, enriched by the admiration and affection of men and women of distinction. She blinked wet lashes.

"Mother would have hated it there," she said softly, "here she has her heart's desire. I must remember that." She sank into the wing chair and tore open the note. From the rug beside the bed Angeline peered at her with jet-black eyes almost obscured by furry white hair.

WENDY DEAR:

If I am not here when you arrive make yourself at home, and I mean home, it is my turn to have you, my one child. Fearing that your luggage might be delayed — my friends have planned countless festivities in your honor — I had the time of my life buying a few frocks for you. They are in the wardrobe in your dressing room. I hope you haven't put on weight, as I had them fitted to myself. Remember the photograph we had taken in color just before you went to South America? Everyone declared we looked enough alike to be twins. Wear the black velvet number with peach — plus your pearls — tonight. I'll wear a model like it with blue — I have pearls now. I want Josh to think we look like sisters, not mother and daughter. Please wear it. Wendy, don't be difficult, and *try* to like my husband.

KIT

Like him. Could she? She had seen the man once, during a college vacation when he had come to the house to escort her mother to the opera, in place of her husband who so often was called away at the last moment to attend a sick child. "Jim never can go anywhere with me." It was his wife's constant complaint. "I'm tired of apologizing for being late to dinner parties."

She visualized Joshua Crandon. "Good old Josh" to his friends, as she had seen him then, was a tall man with a hint of heaviness, bold features, iron-gray hair, eyes of no especial color, the shoulder-slapping type indubitably. A transplanted native of the Southwest, a mining engineer who had struck pay dirt early and was now filthy rich, if one were to believe the columnists.

He must have loved her mother, he had fought off matrimony until fifty, when he had married lovely Kitty Adair after her Reno divorce.

That divorce. The demand for it had been as devastating in their attractive home as a bursting bomb. At first her husband had been incredulous, then shocked, furious anger had been followed by bitterness so deep, so corroding that he had consented. She slowly shredded the note, and thought:

I am here. I must not look back. This is the way things are. I can't change them. I don't want, I don't need the clothes Mother bought for me — she'll be surprised when she sees the snappy numbers I'll unpack. It won't do to tell her that Dad insisted that I was to come here with everything I could possibly need. He had used a rough oath, he who never swore, before he declared:

"I'll be damned if that heel will clothe you as well as—" His voice had broken before he could speak his wife's name.

A white paw patted her knee. She caught the poodle's furry head between her hands.

"You're one hundred percent right, Angeline, when you remind me not to play Lot's wife. Something tells me you'll prove a grand companion, someone to whom I can tell my troubles. Did you shake your head to remind me it's silly to anticipate trouble or because I tickled your ear?"

She didn't need either her father's or her stepfather's money. She had earned a living income, her grandmother had left her pearls and a legacy to her namesake, which fact also had provided a bitter talking point for her son's wife.

"Come in," she turned, eagerly, as she answered a knock at the door. Was it her mother at last? The smiling maid entered carrying a corsage box.

"Mr. Propper said a gentleman left this for you, Miss. I guess one of your boyfriends is mighty glad you've come."

"My name isn't on the outside. Are you sure it is for me?"

"Propper said it was, Miss, and Propper never makes mistakes, he knows everything that goes on inside this house and outside. He's only been here a month. That's longer than most of them stay. I thought he'd walk out when he and Madam had a fight about his wristwatch. She said t'wa'n't right for a butler. He wears it just the same. I wonder how long he'll put up with—" A sniff finished the sentence.

There was no one in the city who would send her flowers — unless — it could be a message from — excitement set her cheeks burning.

"Thrilling, isn't it, Blossom? Thanks for bringing it. That will be all."

"Aren't you going to open the box?" The question was drenched with disappointment.

"Not yet, it's fun to wait and wonder who sent it."

"Okay, come along, Angie, and get your supper."

She didn't wait a split second after the door clicked behind the disgruntled maid and the capering dog before she pulled tape off the brown cardboard. With an ecstatic "O-o-o" she lifted a spray of green orchids from its cellophane box, on the bottom of which lay an envelope. She ripped it open, read the words on the enclosed slip of paper, read them twice. It was a receipt from the official at the Department of State to whom Steve had wanted the "dynamite" delivered. That chapter was successfully closed.

She peered into the envelope, shook it. No card, no message from Van Tyler. Did that mean the end of their friendship? It had been friendship for a few hours.

That seemed to be that. Time was flying, better begin to unpack, first the overnight case. She opened it. Stared down unbelievingly. Clothes and toilet articles were mixed as if they had been hurriedly handled; that wasn't all, the blue lining had been cut and ripped loose.

She sank to her knees and pulled the case to the floor beside her. Who had opened the bag and when? Must have been while she was at lunch at the Mayflower. She had left it in her room, it had been intact when she had closed it after changing her blouse, it hadn't occurred to her to open it again. She frowned at the torn lining. Who had suspected she was carrying important papers? The man who had been shadowing her? "These S.A. guys are cagey," Steve had warned. Cagey or not, they hadn't found his papers — but — they might believe she still had them. Cheerful thought. Would she have to walk with her head over her shoulder while in Washington to make sure she wasn't being trailed?

If only I could consult Van Tyler. What sort of woman is his wife? When I offered to explain to her about my crazy statement he said, "Forget her." Better stop thinking of my brainstorm, dress and be quick about it.

Wearing a white net frock the full skirt of which floated and sparkled with brilliants with each movement of her slender body, she regarded the result in a long mirror. She had tried to wear the black velvet and peach, but it had been much too revealing for her taste and luckily too large. If her mother had had it fitted to herself she must have put on weight during the last two years. She had selected the white from the frocks hanging in the wardrobe, it was smaller than the others and made a perfect background for the spray of green orchids pinned to her shoulder. Lovely as it was she hated to wear anything provided by Crandon money — it seemed traitorous to her father — but while here she couldn't hurt her mother — the wishbone motif again — appeasement was her role.

The clock on the mantel with its glittering rhinestone pendulum chimed the half-hour. It had been a wedding present to her parents. Good heavens, will I suffer an attack of nostalgic sickness at my stomach each time I recognize something that was part of my old home, she asked herself. Too early to appear in the drawing room, so characteristic of me to be early. Because I believe it is stupid to be late for an engagement, I am always a little ahead of time.

"There is another school of thought, Wendy," her father's voice echoed through her memory, "which claims that the too early person wastes a lot of time."

Perhaps she did, but one had to have a design for living and being prompt was part of hers. To be honest, the reason she was lingering in her room wasn't because she was too early, it was because she dreaded meeting her mother and her mother's husband.

At a long window she looked down upon a rambling garden denuded of bloom, but still green. The two red brick terraces which gave the place its name, one below the other, were flanked by mammoth oaks from which lingering, rosy-brown leaves swayed lazily. At the head of connecting steps candles flickered in tall hurricane lamps to mark the path to the pool beside which musicians in aqua and silver were tuning brass instruments that glittered under floodlights. Nearby a bronze nymph held a birdbath in upraised hands.

Who searched my overnight case? The question surged to the top of her mind as it had surged on the average of five-minute intervals while she was dressing. Who had been wise to the fact I was carrying important papers? Had the driver of the embassy car suspected? Suspected. He must have known that I was too unimportant a person to be transported to a distant airfield unless there was a vital reason. Was he one of a network of spies masquerading as a U. S. government employee? Steve must be warned — How? If I write, the letter might be opened. A telegram would meet the same fate. Better consult Van Tyler—

The clock chimed a reminder. Time to go down. She caught up a sparkling white bag from the top of the dressing table now laden with her silver toilet appointments, and flung a stole of tourmaline-pink malines across her shoulders. Before the long mirror she shook her head at the dark-haired girl who shook hers in response, said softly:

"How big your eyes are, Miss Adair, how pink your cheeks. No wonder. Looks as if you were trapped in international espionage. Boy, no wonder you shiver and set every sparklet on your frock a-twinkle. The Red Cross never turned your blood so icy even in its most exciting crises. Watch your step, gal, watch your step." The looking-glass girl's dark blue, heavily lashed eyes indicated that she would.

"And remember," she spoke again to her reflection, "if you don't like the head of this house, you must pretend you do, or life here will be a battle and you know how you loathe domestic battles."

Her mother in a black velvet frock with pale blue satin strapless bodice stood at the threshold of the drawing room as she ran down the stairs. She covered the last three steps in one jump and caught her close.

"Mother! Mother!" she steadied her voice. "It's wonderful to be with you again."

"And it's high time you were here, Wendy. Why didn't you wear the black velvet and peach model like mine?"

The petulant inquiry had the effect of an ice-cold deluge. Separation hasn't changed the clash of our personalities and ideals, she thought. Her arm dropped, she tried to cover her recoil with a laugh.

"Believe it or not, Kitty Ada — Crandon, it didn't fit, I've thinned to a rail during this last year. Must have been the South American climate. After all, I'm just a little New England gal." She hadn't lost weight, but it was a more tactful suggestion than that her mother had gained.

"Come into the drawing room where I can really see you, Wendy."

As she followed her mother she had a sense of many soft lights and pale yellow flowers, mammoth chrysanthemums in floor vases, button variety in bowls in a long room

57

with dark green walls and matching hangings. Furniture coverings were in the same shade with glints of brilliance in the brocade. Dark effect, but distinguished, brightened by a portrait of her mother in shimmering avocado-green satin above the fireplace and the Chinese bride chest and colorful *chinoiserie* lamps. Her eyes winced away from the Coromandel screen halfway down, an Adair family heirloom.

"That's a honey of a frock. Who sent you those beautiful orchids?" She recognized the sharpness in her mother's voice. She had been up against her jealousy before.

"No card came with them. I thought perhaps you—"

"I didn't. It might have been Josh. He used to think of things like that. I know who it was." Her eyes brightened. "I have a husband picked out for you, a pal of Josh's, it must have been he."

"How forehanded of you, Mother. Does the gentleman know that he is to be so honored?"

"Don't be difficult, Wendy. Of course I haven't said anything to him about it, but I have told him a lot about you. He loves music and I've given your voice a rave notice. He has been away for a month. Went home to vote, he must be back or the flowers wouldn't have come. He's rich, Western oil tycoon, and he's brilliant, a coming man. He's dark and handsome, movie-star type."

Of course the prospective bridegroom hadn't sent the orchids, only one person could have enclosed that receipt, better to let her mother think her paragon had been the anonymous donor.

"I'm in a tizzy to see your dream-man, Mrs. Crandon."

"You're ribbing me, that sounds just like your father, I don't mind. Wait till you see him. Nothing of the cold-blooded New Englander about him, he's like Josh, breezy—"

"Hi, Kit," a man hailed as he entered. The Joshua Crandon whom she remembered had fulfilled the promise of more weight. He was colossal in the black and white of faultless evening clothes, lapels long, trousers narrow and waistcoat with a collar. He caught his wife by one shoulder, swung her around, shook his head.

"You're too hefty, Missus, for that low and behold neckline."

"Josh, you brute! Wendy is here."

He turned. She found herself giving back smile for smile. Father was right, the man has a magnetic personality, she thought.

"Gosh, Wendy, I guess you've saved me

from a going-over — my Kitty has sharp claws, your mother doesn't like criticism. Glad you're here." Her hand responded to the warm, friendly pressure of his. "Hope you'll stick it out. We need someone young and gay in the house." He smacked his lips before each sentence as if about to savour a particularly delicious tidbit of his own wit or wisdom.

"I think we're young and gay. Our—"

A man crossed the threshold and interrupted Kitty Crandon's reproach. He caught the hand she eagerly extended in both of his.

"You've come! Thanks be. This is Josh's friend about whom I was telling you, Wendy. My daughter, Mr. Ruggles."

She didn't hear the name, heard only her own fatuous, "Van, darling," to the accompaniment of her heart making the sound of surf pounding against a ledge as she looked up into dark mocking eyes of the man who had stopped at the table. Perhaps he hadn't heard her patter about a marriage, perhaps he hadn't searched her overnight case — or ordered it searched, but, if he had he must not suspect that he was more than the acquaintance of the past minute. All hands to the pumps, she rallied her shocked senses.

"Mother has given you a tremendous

build-up, Mr. Ruggles," she declared with provocative gaiety. "Living up to it will take some doing."

"I'll make good or die in the attempt." Little black devils glittered in his eyes. "Miss, or am I mistaken, is it Mrs.? Has Van Tyler's broken heart been mended at last?"

V

He saw her the moment he entered the green salon at the embassy. Her face which had been in his thoughts since they parted at the cab door was as he remembered it, lovelier, perhaps. Delicately tanned, smooth skin the color of a dusky peach at the cheekbones; heavily lashed eyes under beautifully arched brows; perfect nose and adorable mouth. A deep dimple dented her left cheek when she smiled. Her bare arms and neck were the same lovely color as her face. Short, wavy hair shone under the lights like blue-black satin. She was wearing green orchids at the shoulder of her sparkling white frock. His?

The woman beside her in black velvet and pale blue was her mother, undoubtedly. Except for a difference in age, not too apparent under the flattering lights, they looked enough alike to be twins, noticeable for beauty, charm of manner and exquisite frocks even in this assembly where chic, lovely women were the rule, not the exception.

When she had said that Joshua Crandon was her mother's husband, he had not told her that he had met "good old Josh" through a Congressman. What luck, Crandon was joining the two women. Now, he could be formally presented to the stepdaughter. It couldn't be, it was, Russ Ruggles greeting the girl as if they were old friends.

Anger set blood burning in his cheeks. He had been right when he thought she was working for his enemy. "Mrs. John Smith" had fooled him to the hilt. She had known who he was when she dashed into the compartment and —

Back up, back up, common sense advised. She said she suspected she was being trailed because she was carrying papers to be delivered to the State Department. You believed her and changed your seat in the Pullman to be Johnny-on-the-spot if anyone disturbed her or the beret in her lap, didn't you? You delivered those papers to the high-up for whom they were intended, heard his fervent "Thank God, Graham got them through." You sent the receipt with the orchids she's wearing. Calm down.

He had been approaching the group of which the girl was the center while listening to the inner monitor. Crandon saw him and extended a welcoming hand, clapped him soundly on the shoulder with the other.

"See who's here! Tyler, meet the wife. Kit, Van is a bright and shining star rising in the Congressional sky, with a war record that's nothing short of sensational." He smacked his lips. "If that isn't enough of a recommendation, like all Westerners he's a two-gun man, quick on the draw, knows everyone in this town worth knowing, goes everywhere worth going *and* is a rock-ribbed, girl-resistant bachelor."

"After that solid gold case history — " Mrs. Crandon left the rest of the fervent sentence in the air and held out her hand. She looked up with wide-eyed, "Wonderful man, whyhave-we-not-met-before" expression. He had seen the technique used often but never more convincingly. She drew her hand from his slowly.

"This is my daughter, Miss Adair. Wendy, Mr. Tyler. Mr. Ruggles, Mr. Tyler."

"Van and I don't need an introduction, I know him, don't I, fella?" Ruggles's assurance was accompanied by a significant leer which fired the recipient with an urge to knock his ears together. From the ballroom drifted the alluring strains of "Roses from the South."

"Hear that tempting waltz?" Wendy Adair's question cut off his reply to Ruggles's taunt. She tapped the toe of a silver sandal in time to the drumbeat. "How can you people stand here like dummies? Something tells me I must take the initiative if I want to dance — and I do. Mr. Congressman, may I have the pleasure?"

"Wendy!"

"Have I made a social blunder, Mother? Sorry, I—"

"Take it from me, you haven't," Van responded fervently. "Let's go, Miss—"

"When I saw you two together on the train it was Mrs.—"

"But, Mr. Ruggles," the girl's breathless protest cut off the name. "When you told me at Mother's cocktail party that you recognized and spoke to me in the dining car because I looked so much like her, I explained that just as you stopped at the table I was repeating to Mr. Tyler lines from a play I had been rehearsing in which the lead's name was Van. An unbelievable coincidence, but once in a lifetime it can happen that way."

"You talked with Mr. Tyler *in a dining car* — " her mother bridled with maternal condemnation. "A man to whom you hadn't been introduced until a few minutes ago? Wendy, I hope you didn't acquire the habit of picking up strangers in South America?"

"I wasn't a stranger, Mrs. Crandon." Van moved up his guns, "that is, your daughter wasn't a stranger to me. We met for a moment only, I admit, at a wedding in B.A. where I was best man. When I saw her in the Pullman I had the nerve to remind her of the meeting, and suggest breakfast. Miss Adair, we are losing the best of the music."

"I was wondering why you were wasting time establishing your credentials. I haven't questioned them." She turned in time to cut off a protest from Ruggles.

In silence they edged through the crowd in the green salon with its masses of white flowers, past men who hailed him cordially; past women who smiled invitingly; past one who called softly:

"Van, come here!"

"This is a distinguished gathering even for Washington," he declared in the hope of erasing from her memory the low, impassioned voice, a voice he had been avoiding since his first term.

"Each one a VIP?"

"Not only a VIP but many TIP, which last, in case you don't know, stands for Terribly

Important Person. Most of the U. S. Government Royal Family below the president is here, plus ambassadors and wives from all over the world; chiefs of foreign diplomatic missions; army and navy brass by the gold-braided score; justices, senators, representatives and dozens of mere millionaires and socialites."

"It is thrilling to see them. The saris worn by the East Indian women add theatric splashes of color. I love that pale blue with the glinting gold band on the skirt and on the throw across the shoulders. I am amazed to see so many of our uniforms, almost as many as one saw during the war."

"Officers who were out of the service have been asked to return to instruct the men being inducted."

"It is a curious feeling not to know anyone in a gathering as large as this. I feel as alone as if a plane I had been piloting had pancaked and left me sole occupant of a desert isle."

"I'm a pilot, still in the Reserve, it's up to me to rescue you." They were crossing a library walled with choicely bound books, rosy with glads running the tints and shades of red, from soft peach to deep carmine.

"What a beautifully proportioned room. Who was it said, 'Money invested in a library gives much better returns than mining stock'?"

"I don't know the author, but I approve the sentiment, Miss Adair. However, it isn't fair to lose sight of the fact that often it is the mining stock which has made the library possible."

He stopped at the entrance to the ballroom with its daffodil-yellow damask walls, powder-blue velvet hangings at long windows on one side, and a stage where men in white and gold uniforms made music under a bower of acacia branches in full bloom.

"Shall we dance or find a place where we can talk?" he suggested. "We ought to get together on where we met first, what my role is to be in the immediate present. I'll do the worrying about the future."

"Dance, then talk. I didn't know I had such a talent for prevarication. I got in deeper and deeper with my explanation to Mr. Ruggles, must be an inheritance, like her name, from my novelist grandmother."

"I did my part in landing us in a quicksand by declaring we had met before today. Today!" They had joined the dancers. "Was it only this morning that—"

"You thought I was a *femme fatale* set on your trail for the purpose of allure."

"Forget it. You dance like a dream-girl."

"Don't feel you must compliment me so fervently because I dragged you to the ballroom."

"First, I was not dragged. Second, when I start out to compliment, lady, I never shortchange."

Her laugh was young and gay with an exciting lilt quite different from that of the girl on the train.

"You know all the answers, don't you? A rock-ribbed bachelor would. That reminds me, at breakfast you said you had a wife?"

"I said, 'Could be,' didn't I?"

"That's right. If you know of a spot where we can hear one another's voices above the music, I have an exciting development to report." She nodded and smiled at a slender exotic brunette in crimson velvet, who was dancing with a stout, short-necked man who wore the broad blue ribbon of a diplomat across his white shirt front.

They stopped at the door of a chintzy sunroom fragrant with roses red as the blooms on hangings and slipcovers, crossed to a long open window, through that to a spacious porch with wrought-iron trellises from which vines swayed in a soft breeze.

"How is this for our conference, Miss Adair?"

"Perfect for anything. Will I touch off an

69

international incident if I perch on that inviting stone wall?"

In answer he placed his hands at her waist and swung her to the broad top.

"Good heavens, you're a quick thinker."

"It's the quick thinker who wins the jackpot before the bell rings. You said you knew no one here. I was surprised when you bowed to that striking brunette in the ballroom."

"I was surprised to see her here. We sat side by side on the plane from S.A."

"Did you talk to her?"

"Not very much. With Steve's 'Watch your step' clanging through my mind every few minutes, and jittery-aware of the dynamite parked in my beret, I was afraid to talk. She was charming and friendly, breathtaking to look at in a smart, pale gray outfit. I felt like a cheat when, in response to her questions, I told her I was Mrs. John Smith."

"Did she reciprocate with her name?"

"I didn't ask her, the question might lead to conversation and I was afraid of conversation. I did tell her I planned to stay with friends in New York."

"No mention of Washington?"

"Definitely *not*. Now that you've recalled her to my memory, I remember that I almost lost my overnight case. When we started to leave the plane, she picked it up. 'That's mine,' I declared, and in my state of excitement grabbed the handle as if I suspected she was a bag-snatcher. For a minute I thought she intended to argue, then she laughed and explained.

" 'It's exactly like mine, for a second I forgot that I didn't bring it.' She was so charming I was ashamed of my frightened grab."

"Was that the last you saw of her?"

"As we parted, she called, 'Good-bye and good luck, Mrs. John Smith.' Her loud voice attracted all eyes to me. I wonder if she lives in Washington?"

"She was dancing with a foreign diplomat, she may be a visiting VIP. Don't you need a wrap?"

She shook her head, and drew the gauzy tourmaline-pink stole across her bare shoulders. He leaned against a trellis, his face in shadow. A moon round and shining as a newly minted copper penny emerged slowly from behind the silverf-luted edge of a snowy cloud and poured its radiance over the slender figure in the glistening white frock as if slap-happy that it had discovered an object worth illuminating. She drew a deep breath.

"Smell the spicy scent the breeze is shaking from the box hedges. I love it."

"I prefer the perfume you are using. What is it? Do I detect sandalwood?"

"Right. It was blended to suit my personality, I having been born under the sign of Virgo need a touch of the Oriental — the *parfumeuse* speaking. A lot of hooey, if you ask me, and I *didn't* smuggle it from South America."

"Do you never forgive and forget?"

From inside the house came a woman's voice singing:

"Wonderful Nights Don't Last Forever."

They were silent until the last lovely note drifted out and was lost under the stars.

"Beautiful voice," she said softly. "It's true, a wonderful night like this won't last."

"There will be others — " he cleared his husky voice. She would think he'd lost his mind — he wasn't so sure he hadn't — was a practised philanderer if he finished the fervent sentence. In place of it he suggested:

"To return to the subject of quick thinking. When a girl wishes to elude a certain person—"

"She dashes into a Pullman compartment, formerly called 'drawing room.' In spite of the fact that I explained at length the why and wherefore of my panic a splinter of suspicion of me still pricks, doesn't it? A rhetorical question. Don't answer. I'm glad of this chance to thank you a million for de-livering Steve's papers, and for these—" Her fingers with shell-pink nails touching the or-chids at her shoulder stiffened:

"Look! *Look!* Crossing the garden! Did you see him?"

"Him? Who?"

"The man who followed me to the train."

VI

He almost pitched over the wall in response to her excited whisper.

"Which way did he go?"

"Not so loud, he may be listening. He turned and looked at me before he disappeared among those tall poplars. In the dim light his face was spooky, his eyes glittered. Gave me the shivers. Is *he* on my trail again?"

"*No.*" He perched on the wall between her and the direction in which she had said the man disappeared. "I'll bet you were looking for trouble and imagined him."

"He was real — even the memory of that face makes my nerves go creepy-creepy like the jointed legs of a centipede up my spine."

"Forget him."

"I'd like to. Thanks for going on sentinel duty while I slept on the train. The porter told me you changed from the compartment to a seat."

"That porter talks too much. Your beret needed watching. I seen my duty an' I done it."

"You can laugh about it. I wish I could, but every little while I have a breath-snatching suspicion that the delivery of those papers didn't end my connection with the revolution. We'll forget that, too. This must be Indian summer, it is so warm. The maid at Mother's told me that blossoms had appeared on the famous cherry trees. It's a heavenly night."

"It is. Others are bound to discover it. How about reporting the important development while we have the porch to ourselves?"

She told him of the ransacked overnight case.

"Why that long, low whistle?"

"Habit of mine when surprised." Better not tell her of the suspicion which had flamed to conviction. "What do you make of it?"

"Someone in this city must have been tipped off that I was carrying secret papers. What other explanation can there be? Not having found them, are they trailing me? Was the man who flitted across the garden—?"

"Wipe him off the slate. What you saw

could have been the shadow of one of those tall poplars bowing in the breeze. There is no longer a reason for you to be trailed. Graham's message got through. The interested parties will find out that it has been parked in the Department of State where it can't be reached, they have contacts in high places, unfortunately. Forget it. You could have knocked me over with a feather when Ruggles spoke to you in the green salon."

"And that splinter of suspicion pricked. When you joined us I knew by your expression that I was in the doghouse again, that you were sure your political rival was behind my sensational 'Save me! Save me!' appeal."

"Guilty, but only for a split second. Would you mind telling me why you appeared so fratty with him?"

"It was the triumph of will over instinct. I don't like the man. In spite of my explanation he makes me feel that he believes you and I were secretly married. He must know it isn't true, but for some reason he's trying to scare me."

"We could make it true and wreck his scheme, if he has one."

"Now you're laughing at me. Perhaps sometime I'll learn not to put my secret thoughts on the air. To return to Mr. Ruggles. I don't like him, even on this short acquaintance. I distrust his eyes, but, he is a friend of Mother's husband. Apparently she admires him and I made a compact with myself before I came that I would do everything in my power to keep peace while here. After this visit I intend to give shape to my life, stop being pulled in different directions, settle on a definite objective."

"I approve that intention. Call me in as consultant on the shaping, will you? I have ideas. Meanwhile, you don't have to appear as if Ruggles were your hero returned from the war, do you?"

"Was I that good? Here's where I shyly flutter long lashes, my maternal parent has selected him as a husband for her only chee-ild." Moonlight accentuated the brilliance of her laughing eyes.

"No kidding!" Should he tell her that Russ had been married and divorced? Not now.

"That's her story. He doesn't know the awful fate being planned for him."

"Do you *want* to marry the guy?"

"What a question to ask after I told you how I distrust the man."

"Mothers have been known to be very persuasive. What say we work as a combat team against her plan?"

"The suggestion has possibilities. Time is

flying. Let's get back to our reason for this heart-to-heart."

"Want my first reason?"

"I am referring to your statement that we had met before today."

"Afraid to hear the first, aren't you?"

"I am not afraid of anything."

"No?"

There was sufficient light to betray the surge of delicate color to the lovely line of her dark hair.

"Now you are the one who doesn't forgive and forget. I told you what happened at the hotel to my overnight case, you'll have to admit that I had reason to suspect I was being shadowed this morning."

"You had. My apologies for teasing you. Since your arrival in the city have you seen the man you thought was trailing you?"

"Not until I saw him — it may have been his ghost — cross the garden. He must have arrived by air, how account otherwise for the search through my overnight case? How could he get into my hotel room? How could he know which it was?"

"Finding out would be ABC for an expert. He heard your name called when you deplaned. In spite of the porter's bluff he was sure you were on the train, flew to Washington, and was in Union Station when you arrived. Not having seen me he didn't attach importance to the fact that I shared your taxi — he missed that trick — and followed to the hotel. You registered as Mrs. John Smith. He saw you go to the dining room for lunch, stepped to the desk and inquired for you. Stood near enough to hear the clerk tell the switchboard operator to call — whatever was the number of your room. A passkey and there he was."

"Shade of Sherlock Holmes! You take my breath. Are you a whodunit author in disguise?"

"I've had a yen to try my hand at it. We'd better settle on the place of our first meeting."

"You *said* you went to South America to best-man a pal. I can carry on from there. An attaché of our embassy married an Argentine girl in Buenos Aires. His name was Hugh Sinclair. I won't attempt to pronounce the bride's. I have the invitation among my papers at Red Terraces. I will mail it to you. You can make yourself letter-perfect."

"That will help. I did fly to South America this last summer, and I was best man for a pal."

"That bases our fabrication on truth. I hope that coming to the rescue of a damsel in distress won't land you in a shell-hole of trouble with your friends — or enemies. As we came through the rooms I decided that Mr. Crandon's fanfare about you is true. You do know everyone, go everywhere. You left a trail of frustrated female admirers."

"That stuff 'good old Josh' got off was a lot of hooey. I do *not* know everyone, I do *not* go everywhere, how could I? Don't you realize that a man in Congress has to *work*, that the years ahead will be critical in this profoundly exciting era in our history; that every department of the government, executive and legislative, will be taxed heavily with problems?"

"If I didn't, I do now. I don't wonder you won the fight for a seat in Congress. Your eloquence would fire the imagination and patriotism of your listeners."

"Sorry I mounted the soapbox and cut loose, but I feel a tremendous sense of responsibility."

"Why be sorry? I am proud that you trust me enough to 'cut loose.'"

"*Trust you?* More about that later. I started to explain the source of your stepfather's 'fanfare,' as you called it. My acquaintance in the Capital is large, my family had a winter home here for years while Father was a member of the Senate. I still own the house and—"

"Van!"

The call came from a girl standing in the embrasure of a long window. Light from the room behind turned her blonde hair to gold and set each sequin on her all-black frock glinting.

"Thunder!" Van Tyler's low protest was followed by "Here, Clare."

She ran across the porch, stopped with a startled "Oh!" when she saw the girl on the wall.

"I — I thought you were alone. I have something terribly important to tell you, Van," she added in a whisper.

"Don't go!" He caught Wendy's arm as she moved. "Miss Adair, Mrs. Clare Sanford. What's the excitement?"

"Russ is here. Don't glare at me as if I were the man himself, it's ungrateful of you when I ditched a fascinating admiral with whom I was dancing — and can the navy dance — to find and warn you."

"Mighty noble of you, my girl, but why the hectic warning? That you may be able to follow the plot of this thriller, Miss Adair, here's the line-up. Mrs. Clare Sanford, her brother Rolfe, and Ruggles, heretofore mentioned as Russ, and I hail from the same part of the country. Our forebears were transplanted New Englanders."

"You are making fun of my warning, Van. It may not seem so amusing when you meet him."

"Clare, you terrify me. My political opponent isn't looking for me with a gun in his shoulder holster, is he?"

"My *political* opponent, says you, as if that were all. You are determined not to take me seriously, while I am trying — with darn little success — to put you on guard. He is fairly dripping with brotherly love and when R. Ruggles drips sweetness and light it's time to run up storm warnings. Who knows that better than I?"

"Clare, don't be so breathless. Stop and—"

"How can I stop when I am so worried about you? He told Rolfe this afternoon — he came in on an early train — that he intended to look you up, hoped to bury the hatchet — bury it in your back, I'll bet. My sixth sense tells me he believes he has something on you — he's been watching for it like a cat at a mousehole — something to your discredit. He hasn't, has he, dearie?" Moonlight revealed her eyes, green as emeralds glittering behind pools of tears.

He shut his teeth hard to hold back a furious protest. She stepped out of my life.

Why won't she keep out? If she calls me "dearie" in that tone once more I'll be tempted to wring her neck.

Wendy Adair slid off the wall. Her troubled eyes met his. Was she thinking that the something to his discredit was tied up with her announcement on the train of their marriage? She had said that Ruggles was pretending he believed it. He made a slight negative motion with his head in answer to the question in her eyes and laughed.

"Clare, cut your consumption of mystery yarns, they are getting you down. You see a menace behind every parking meter. Here comes your brother. Boy, am I in for another warning? Who's the foreign-looking guy with the eyebrow mustache twirled to sharp points he has in tow? I'll bet he's Spain out of Hollywood." Clare Sanford's laugh was hysterically high.

"This appears to be old home week, Rolfe," he suggested as the two men joined them. "Miss Adair, enter another of my neighbors from the great open spaces, Rolfe Sanford."

The eyes of the wiry, lean-faced man with short, sandy hair twinkled behind bifocals as he acknowledged the introduction with a bow.

"I've heard you are the spittin' image of

your beautiful mother, Miss Adair, now I know it to be true. May I present Señor Antonio Cardella — he claims that you and he have many mutual acquaintances below the equator. My sister, Clare, our Congressman — Vance Tyler, Señor."

The slim dark-haired man bowed in acknowledgment to each in turn as with the fingers of his left hand he twisted an end of his mustache. Van Tyler glanced quickly at Wendy Adair. Had her face whitened, or was the moonlight playing tricks?

"It would be a great pleasure to speak of these many friends to you, Señorita Adair. I am a stranger in your great country. May I have the honor of this dance?" His voice was as satin-smooth as his hair, his large eyes soft as black velvet hinted a tragic personal secret.

If Van had been uncertain of Wendy Adair's change of color when the Señor was presented, the clutch of her hand on his arm was not to be misunderstood. Fright was indicated.

"Thank you, Señor Cardella, the talkfest is tempting, but just before you came I promised the dance to Mr. Tyler. Let's go, Van, the music is too alluring to ignore."

As they entered the chintzy sunroom a-bloom with red roses, oboes, flutes, clarinets and bassoons were crooning, "My Darling! My Darling!"

"Now, perhaps you will believe I saw him cross the garden," she whispered. "Señor Antonio Cardella is the man who has been shadowing me. I feel as if a delayed action bomb had gone off. What do we do next?"

"We dance." He slipped his arm about her, swept her into the softly lighted ballroom. "Remember, we're a combat team."

VII

Vance Tyler stood at the window of Rolfe Sanford's office high above a street teeming with traffic, staring out at the Monument, Reflecting Pool and the Lincoln Memorial, which in the distance looked like reproductions in miniature, thinking.

Who is Señor Antonio Cardella? Has he been shadowing Wendy Adair or has she imagined it? Having been warned by Steve Graham to watch her step, that S. A. guys were cagey, it could easily be that she had seen trouble where no trouble existed. There had been no chance to question her further, no opportunity to make a date with her. Good old Josh had appeared at the door of the ballroom to report that her mother was eager to go home.

Cheerio, this is only the next morning. Before you see her again — I can't see her for a week. I've got to start west this noon.

How can I leave with Ruggles — if Clare's supposition is correct — watching for a chance to spring a trap and Cardella following her? When she looked up and said, "I suppose it could be admiration?" something happened to me. My heart picked up, my blood rushed through my veins — as I had thought it never would again — in short, I made a crash landing at her feet. Something tells me I'm grounded for keeps.

He forced his thoughts back to the reason for coming to Rolfe's office, it was to find out from him where and how he had contacted the smoothie. The South American — if he were a South American — wasn't his only reason for being here. He was uneasy about—

"Greetings, *Mister* Tyler." The mocking voice swung him from the window. He faced the girl leaning against the door. Her black jersey frock accentuated the lovely lines of her body, the gardenia whiteness of her skin, the gold in her hair which hung to her shoulders. Her brilliantly rouged lips drooped at the corners, her eyes were brilliant as green peridots. She held a notebook and pencil.

"Greetings, Mrs. Clare Sanford," he responded, and thought, You are beautiful, but "if she be not so to me, what care I how fair she be?" Where did those lines come from?

Must be a fragment of English A which had detached itself from the deeply buried course to float to the top of my mind.

"You're looking at me, but I'll bet you are seeing the girl perched on the wall last night," she accused bitterly.

"On the contrary, my thoughts were entirely on you and how lovely you are."

Bright color burned under her skin. She took an eager step toward him.

"Mean that, Van?"

"Of course I mean it. You know you are beautiful, don't you?"

"Yes, but hearing you say it is something else again. It means you have forgiven me, dearie?"

"Get this straight and for all time, Clare. I have nothing to forgive. You broke our engagement to marry a man you preferred—"

"I divorced him after a year. The court allowed me to resume my maiden name, I couldn't bear to keep his."

"That means nothing in my life, *nothing*."

"Van, don't be so hard. I found I loved you. You loved me once."

He forcibly removed the white hands gripping the lapels of his coat.

"But not twice, Clare—"

"Sorry to keep a busy man waiting," Rolfe Sanford glanced from his sister's face to Van

Tyler's. "Clare, why are you here? You've been told time and again you are not to enter this room unless I call you." He held open the door. "Exit my number one secretary. Go out to lunch."

"Lunch! I know a brush-off when I hear one." With an indignant sniff she crossed the threshold, caught the handle from him and slammed the door behind her with a force that set the telephone receiver jiggling in its cradle. Her brother dropped a bulging briefcase to the top of the broad desk and sank into a swivel chair with a tired sigh.

"Sit down, fella. I know from your burning ears you were let in for a scene." He ran his fingers through his sandy crew-cut till every individual hair stood on end.

"Gorry-me, what can we do about that kid?"

"She isn't a kid, she's a married woman."

"I know, Van, I know what she did to you when she walked out on you. You can't by any chance forgive her, can you?"

"It isn't a question of forgiveness, chief. I feel no bitterness toward her, she's absolutely out of my life."

"As if I didn't know that. The smart thing for you to do is to get engaged and married to another girl — and quick. Sometimes I think I should send her home but, oh, hell, that's my problem, not yours. Got held up in Committee. Auto-Sales-Gouging Division. On top of that the spy-ring horror has boiled over again. We've been drifting when we should have been breaking our backs rowing against a pernicious current." He rose, walked around his chair and sank into it.

"Let's forget it. What can I do for you? Smoke?" He pushed an open box of cigars across the expanse of shining mahogany desktop between them.

"Thanks, no. They look deadly."

"Sissy! You can't take it." He grinned and returned the box to a drawer. "What say we have a bite? It's early, but I can always eat."

"I'd rather talk here. You are a man of importance — no danger that your resignation will be asked for by the new administration — what you say, if overheard, would be used as headline stuff."

"Why the build-up? You don't waste time on words as a rule, Van. What's the pitch?"

"Where did you pick up Señor Cardella?"

"So, he is the occasion of this call? He dropped in here yesterday, after having flown from New York. Presented a letter from his Consul. He's South American Spanish. Apparently he was tipped off to clear through this office. He laid his cards on the table, claimed that he and Miss Adair who arrived here recently had slews of mutual friends in his home city who wanted them to meet. He didn't express himself in straight U. S. like that, but I've given you the gist of his flowery discourse."

"If that 'mutual friends' stuff is straight goods, why didn't he bring letters to her?"

"You're asking me. What have you against the guy? Isn't he regular?"

"I'm here to find out. While we were dancing Miss Adair declared she was sure he and she hadn't a friend in common."

"Thought his yarn a phony, did she? Bright gal. So did I, but it was my job to find out what was behind it. When she gave his invitation to dance the heave ho, her voice was so icy I saw frost glint on his mustache. When did you meet her?"

"I'm here to tell you. It's strictly confidential."

"Wait a minute." Sanford touched a button and spoke into an interoffice phone. "I'm in conference, Hood." He settled back in his chair. "That will prevent interruption. Strict confidence is my meat. You and I worked together for years in ACIC, Army Counter Intelligence Corps, if you insist upon the full title. You went in as green an amateur as I've ever seen and came out my head man."

91

"Credit my success to the correspondence course to which I subscribed at the age of twelve, 'How to Be a Detective in Ten Lessons.'"

"It's a mean break you didn't keep in that line of work."

"I heard the stentorian voice of Politics calling, working for the best kind is in my blood."

"You were tops in the other job. Being an ace pilot helped. I'll say you've been working. You went to the voters over the heads of political machines, bucked 'em with one hundred and ten speeches in thirty days, all emphasizing the needs of our district. You crossed mountain passes and covered miles of sagebrush and licked your opponent to a standstill. And for what? representative to Congress. Where and what will that get you? Perhaps the chairmanship of a committee if you live long enough — the seniority system is the only way you can make it at present. Special ability or qualities of leadership won't do the trick."

"I don't intend to remain a Representative for life, chief. Our state can use another good governor in a few years, after that — there's always the Senate."

"You'll get there. You've been a fighter for the conservation of our national resources from the moment you became a rookie Congressman. T. Roosevelt started it. I know by your grin you're thinking that my grousing about your choice of a career is an oft-told grievance, charge it up to the fact that I'm still sore at losing my best agent — and, boy, can we use a few now. Forget my peeve. Get on with your story."

Van told of meeting the girl on the train, his suspicion of her, his uneasy feeling after she left the compartment that he had been brutal to a woman who was really frightened, his olive-branch invitation to breakfast, the appearance of Ruggles beside their table, her whispered confidence that she was carrying secret papers, the delivery of them by himself, her discovery that her overnight case had been searched.

"There it is in tabloid," he concluded. "Now for the climax, Cardella is the guy who tried to speak to her at the airfield and at the station."

"If I followed your story, Van — and believe me I did, it makes highly interesting listening — that isn't the climax, that's merely a crisis. Did you contact the right guy when you delivered the papers?"

"I did. When it seemed that I had run into a bottleneck, I mentioned my name and outfit. It proved an open sesame."

"It would. Who in the upper brackets of government doesn't know how you won that ribbon? So far Miss Adair's story is plausible. When did she discover that the overnight case had been searched?"

"After she reached her mother's house."

"Is she sure it wasn't opened there and not at the hotel?"

"I asked that question. She answered that immediately on her arrival at Red Terraces — that's the name of the estate Crandon has leased—"

"I know. Go on."

"The maid carried the bag to the room assigned her, that it wasn't out of her sight from that moment until she opened it."

"That ties it at the hotel. To prove that I haven't gone stale on my job — I spent some time at midnight pondering the dapper Señor's story, Miss Adair's frightened eyes, her icy voice when she turned down his invitation to dance. It got such a hold on me that this morning I had the girl's background looked up." He drew a paper from a drawer of the desk. His eyes were on the written script as he talked.

"She told you of the break in the family, that she had been with her distinguished father two years — among other activities she doubled as receptionist in his office and nurse's aide at the hospital. Did she confide that it is the consensus among their friends that she is as good as engaged to an attaché of our embassy, Steve Graham?"

"She did *not.*"

"I judge by your expression that you are surprised unpleasantly. She received a legacy of fifty thousand dollars from her paternal grandmother. When I saw that statement I thought I knew why the slick Señor was in pursuit of the girl, that he had an urge to acquire a little fortune by marriage. Fifty thousand may not be spectacular, but it ain't hay. Having heard your story, I'll reshift my facts and begin again, assuming that he is interested in the papers she was carrying. Why? There is one angle we've neglected. Russ Ruggles."

"Ruggles! I told you he overheard Miss Adair's goofy statement in the dining car that we were married, and the explanation she gave him of the yarn later at Red Terraces. I don't see where he comes in."

"He'll come in anywhere he thinks he can do you dirt. He came in last evening after you and Miss Adair left to dance. He appeared from the shadows, immediately introduced himself to the Señor — I'll bet he had overheard our conversation — buttered him to the gills. After a few minutes arm in arm they left the porch for the champagne cocktail bar. I saw them there later. I didn't think of it then, Russ is always taking up with strangers, but since I've heard your story, I'm wondering if in some dour, dark and devious way he is planning to hurt you through the girl."

Ruggles going all out to be fratty with Cardella, a man whom Wendy suspected had rifled her bag — that angle would bear following up.

"Could be. In that case Miss Adair needs protection. Put one of your best men on the job, will you? I'm off this afternoon for a week. Keep him on till I return."

"Sure. And when you get back you take over. In the war ostensibly you were a pilot, few knew that you were an agent to catch agents."

"Suits me. The new Congress doesn't convene till January. Long before that we ought to have the matter cleared up. I can't be her shadow all the time, Mrs. Crandon won't stand for too much of me at the house. She has picked Ruggles for a son-in-law."

"With an eye on his oil wells? Her plan makes the fight more interesting for you."

"What fight?"

"Keep your shirt on, fella, that was a mere figure of speech. We'll screen the smooth

Señor to his backbone. Sure you've given me all the data?"

"One fact more. Madame Zaidee Latour arrived from South America yesterday by plane."

"You're telling me. I was informed the very hour she left for home."

"Then of course you know, wise guy, that Wendy Adair, carrying secret papers, was her seatmate all the way, that when they started to leave the plane Zaidee picked up Miss Adair's overnight case, that when the owner seized it she laughed, and explained that it was like hers, that for a moment she had forgotten she had left hers at home. You might turn your X-ray eye on that situation. I have a hunch it will fit into our picture puzzle."

"That was the overnight case that later was searched?"

"Yes."

Sanford drummed on the desktop with long bony fingers and gazed unseeingly at the photograph on the wall of a new riot squad armed with thirty-inch batons and tear-gas grenades. Wearing gas masks, they were weirdly suggestive of Martians on parade.

"Encourage Miss Adair to meet the alluring Zaidee again."

"You're crazy, Rolfe. That woman was suspended from an eight thousand a year job because of suspected disloyalty."

"That's right, *suspected,* nothing was proved. It could be a shocking miscarriage of justice. She's still in circulation, newspaper reporting. Many think her a martyr. Time and investigation will tell. I'll suggest to Mrs. Crandon that scuttlebutt whispers she is royalty incog, and Mrs. Josh will go all out to entertain her — she eats up celebrities."

"Didn't realize you knew the Crandons socially."

"Sure I know them. I'll admit that I'm more popular with the fair Kitty than with her spouse, he gives me the impression that he suspects I'm about to spring a trap."

"Good old Josh? What could you have on him?"

"I didn't say I had anything. I was reporting his reaction to me. Miss Adair may help prove me right or wrong about Latour. I hear she sings — Wendy Adair, not the exotic Zaidee — added to other interests she had a radio program for kids in S. A."

"She didn't tell me that."

"From the slight opportunity I had to observe her, I judge she has learned not to tell all she knows. I have an open line into a broadcasting studio. I'll get her a job. It may interest her — she won't be happy long where she is — her mother is not sweetening with age, I hear."

"Okay to that, but for Pete's sake, chief, why drag her into the Zaidee Latour complication, she has enough on her mind with the mystery of that ransacked overnight case to solve."

"It was your suggestion that the two situations may interlock, wasn't it? Don't have Miss Adair's safety on your mind. I swear she will be protected."

"On that assurance, I'll take off. Remember, I'll be back in one week, earlier if I can make it. I hate like the dickens to go. Brief me soon as to my part in your program. I'll be seeing you."

In the corridor outside the office he stopped as Rolfe's question shot to the top of his mind.

"Are you sure it wasn't opened *there* and not at her hotel?"

Does that mean that Red Terraces is under suspicion? Is that why he knows so much about the Crandons? Could be. In these hectic days anything can happen, anything at all.

VIII

Dusk hung in the offing as if waiting for the sun to drop below the horizon before flinging its lavender veil over fields and river. Wendy touched the horse with her heels and leaned forward in the saddle to pat his sleek neck. In answer his pace quickened. Her heart which had been heavy lifted in swift response to the beauty of the country through which she was riding; her voice rose in the lilt of Edward Lear's nonsensical little song she had set to music for her broadcast program.

> They went to sea in a sieve, they did,
>   In a sieve they went to sea;
> In spite of all their friends could say
> On a winter's morn, on a stormy day,
>   In a sieve they went to sea.

The fiery top of the sun disappeared behind a hill. The world turned rose-color.

It was still light enough to see the black gums brilliant with red; the sweet gums touched with maroon; the yellow of silver maples; the orange of wild cherry. Irregular wine-red branches of sumac, with seed-spikes rising like brilliant flames bordered the choppy river, each dark ripple topped with a lacy-white nightcap. A lone fisherman on the bank reeled in his line and trudged homeward along a well-worn path, his drooping shoulders registering discouragement. From somewhere near rose the smoke of a picnicker's fire and the appetizing scent of crisping bacon.

A flock of geese in full southward cry high against the purpling blue of the sky vanished into the haze. A shot sounded from what appeared to be a stationary raft about fifty feet off shore, but the birds flew on. A chipmunk scolded noisily from the limb of an oak, and a gray squirrel which had been furtively digging for its hoard scampered across the road.

> Far and few, far and few,
>   Are the lands where the Jumblies live;
> Their heads are green, and their hands are
>   blue;
> And they went to sea in a sieve.

Her song and the vivid thrust of happiness died. Doubt settled over her spirit, doubt as to the security of her mother's marriage, a disturbing sense that the appearance of Señor Antonio Cardella in her own life meant trouble. She had been at Red Terraces a week. A week of impressions the memory of which kept her awake at night. Something was wrong, terribly wrong.

"In a sieve they went to sea." The words surged through her mind: was that the answer? Was a marriage like her mother's a leaky contract that wouldn't outlive a storm? The historic Potomac estate was the center of a brilliant social life. What could be wrong? She answered her own question.

I don't know, I honestly don't know. I just sense it. It isn't because of Mother's bursts of temper though they seem more frequent and violent than when she was Kitty Adair; it isn't that I don't like Joshua Crandon because, much as I hate to admit it, I do; it can't be because I distrust his sidekick, Ruggles, who seems to be everlastingly underfoot. My excuses for refusing his invitations are worn threadbare.

"Why, why do I feel as if I were walking over mined territory, that at any moment the surface calm, color and luxury of life at Red

Terraces may be blown to smithereens?"

The roan turned his head, regarded her with one enormous eye, and whinnied. She laughed and patted his smooth neck.

"Was I talking aloud, Scotty, old dear? It's a habit I have you'll discover. Why those pricked ears? I hear it now, too, the tap, tap of hoofs behind us. Someone's coming, coming fast. Who? The sound gives me the chilly-willies. Let's get well ahead. Step on it." The roan stepped. Her thoughts kept pace.

Is it Cardella? Don't be goofy, gal, you haven't seen him since the evening of the embassy reception. Van Tyler was right when he said that the person who had tried to intercept the papers I was carrying would lose interest in me when it was discovered they had been delivered.

Where is he? He has dropped out of my life as completely as has the smooth Señor. It's a blow. The evening on the embassy porch I nobly resisted the urge to tactfully find out what Ruggles meant when he sneered, "Has Van's broken heart been mended at last?"

He is the one person in this seething city upon whose friendship I had counted, had counted is right, I haven't been so sure since I heard the green-eyed Clare call him "dearie." He told me he liked 'em blonde. She's blonde enough to suit the most exacting blonde-complex. She can't be the person who broke his heart, it's as plain as the nose on her face that she'd fall into his arms at the crook of his little finger.

"Hey! Where's the fire? Wait for me." The shout came from behind.

Steve! In response to her jerk on the reins the roan stopped so quickly she almost pitched over his head. Her left hand went out in eager greeting to the hatless man on the dapple-gray horse.

"Steve! Steve, *dear.* I'm so glad to see you I could cry."

Color rushed to his smooth silver-blond hair, his blue eyes flamed with triumph.

"That's telling me, Wendy. This is one time when absence made the heart grow fonder. You've discovered you love me. Do I get a kiss of welcome?" He tried to draw her toward him; she twisted her hand free.

"Not that fond, Steve. Sorry, if I misled you. I am terribly glad to see my *friend,* that's all."

Oh, dear, had her excited greeting undone what she had accomplished? When she left South America, she was sure she had made him realize she did not love him enough to marry him.

"Okay, as long as you love me a little I shan't give up hope, lovely."

"It's getting dark, let's go on. We can talk while we ride toward home." The two horses moved forward side by side casting wary glances at each other.

"How did you know where to find me?"

"That movie butler at your mother's told me you were riding. When I heard you caroling the Jumblies at the top of your not-too-bad mezzo, I figured he was right when he said you always took the river road."

"*How* can he know that?" Memory played back a recording of Blossom's voice:

"Propper said it was, Miss, and Propper never makes mistakes, he knows everything that goes on inside the house and outside." At the time she had been too excited over the orchids to sense the maid's comment.

"As I've never seen the guy before, I can't tell how he knows your schedule," Steve was answering her question. "But from the glimpse I had of him, I'll bet he has see-all eyes and hear-all ears. He suggested that I take a horse from the stable and try to find you. An understanding fella if he is nosy. I must be an honest-looking lad, apparently he believed me when I told him I'd brought a letter from your father in S. A."

"Did Father send a letter by you, Steve?"

"Sure. A bulky one which I left at the hotel until I located you. This is the best chance I'll have to tell you why I'm here. To be honest I didn't fly to Washington just to see you, I was ordered here by my boss. He wants a first-person account of what happened to the message you carried."

"Didn't it reach the high-up to whom it was addressed?" For a hectic instant she doubted Van Tyler's assurance that he had delivered the papers.

"Sure it did. What's there about my question to make you jump as if I had drilled into a tooth nerve? I told you not to write about it. Now, I want the low-down on what happened."

She began with a description of the man who had tried to speak to her as she deplaned, reported each event of the next day and evening inclusive of Señor Cardella's introduction on the porch of the embassy, of her recognition of him as the man who had shadowed her.

Night, a brilliant night had taken over the country, stars appeared like a golden shower of rocket sparks before she finished the story. They dismounted in the hay-scented stable at Red Terraces. Outside Steve caught her arm and drew her into the shadow of towering rhododendrons.

"Wait. I want to ask a few questions before we get to the house. What did you know about this man Tyler when you entrusted the papers to him?"

"Only what he had told me which intuition declared was true. That last won't sound so crazy after you've met him." She repeated Joshua Crandon's words when he presented Van Tyler to his wife.

"He's the guy? I've heard of him. He was a daredevil with the CIC, I'll bet he packed two guns then. If it will make your mind easier, dollars to dimes Cardella wasn't after the papers you carried."

"Then why was my overnight case searched?"

"Are you sure he did it? If he did he was looking for a sensational lot of diamonds being smuggled into this country for sale."

"Smuggled!" Van Tyler had asked her if she were frightened because she was smuggling. Had he known then that jewels had been stolen? *"Diamonds!"* she repeated.

"Softly, lovely, softly. Keep your voice down, remember what I have told and may tell you is strictly hush-hush. These shrubs may have ears *and* a hand with a long, keen knife in it. Br-r-r!"

"That's a cheery suggestion, Steve. We'll walk in the middle of the drive to the house.

Where did the jewels come from? To whom did they belong?"

"To the government, old Spanish loot. You saw them displayed under guard, Tower of London style."

"Some of the single stones must be worth thousands."

"You've said it. Came the revolution in which you were caught and the long-planned plot to snitch 'em worked."

"Why suspect *me?* Why search *my* luggage?"

"Hold everything, Wendy. You're getting hysterical."

"Wouldn't you be hanging on the ropes if you were suspected of transporting fabulous loot? 'Hand with a long, keen knife. Don't get hysterical!' My word! Go ahead, laugh your head off, but I don't get the humor of the situation."

"Right, there isn't any, but you are so adorable and funny when you're excited that if I didn't laugh I'd have to kiss you. Under existing conditions my danger-scout warns me it is safer to laugh."

"Tell me more about the stolen jewels."

"Flashing the stop light on sentiment? I get it. The theft was discovered at the peak of the outbreak which increased in fury after midnight. It took time to round up loyal police to hunt for the thieves. Finally a smart aleck — I suspect the smooth host at your hotel — remembered and reported your departure in an embassy car."

"They don't suspect this country of having gone into the jewel-stealing business, I hope."

"No. They suspect you took the loot out for the rebels, they declare there is evidence that a woman was involved. Did you talk with other passengers on the plane?"

She described her seatmate, told of the confusion as to the ownership of the overnight case.

"You mean the woman tried to snitch your bag?"

"No, Steve, no. Didn't I make it clear that she explained her mistake? She owns one like mine, forgot for a minute she hadn't it with her. Van Tyler and I decided she was a VIP when we saw her at an embassy reception."

"On the plane did you tell her who you were and whither bound?"

"With that 'Watch your step' warning of yours going round and round in my mind like a revolving door gone crazy? I did *not*. When she asked my name, I said 'Mrs. John Smith,' that seemed on the conservative side. I didn't ask hers. Here we are at the house — wouldn't the antiquers we know at home lose their minds over that glass-paneled door? Note the pineapples above? In these parts it is the emblem of hospitality. You'll stay for dinner, of course."

"I'll beat it back to the hotel and dress. I wouldn't dare face your mother like this. That convertible in the road is the 'Drive-Yourself' I hired. I'll be seeing you."

Light flooded her as she watched him sprint toward the car.

"Isn't the gentleman coming in, Miss Adair?" Propper's concerned question came from the open doorway.

"He'll be back in time for dinner. There won't be other guests, I hope?" she inquired as she entered the hall. He closed the door.

"Sorry to disappoint you, Miss Adair, Madame Latour, Mr. Rolfe Sanborn and his sister are coming."

"Does Mrs. Crandon know *them?*"

"Certainly." Propper's voice was drenched with surprise. "Everyone knows them. We are lucky to have secured them as guests. Mr. Sanborn is an important man in the government, he was something big in Intelligence during the war. Mrs. Clare Sanborn, she's a divorcee — the court gave her the right to resume her maiden surname — is considered a great beauty; though I don't care for her type myself. I prefer brunettes."

"Will my unexpected guest upset the seating at table?"

"Not at all. We always prepare for extras. Mr. Crandon insists upon having the establishment run that way. He likes people round. Mr. and Mrs. Brown, neighbors — they live in what used to be the overseer's cottage on this estate — are likely to drop in for coffee and cards after dinner. Nice young people."

"I've seen her. I was exercising Angeline. The dog caught a glimpse of the Browns' black cat, dashed across the lawn dragging me at the other end of the leash. My first contact with Mrs. Brown was a collision, *not* a meeting."

"That dog and cat sure hate each other, sometime they'll make serious trouble for somebody." From an intricately carved black teakwood table he picked up a slip of paper.

"A gentleman phoned. Gave this number. Said for you to get in touch with him the minute you came in, Miss Adair."

"I'll call from my room, Propper." She started up the stairs, hoping that the message was from Van Tyler, humming:

"Wonderful nights don't last forever."

"Give me a minute, will you, Wendy?"

111

Joshua Crandon's voice stopped her upward flight. Dressed for dinner he was standing at the threshold of the smoking room. "Come in here?"

What's happened now? she asked herself as he closed the door behind her.

"I won't keep you but a minute. Help me out, will you? I want to go back to my ranch; I hate this hectic life and the mad social merry-go-round is bad for your mother. Her bursts of temper are getting more frequent and violent. I can't take it."

That smack of his lips would drive me crazy if I had to live with it, she thought before she reminded icily:

"You weren't *asked* to take it."

"I know, I know. The wonder is that during the year I saw her so frequently—"

"During the year you were breaking up our home."

"That's right. I haven't a word of apology to offer for myself. I lost my head over Kitty Adair, over what I thought she was, she seemed to have a wonderful disposition. She sure fooled me. If she had been what I thought her, she wouldn't have fallen for me. At times I wonder if it was money — not the man."

"They went to sea in a sieve they did," the song surged to the top of her mind.

"I won't listen to criticism of my mother."

"You won't have to. I'm through with that. I've had a lot on my mind. I'm worried. For the first time in my life I've taken stuff to make me sleep. If I could get Kitty to the ranch for even a few months, I'd get my grip again, and it would do her a world of good. You hate me, but help me for her sake, will you?"

"No. I won't touch her life or yours even with the tip of a finger, but, I don't hate you."

"Thank you for that much," he answered gruffly.

To break the emotionally charged silence she looked around the room.

"What beautiful books."

"All first editions," pride brightened his voice and eyes. "A rare set of Dickens is to be delivered tomorrow."

"I adore Dickens. I've read part of the *Christmas Carol* to the kiddies on my broadcast. I'd get a thrill as I tried to put across the meanness of old pinchpenny Scrooge and then his change of heart."

"Then you'll go all out for the edition coming. I'll let you know when I open the box. We'll make a ceremony of it. Thank you for what you haven't said." He opened the door. "Let's be friends, please, Wendy."

IX

She went up the stairs slowly, thinking that one never could tell, she had thought Josh Crandon was insensitive to literature and art and he was collecting rare editions, wondering what his problems were, by what he was worried. Could it be money? As she entered her room she became aware of the slip of paper gripped in her fingers and flew to the telephone.

"I've been sitting practically in the lap of the phone waiting," Van Tyler's voice answered her call. "What were you doing out so late alone?"

"Perhaps I wasn't alone." She could see the girl in green cardigan and tan jodhpurs smiling back at her in the mirror.

"Could be, we'll take that up later. How about dining and dancing at a nightspot with me?"

"This evening?"

"That's right."

"I can't. I would—"

"Hold everything before you turn me down. I know this seems like a last-minute invitation, but I've been out of town for a week. I've spent every second since my return an hour ago waiting to contact you."

"I was about to say, when so rudely interrupted, that I would love to go but Mother is entertaining distinguished guests at dinner, Steve Graham arrived, and—"

"So, that's where you've been. Out with him."

"You must be psychic. Steve is dining here. I'd love to have you join the party at seven, if you would care—"

"*Care!* Lady, you don't know the half. Black tieish, I assume? I'll be with you."

She phoned Propper that there would be another guest and was relieved at his cheery, "Very good, Miss."

Later, she shook her head at the looking-glass girl who wore coral-colored chiffon sprinkled with minute gold stars, a lustrous string of pearls and matching studs in her ears.

"Sister, you sure dawdled over dressing," she accused her reflection. "Couldn't decide which costume would make you a match for the devastating Clare, could you? Cheerio, gal, even if Van likes 'em blonde, Propper doesn't care for her type." Laughter highlighted the eyes of the girl in the mirror. "I take that as a subtle compliment to you and myself." The clock on the mantel struck the hour.

"My word, I'm late."

She caught up a bag fashioned of gold kid like her sandals and tried to slip a huge old-fashioned diamond dinner ring which had been her grandmother's on the third finger of her right hand. Ooooch! Too tight. The left hand? Better.

She flew down the stairs, stopped suddenly halfway as she heard Rolfe Sanborn's voice and his sister's high laugh.

Why didn't I tell Van Tyler they were coming to dinner? Why this curious presentiment that he may not care to meet them in Mother's house? Too late to do anything about it now.

Exuberance wiped out by the thought, she finished the descent of the stairs slowly.

A muted radioed voice was singing, "Listen, Love Is Calling" as a few minutes later she and Van Tyler stood near the gold-leaf-paneled portable bar behind which Joshua Crandon presided. She saw Steve enter the front drawing room.

"Who's the Johnny-come-lately your

mother appears so tearfully glad to welcome?" Van inquired.

"Steve Graham. He was our neighbor for years, almost like a son of our house."

"I didn't know a man's hair could be so blond, so smooth." He brushed his left hand over his dark head as if to press down the one deep wave. "The boy from South America? Right? I caught the shimmer of star dust in your eyes when he appeared."

"Quote, I like 'em blonde, unquote."

"I'm glad you remembered what I said if it is hopelessly old hat. I'm sold on brunettes now. We'll file that under unfinished business for the present. I've been in my home state for a week."

"Was it a successful trip?"

"One hundred per cent. I returned firmly convinced I had found the solution that will straighten out a few misunderstandings with the leaders of my party. I wanted my position on certain issues completely understood."

"Was your opponent Mr. Ruggles the reason you had to do some straightening out?"

"Russ? Certainly not. Where'd you get that idea?"

"I feared he might have used my phony marriage story against you."

"So what? Suppose he had repeated it?

Suppose it were true that you and I had been secretly married? What's scandalous about that? Sounds out of this world to me."

It isn't so much what he said as the way he said it that makes my face burn and sends my heart to my throat, she thought. Why do I keep forgetting that remarks lightly thrown in are part of a gilt-edged bachelor's technique, especially a Washington bachelor? My mind has gone blank, I can't think of anything to say.

"Has Cardella made a move to see you since I've been away?"

His question broke into what had seemed a desert waste of silence in which there was not even the footprint of an idea.

"No, I have neither seen nor heard from him, which fact gives me the creepy feeling that he is lying low, making ready to spring."

"That's a cheery thought. If he writes to you or tries to see you, get in touch with me instantly."

"Where?"

"I'll give you three numbers — the House Office Building, my apartment, and Rolfe Sanborn's office, he would know—"

"Van, dearie, you're taking me in to dinner." Clare Sanborn, with an elaborate high hairdo, in a frock of tissue that shimmered like the scales of goldfish, slipped her hand

under his arm and gazed up at him ador-
ingly.

No wonder the femme is sure of her appeal, Wendy decided. Who wouldn't be with
her beauty, breathtaking frock and that sensational flat necklace of uncut emeralds?
Long earrings must be in again, hers dangle
to her shoulder.

"Clare, if you call me 'dearie' once more,
our friendship is done, finished," Van
protested lightly and firmly released his
arm. She wrinkled her nose at him.

"I'm still loving him after years of expo-
sure to his brutal indifference, Miss Adair."
Her green eyes narrowed in competitive
challenge, contradicted the amused asser-
tion.

"That sounds as if you were staking a
claim, Mrs. Sanborn."

"I am. Glad you recognize it. Come over
to the portrait above the mantel, Van. The
artist who painted Mrs. Crandon wants to
paint me. I would like your opinion of his
work."

If he is as furious as he looks why doesn't
he finish that friendship as he threatened?

"Been trying at intervals all day to contact
you on the phone, Miss Adair." Rolfe
Sanborn's voice broke her train of indignant
thought.

"What have I been doing?" she demanded in mock fright. "I'm shaking with terror. Propper told me you were something big in Intelligence during the war."

"I'm no longer connected with Intelligence, I'll clear that point with your mother's butler." He was palpably annoyed. He twisted the cocktail glass in his right hand and frowned at a prune wrapped in crisp bacon impaled on a wooden toothpick in his left.

"Why did I take these, I hate the stuff." He laid them on top of the bar behind him from which the host had departed. "That's better. I dislike having my hands full when at a party, perhaps I talk with my fingers, I wouldn't know. You haven't done anything yet, Miss Adair, but I'm hoping to interest you in a job."

"It won't take much persuasion. I'm accustomed to being useful and after but a week of it, I'm fed up with a round of debutante and embassy teas, cards and cocktails which I don't drink."

"Something tells me I've appeared at the psychical moment to sell you on my plan. I hear you had a radio program down yonder which was a knockout."

"You mean my 'Let's Sing for Our Supper' broadcast? Fans from six to sixty adored it and — if I say it who shouldn't — me." She finished her sentence with a laughing upward glance.

"Shucks, your eyes talk. I suppose you've heard that one before. To return to the program, I'm interested in a studio here. There is a vacant half hour at five-thirty one afternoon a week. Would you care to audition for it? It would be a formality, that's all. We know you're good. How much were you paid in S.A.?"

She told him.

"I'd be glad to do it for nothing just to have something really interesting and useful to do. I'm taking in all the time. I'd like to give out to others."

"Never offer to work without pay, your program won't be prized nearly so much. Charity is one thing, business is another. This is business. We will pay what you've been getting. If 'Let's Sing for Our Supper' goes over big we may land a sponsor, then you'll get more. We may televise you. Report at five tomorrow."

"Yes, sir. Your maybes fly so fast they take my breath. Are all Northwesterners quick thinkers?"

"What others do you know?"

"Mr. Tyler."

"Van? He's a ball of fire. When I lost him

121

— that's another story. I'll tell him to bring you to the studio tomorrow."

"Can't I find it myself? Is it necessary for me to be personally conducted?"

"What's the matter? Don't you like Van?"

"Certainly I like him, but I don't like being considered so brainless that I can't find my way alone after dark."

"No question of your intelligence involved. Your mother is looking at me, she has talking eyes, also. In that pinkish net over silver isn't it, she looks almost as young as her daughter. I'll be d — Ahem, how did Zaidee Latour manage to crash this party? Always wears red, doesn't she? Pardon my surprise, Miss Adair, I'm just a Western roughneck without manners."

"You are not as surprised as I was when she entered the drawing room. Propper told me Madame Latour was coming, but the name meant nothing in my life. She and I flew side by side from South America, but I didn't know her name. She is so dark and in spite of being slender so regal I imagined she was a Spanish grandee."

"There is a whisper that she is, though she claims she's French. She has lived in Washington off and on for several years. Don't forget our date. *Promptly* — and promptly means at five and not one minute after."

He was gone before she could tell him that having worked in a broadcasting studio for a year she knew that five o'clock meant five o'clock and not one minute after.

"How come the daughter of the house is standing deserted and alone?" Steve Graham inquired gayly.

"Thanks for reminding the daughter of the house that instead of standing here she should be making herself charming to the guests."

"You may concentrate on this guest at present. I'm taking you in to dinner. We'd better step on it. Your mother has led the way with that man Sanborn."

"Wonderful to be with you, Steve. I'm all excited about it."

"Like crazy you are. Quite an establishment the late Mrs. Adair carries on here. I can't see the Doc in it."

"Steve, please don't mention Father. I'm trying desperately to forget, to be a sport, to take a modern view, but—"

"Don't cry, lovely, don't cry." He laid his arm across her shoulders. "I'm sorry, but I get so mad when I think of him alone — Here, let's mop those sensational wet lashes—"

Darn, why at the moment Steve dabbed at my eyes did Van Tyler have to look back at us, she thought furiously.

"*Steve*, put that handkerchief in your pocket, it's big as a sheet. I've no intention of crying."

"Don't get mad about it. When your voice laid down and died, I thought—"

"I'm not mad, Stevie, I'm not, but, I'm keyed emotionally to the snapping point. Give me time, I'll get adjusted, now that I have a job in sight."

"What kind of a job, not getting married, are you?"

"Me, married, with the family smash as a horrible example? Not a chance. Intend to be a career woman, earn a spectacular income, live alone and like it. Come on, the others have gone in while I've been sobbing out my troubles on your shoulder."

"What's my shoulder good for unless as a wailing wall for you, lovely? It was made for it. Any place to cache this? That brought out the smile."

She eagerly seized the fat letter, doubled it and tucked it into her gold bag.

"Thanks a million, Steve. I can't wait to read it. Come on, or Mother will send Propper scouting for us. You love to eat, you are about to fall and fall heavily for her cook,

Chef to her. You never tasted anything so luscious as his breasts of chicken *en supreme,* with big fat mushrooms."

"That-a-girl. The lift is back in your voice. Breasts of chicken *en supreme* with big fat mushrooms! Lead me to 'em!"

X

After dinner she snuggled deeper into a high-backed chair before the fire in the cypress-paneled book-shelved library fragrant with the spicy scent of white carnations in a silver bowl on top of the grand piano. Voices, laughter and the click of cards came through the doorway which opened into the back drawing room. She reread the closing lines of her father's letter.

If your mother is difficult, Wendy, remember that even three years isn't time enough for a woman who grew up with ideals of honor and justice to make peace with her conscience for having pulled up those same ideals by the roots, because she wanted more "money and real living." If she *loves* the man I have firm faith that eventually she will be the grand person I saw in her when we married.

She smiled as she read:

You still hold the record for shooting in our Clay Pigeon Club. Much as they admire and miss you, the members are pretty sore that a girl beat them.

She leaned her head against the high back of the chair, watched the low red and yellow and green flames lick the logs and thought of her life in South America.

The Clay Pigeon Club was fun. I wonder if there is anything like it here I could join to keep in practice? How did Father know that Mother is more difficult? I didn't mention her in my letter, even if I had he wouldn't have received it yet. Difficult, he doesn't know the half that "good old Josh" takes. My heart still smarts from her swift, *sotto voce* jabs when I refused to join the game tonight. "You're just like your Grandmother Adair," was the bitter conclusion. I never have played cards for money, why begin here? I've made a certain plan for living, why not stick to it?

The sound of one of the long windows opening broke into her troubled thoughts. Someone coming in from the terrace. I won't stir, it may be Ruggles arriving late. I hate him.

"How the dickens did you get into this house, Zaidee?"

Not Ruggles speaking. It was Joshua Crandon.

"Your wife invited me. When I met her at an embassy tea and told her I flew from South America with her charming daughter, Wendy Adair — I didn't tell her I had been alerted that the girl was traveling as Mrs. John Smith — she insisted that I must dine here. I won't say I didn't engineer the invitation. I confess I was surprised it came so easily. Your Kitty is reputed to be choosy socially. You won't answer my phone calls or my letters, Josh. I had to see you to ask you once more to come back, to help me now."

"I told you six years ago I was through, that stands."

"I can make trouble—"

"Okay, you can make trouble — I'm still through. We'll join the game now."

Wendy heard the two hailed by the card players and drew the first long breath she had drawn since she had recognized Crandon's voice.

Thank goodness they didn't see me, she told herself. I would have made my presence known had they settled down to talk. Joshua Crandon has been "through" with the exotic Zaidee six years, that means before he married Mother. Did their previous companionship account for Rolfe Sanborn's surprise at the woman's presence in this house? Her thoughts picked up speed and a hint of suspicion.

Is she the worry Josh mentioned in the smoking room before dinner which he wants to escape? "I'm still through," he had answered her threat to make trouble. Is she trying to get him back? Good old Josh. Apparently he has a pattern for living which he doesn't intend to wreck. I'll like him even more after this.

Madame Latour said she had been alerted to the fact that I, Wendy Adair, was traveling under the name of Mrs. John Smith. *Alerted.* The word dumped a tray of ice cubes down my spine. Is she in league with Cardella? That's a shivery thought.

"I've come to remove the coffee tray, Miss Adair." Propper's deferential voice brought her to her feet. "Sorry if I startled you, Miss."

"I must have been half-asleep. It's too warm for that fire."

She crossed the room to the piano, ran her fingers over the keys and sang softly, *"Connais-tu le pays où fleurit l'oranger?"*

Song and music ceased as the butler, holding a laden silver tray, stopped beside the bench on which she was seated.

"'Know'st thou the land,' from *Mignon* is my favorite operatic melody," he approved. "I know them all. I was in the chorus at the Metropolitan one winter. Don't you like the game of Canasta, Miss Adair?"

"Very much, Propper, but the table was full. As you prophesied, Mr. and Mrs. Brown dropped in after dinner, eager to play. Being the daughter of the house, naturally, I gave my place to a guest."

"I understand, Miss. I don't approve of gambling myself."

Her eyes, wide with surprise, followed his dignified exit to the hall. After her logical explanation how could he know—

"Why so exclusive?"

Van Tyler stepped in from the veranda and closed a long window behind him. He leaned against the piano and regarded her with appraising eyes.

"A lovely girl in that luscious coral frock shouldn't cultivate a recluse complex. Why are you here alone?"

I wonder why some men fuss about wearing dinner clothes? I've never seen one to whom the outfit isn't becoming, she thought irrelevantly before she answered.

"I snuggled into the deep chair in front of the fire to read a long letter from my father."

"All okay with him, I hope." He had a gift for sympathy which was like wings buoying her troubled heart.

"Yes, too busy to feel lonely, he wrote. He did acknowledge that the clay-pigeon contingent missed me. I loved it, the shooting, I mean. Know of a place where I could practice?"

"Sure. I have a blind on the bay. The first cloudy, windy day — a chilly, penetrating drizzle would make conditions perfect, if you can take it — we'll corral Rolfe Sanborn and try for some ducks." A burst of laughter attracted his eyes to the open door. "Don't you like cards?"

"Love 'em. Just between you and me I'm a whizz at Canasta."

"Why didn't you join the game after you finished your letter?"

"No room at the table. Why aren't you there?"

"I've been waiting in the smoking room for long distance. The first editions the head of this house has collected are something to write home about, aren't they? I left word at the Club to contact me here if a call came. My state boss wanted me. It took an infernally long time to get a clear line. There are a few matters I wish to discuss with you. Come outside, it's warm as summer."

"I like it here. Why don't you join the card players?"

"I like it here. What did Graham say in the drawing room before dinner to make you cry?"

"I wasn't crying."

"No. Then why not look at me when you deny it instead of at your fingers? You don't have to watch the keys as you play. Did he put that whopping ring on your left hand? Cinnamon, canary and white diamonds. Sensational. I'm old-fashioned. I prefer a solitaire for an engagement ring. I saw him mopping your eyes with the outsize white handkerchief. I suggest that he carry a smaller one for an emotional crisis, it would be less conspicuous."

She ended the running accompaniment to his voice with a soft crash of chords.

"Suppose you stop being personal? I suggest that you return to your adoring Clare and ask her the question for which evidently she is waiting. My mistake, doubtless you asked it and presented your favorite solitaire when you two vanished to the veranda after dinner."

Ooch! How crude. No wonder your cheeks burn like fire, Wendy Adair, she scoffed at herself. Why disclose the fact that you saw them go? What's happening to me?

I was right when I told Steve I was emotionally keyed to the snapping point.

"Who's being personal now? It's okay. I asked for it." His voice was amused, not angry. "I assume you refer to Clare's absurd declaration of devotion. She has a flair for melodrama. Just to keep the record straight, she is not, never will be 'my Clare.' Before we leave this subject forever, I hope, I'd like you to understand that I am averse to forcefully correcting an error of statement by a woman in the drawing room of my hostess. The veranda had no other occupants, we fought it out there. Why were you riding on the river road so late?"

"You're a quick-change artist in conversation. One's mind has to be fast to follow. Give me a moment in which to think." Under the touch of her fingers the enchanting music of Debussy's *La Mer* flowed softly.

"Do you have to think up an explanation?"

"No, just think back. It wasn't late. The sun was sinking behind a hill when Steve caught up with me, the western sky was pink."

"Steve again. Did you meet anyone on the road before he joined you?"

"The only living person I saw was a man fishing. It was the second time I've seen him standing on practically the same spot. I recognized him tonight, it was our neighbor whom Mother introduced as Gib Brown. He must have another name."

"He has, Gibson Gary. You ought to know the name, he is an ace news photographer, did sensational work during the war. His wife grew up in our part of the country. I've known Lucie since she was a small girl. She's a good little sport. You'll like her. They have two corking kids."

"I have made friends with 'the adorables.' Their black cat, Sambo, is allergic to our poodle, Angeline, a feeling which is one hundred percent reciprocal. I love children. What luck, Mr. Sanborn?" she inquired as he entered from the card room.

"Rotten. How are the mighty fallen! I've rated myself an ace at Canasta, but the fair Zaidee took my shirt. I've said good night to your mother, Miss Adair. I like her parties, but I'm a workingman and those card addicts may whoop it up till dawn. I can't sit up all night, I leave that to playboys like Van. Five o'clock tomorrow, sharp, remember. Our representative to the Congress of the United States has been briefed as to his duties."

"But Mr. Sanborn, I don't need an escort to the studio."

"But you are to have one. We'll call that settled," Van Tyler assured. "I'll say good night to my hostess and go along with you, Rolfe. Thunder, is Clare leaving now?"

"Relax, she is not. A lad named Graham is taking her home later via a night spot. Coming, fella?"

"Sure." He caught Wendy's hands in a grip which made her wince. "Sorry, it was the ring which hurt, wasn't it? Better take it off, it hurts me where it is. Until five tomorrow. Good night — Mrs. Van."

XI

"Good night, Mrs. Van."

The words bobbed up in her mind as perched on the arm of a chair she kibitzed at the game. If the tensity of her mother's mouth was an indication the stakes were high. The Browns, the tall, rangy tight-lipped husband and the pretty auburn-haired pencil-slim wife, were playing cautiously, Josh Crandon recklessly, Madame Latour with exceeding care. Steve and the fascinating Clare had departed for a nightclub, Steve pretended he had gone all out for her. Perhaps it wasn't pretense, perhaps it was the real thing. I don't want him, she reminded herself, why feel so aggrieved?

She left the card players, too absorbed in the game to know whether or not she was present, and went to her room. Angeline on a floor cushion at the foot of the bed opened one eye and languidly wagged a short tail tipped with a fluffy pompon. Wendy dropped to her knees and hugged the fuzzy white head with its smart Dutch cut. The dog yawned.

"You needn't make it quite so evident that I bore you to tears, Angie. After all, sharing my room was your idea, not mine."

The poodle regarded her with eyes shiny as black jet buttons, widened her mouth in what looked to be an elfish grin before, with a drowsy whack of her tail, she relaxed into slumber. With a laugh Wendy rose from her knees.

"As a confidante, you're an utter loss, Angie. I had a lot of interesting things to tell you. You're missing the boat, gal."

Indifferent to the intriguing suggestion Angeline slept on.

In an American-Beauty satin housecoat over white crepe pajamas, in scuffs of silver threads, she wrote a long letter to her father, acknowledged invitations and busied herself in preparations for tomorrow, hoping to silence the inner voice repeating, "Good night, Mrs. Van." The panicky alibi she had proclaimed for the benefit of the man with mocking dark eyes who had stopped at the table in the dining car might seem a huge joke to Van Tyler, but it was a scorching memory to her.

Forget it, she told herself impatiently. Better look over your broadcast programs and select one for tomorrow.

The clock with the sparkling pendulum softly chimed three as she slipped the chosen papers into her briefcase and thought:

I'll practice in the library in the morning. Even if my eyelids do feel as if they were wired open I'd better get to bed or the audition tomorrow — it's today now — will be a flop.

She opened the door to the hall. Listened. Sepulchral quiet. The guests had departed. The balcony outside the long window tempted, "Come out. Fresh night air may make you sleepy."

The poodle opened heavy lids as she passed and soundlessly tapped the pomponed tail.

"I'll do my darndest not to disturb your slumber, Angie, my love," she whispered and gently nudged the white body with the toe of her silver scuff before she stepped to the balcony leaving the long window open behind her.

Arms folded on the intricate iron railing she drew a deep breath. Heavenly night, more like April than November. Warm. Fragrant. Still. Too late in the season for a cricket chirp. The only sound was the soft rustle of leaves that clung to the oaks which flanked the brick terraces. A gentle breeze scattered spicy scent from box hedges and frilled with white the dark water of the river beyond the garden. The golden glow of a cloud overhead betrayed the hiding place of the waning moon, and gave light enough to outline the bronze nymph holding in up-raised hands the shallow birdbath at the end of the path between the terraces. Stars, millions of them, seemed so close it would be easy to pluck a handful if she but raised an arm.

If not so near they had been equally brilliant when Steve and she had walked from the stable to the house and he had told of the smuggled jewels. "A hand with a long, keen knife," he had said.

Why pick on me as the smuggler? she wondered. There were twenty other passengers. It's as absurd as it would be to suspect orchidaceous Zaidee Latour.

Is that so absurd?

The question blazed in her mind with the clarity and suddenness of an electric sign turned on at high, accompanied by a voice declaring, "When I met her at an embassy tea and told her that I flew from South America with her charming daughter, Wendy Adair — I didn't tell her I had been alerted that the girl was traveling as Mrs. John Smith."

Alerted by whom? Had Zaidee Latour's unnecessarily loud call, "Good-bye and good luck, Mrs. John Smith," been a trick to identify her to the man who had tried to speak to her, whom she now knew as Señor Cardella?

That's a chilling thought. Could be that seizing my overnight case wasn't a mistake, could be she was sure I had the jewels. Are two conspiring against me? What shall I do? Tell Van Tyler what I suspect? Not yet.

She recalled the hint of suspicion in his voice when he had questioned her about the woman at the embassy reception, Rolfe Sanborn's surprise — not quite genuine, now that she thought of it — when he had seen her in Kitty Crandon's drawing room, added to that, the conversation she had overheard in the library not so many hours ago.

"You won't answer my phone calls or letters, Josh, I had to see you to beg you once more to come back, to help me now."

"I told you six years ago, Zaidee, I was through. That stands."

"I can make trouble—"

At the time she had thought it a threat of a personal nature, now she was not so sure. Wendy Adair, you've gone haywire, she told herself. Why would a man like Joshua Crandon, reputed to be "filthy rich," mix up with a jewel-snitching gang? And six years ago at that. He wouldn't, you're on the wrong network insofar as he is implicated.

Voices below, or was it the rustle of leaves? The question wiped all thought of Zaidee Latour from her mind. Cautiously she leaned over the balcony railing. Two dark shapes on the upper brick terrace. Two persons? Were they both from within the house or had one come out for a rendezvous? Whichever it was, it wasn't regular. Was this the explanation of her sense that something was wrong at Red Terraces? If she tried to find out what was going on would she be "nosy" or would she be protecting her mother?

"Angeline! *Angeline!* Your bark will raise the roof!" she protested under her breath. "I didn't know you had it in you."

That did it. A click. One of the long windows of the back drawing room closing. Had Propper gone in? Was he one half of this early morning rendezvous? I wouldn't put it past him. Blossom said he had been here but a month, she wondered how long he would put up with — she left the sentence unfinished, of course she meant Mother's bursts of rage. Has he a reason for staying at Red

Terraces? Is this my chance to solve a mystery?

Hands clasped over her heart for fear its loud beat might be heard, she dropped to her knees. Her hair was dark, the top of her head, which came a little above the railing, wouldn't be visible from below. She could see the lower terrace from between the intricate convolutions of the ironwork. Ears strained to the snapping point, she listened. No sound of voices.

A shadow cautiously stole down the path between the terraces. Paused beside the bronze nymph. Went on. Vanished among the trees. Had it been man or woman? It was too dark to be sure. Had something been left in the birdbath?

She would crouch here till everything was quiet, then steal down the path and take a look-see. If she waited until morning whatever was hidden, if anything were, might be, probably would be gone.

One! Two! Three! Four! softly chimed the clock in the room behind her. The coast should be clear now, clear or not, she must move, her knees pressing against the board floor of the balcony ached unbearably. Hand on the top of the rail, she pulled herself up. Ooch! her legs were stiff as sticks.

In her room she flexed muscles, her entire

body was cramped, so like her to be tense. You do everything hard, Wendy Adair, she reminded herself, and slipped on a dark topcoat. The white poodle watched her with unblinking eyes. She glanced at the drawer in which the automatic was locked. Shall I take it? Now you are crazy, she told herself.

"Go back! Go back! Angie," she whispered to the now wide-awake dog who followed her across the room.

She cautiously opened the door to the hall, closed it soundlessly behind her, barely missing the snuffling nose. She listened. No sound except a low, imploring whine and the creaks and cracks incident to an old house in the silence of night.

Step by cautious step she went down the stairs to the accompaniment of a quickened heartbeat and racing thoughts. Here I go. The Case of the Sleuthing Gal. What a title for E.S.G. Perhaps the celebrated writer of mystery yarns will collaborate with me. Swallow that chuckle, Wendy A. This escapade won't seem so funny if the shadow which disappeared into the house hears you.

The dimly lighted hall at last. Through the dark drawing room. Suppose the shadow which came in were lurking there? Chills. A sound in the wainscoting. More chills. Silly, it's a mouse. Across the veranda. Not even a drift of moonlight now. Fortune favors the brave. Down the path. Golly, I've shed a scuff. I'll pick it up on my way back. The birdbath at last. What's tucked in the nymph's hand? I have it. A sound. Someone walking cautiously? Won't do to run. Perhaps I won't be visible if I huddle against the bronze figure.

She dropped to her knees. Her thoughts pelted on.

The thing I found is a plastic envelope, visiting card size. It's a message, of course. To whom? It will have fingerprints — mine, too. That will help. She held the envelope gingerly between the tips of her fingers. When I get to my room — What's poking my back? A gun? Her heart zoomed to her throat and threatened to choke her with its anvil beat.

Has Cardella caught up with me? What do I do now? Another poke. Why doesn't he speak? If I yell he'll shoot. I'll *have* to turn. Here goes.

"Angie! You pest. How did you get out? Don't kiss me, slobberer. What will I do with you? If I take you along I might just as well go up the path caroling, Here I am."

But the poodle had ideas of her own. Ears pricked, she sniffed. With a "Whoof!" of triumph dashed soundlessly in the direction of the Browns' cottage and disappeared.

Now what? Wendy mentally answered her own thought. Angie is after the black cat, that's what. Josh will want to brain me if the dog is lost. The poodle is so valuable he'll have to pay plenty to get her back — if she is returned. Can't help it. Luckily she didn't follow the shadow that parked the message, if it is a message. He, she, or it, disappeared among the trees. Here's where I make my getaway and quick.

Across the lower terrace. So far so good. Better not crowd her luck by stopping to hunt for the scuff. She would steal out early and look for it.

She kicked off the other and thrust it into the pocket of her coat. Up the path barefooted. Across the veranda. Into the back drawing room.

Did something slip behind the Coromandel screen or was she seeing things? Imagination plus. Nothing moved.

Up the stairs on tiptoe. Into her room. Closing the door as if it were spun glass that might shatter at a touch. Holding the transparent envelope under the light. Words typed on the card within but too faint to be legible through the plastic.

She dropped it to the desk and lifted it carefully with a silver clip. Allah be praised, there was no flap. Could she pull out the card inside without touching the cover? The pesky thing kept slipping back. That did it.

With the card speared on the point of a silver letter opener she read the typed words:

FORD. 13–4. Or else.

FORD. 13–4. Or else. She puzzled over the meaning of the words and figures. Had Angeline's bark sent the person for whom the card was intended into the house before it had been given to him or her? Was it a summons to someone with a Ford car? Could be. Propper owned one. 13–4. A date? Today — it was today now — was the twelfth. Tomorrow would be the thirteenth. Did 4 mean four o'clock? Not too bad as far as it went, but, who was to meet whom and where? Was "Or else" a threat?

The east turned pink while she tried to work out an answer.

XII

In the early afternoon, curled in the chaise longue in her room, she pored over a guide to Washington. 13–4 — tomorrow at four o'clock — still seemed okay as a date, but there might be more in that word Ford than met the eye. It could mean a meeting place and not an automobile. She ran her finger down the page that gave a list of "Points of Interest."

"Lincoln Museum. Ford's Theater" — her heart hopped up into her throat —

It was here on April 14, 1865, the nation's greatest single tragedy occurred, the assassination of President Lincoln by John Wilkes Booth.

Ford 13–4. Eureka! Was that the answer? Had good old subconscious worked on the problem while her conscious mind had been busy with many things? Head back, eyes closed, she lived over the hours since she had watched the eastern sky turn pink, streak with pale green and fuse violet into blue. No sense in going to bed, she had decided, the scuff must be found before the sun came up. She had stolen out in the half-light to hunt for it. No dice. Had it been picked up? What would happen if she had been seen taking the envelope from the nymph's hand? That question gave her the chilly-willies. Blossom's face had registered surprise when she entered with a breakfast tray.

"What's happened to you, Miss Wendy? Your eyes look like burnt holes in a blanket, as if you'd been up all night."

She thought, Sister, you don't know the half. She said, "It may be the start of a cold."

Later she had practiced in the library in preparation for the audition, attended a lecture on the recent additions to the National Gallery, followed that with a Book and Author Luncheon, and here she was with a clue to the explanation of the message she had found this morning. How follow it up? The place must be a Mecca for tourists. If Lucie Brown—

"Come in," she answered a discreet knock at the door.

"I thought you might be worried about this, Miss Adair." It was Propper, Propper with her missing silver scuff in his hand.

"Where did you find it?" The question was a mistake. She shouldn't have admitted she knew it was gone.

"The poodle had it in her mouth when I let her in this morning. It was quite wet, I hope it isn't spoiled, Miss."

"Not a tragedy if it is. Thank you for returning it. Angeline must have picked it up from the floor when I let her out this morning."

"Could be so. She came home with a badly scratched bloody nose. Perhaps sometime she'll learn to keep away from the Browns' black cat, perhaps though she's the kind that won't learn from experience. There are such people." He paused on the threshold. A ray of sunshine highlighted his eagle beak. "It isn't safe for a young lady to be running round this place at midnight. Shall I close the door, Miss?"

"No." Her eyes followed him to the hall.

Another of his cryptic observations. Was the brief lecture on experience beamed at her? Was he the person who planted that envelope, or did he come back into the house?

She closed her eyes to visualize the

shadow. No use, it had been shapeless. It might have been—

"Wendy Adair, are you napping at this time in the afternoon?"

Her eyes flew open. Her mother, in a silver-gray satin frock with amethysts set in diamonds at ears and throat, an amethyst velvet beret with a glistening ornament on her charming head, was standing behind the avocado-green wing chair, arms crossed on top, achieving a ravishing color effect.

"I wasn't asleep. I — I closed my eyes the better to visualize last evening's grand party. Looked like an exciting game. Who won?"

"Madame Latour. Her gold kid bag bulged when she left. I don't care much for the woman. Those red costumes of hers are too harsh. Had Russ Ruggles been here she wouldn't have cleaned up. He's a wizard at cards."

"How come he wasn't here?"

"He wanted to bring a Señor somebody with whom he has been palling recently but Josh said 'No,' an explosive 'No.' I couldn't believe my ears, he never interferes with my guest list, but he hasn't been like himself, lately."

Joshua Crandon refusing to have Señor Cardella in his house. Could he know that the man had followed his stepdaughter?

Didn't his wife realize he was worried?

"Any idea why he did this time?"

"Not the slightest. Russ said that as he had invited the Señor to dine with him he couldn't come without him so that ended that. Josh is beginning to have queer ideas. If you can believe it, he wants to sublease this place — he didn't buy, though I urged it — and return to his ranch. Can you see me on a ranch in New Mexico? It's abominably selfish of him to suggest it."

"He has lived the way you like for three years. The change would do you good, it wouldn't hurt you to relax. Your hands haven't been quiet a minute. Your fingers have been rearranging the exquisite old lace frills at your wrists or twisting those sensational diamond rings."

She was arguing Josh Crandon's case after she had told him yesterday that she wouldn't touch her mother's life or his with the tip of a finger, she reminded herself.

"Nonsense, I don't need a change. I love my life as is."

"Why not give him a break? Let him love his way of life for a while. Don't you believe in reciprocity?"

"Not in this case. I shouldn't have brought up the subject. I might have known you wouldn't understand. Is that open letter

151

on the desk from your father?"

"Yes."

She folded the pages and returned them to the envelope. Head slightly tilted, Kitty Crandon critically regarded her mirrored reflection.

"Lucrece hit the bull's-eye when she designed this beret especially for me. It's perfect on my head. I'd like to read Jim's letter. You needn't stick it into your pocket as if you feared I might grab it. Did he send a message to me?"

Wendy stood up. Experience warned that a battle was indicated. She could fight better on her feet.

"Who's 'he'?"

"Your father, of course."

"No message."

"Didn't he even refer to me?"

"Mother, before I left South America I promised myself that I would write nothing about you and your life here to Father, and would not repeat the contents of his letters to you. Misunderstandings might arise if I did. I intend to keep that pledge."

"You have as many planks in your platform for living as a political party. It wouldn't wreck your code to admit that he inquired for me, would it? He still loves me, doesn't he?"

Unbelievable as it seemed, her voice quivered. Did she still love him?

"That's a question for him to answer."

"Perhaps sometime I'll ask him. You never can tell." Her brilliant lips curved in a tremulous smile. "Why are you still in that beige gabardine? Have you forgotten the tea for the senator's daughter at five?"

"At five I shall be auditioning for a broadcast."

"Wendy Adair, don't tell me you are thinking of putting on that 'Let's Sing for Our Supper' program here?"

"Cheerio, Mother, they may turn me down."

"I hope they do. I don't want you on the air. People will think Josh is stingy and won't let me give you things, that you are obliged to work. I'm sure Russ Ruggles wouldn't approve, and while we are on that subject, you are treating my husband's friend abominably. He says you won't accept his invitations. Why?"

"I haven't been here much over a week. You know, Mother, that I am slow at making friends."

"You weren't slow in becoming pals with Vance Tyler."

"We met under unusual circumstances." Memory set a smile tugging at her lips.

"Don't fall in love with him. You heard Josh say he is a girl-resistant bachelor."

"Thanks for the warning. I'll keep my heart on leash. Going? Wait a minute, you've left your bag in the chair. What a beauty. Petit point with amethysts in the gold frame, real, too, I'll bet. You do yourself proud, Mrs. Crandon."

"Why not? I married Josh for money—"

"But how cagily you camouflaged your motives, Kitty."

Josh! Wendy's heart did a heels-over-head. White and stern, he leaned against the side of the doorway. Her mother had the decency to go red to her hair. Now what. She can't take back words once they are on the air.

Kitty Crandon laughed, drew her husband's head down within reach and kissed him on the mouth.

"You know better than to take that joke of mine seriously, honey. Wendy takes life so hard I can't resist trying to shock her. I married you because I was crazy about you. Didn't I give up a perfectly good husband, home and child—"

"The dramatic approach which I've heard many times before." His curt interruption sent another wave of red to his wife's face. He shook off the jeweled hand on his sleeve.

"Wendy, the case of books has come.

Propper'll be along to open it in about ten minutes."

"That will give me time to collect my hat and coat and check on the songs in my briefcase. I'm all excited about the Dickensiana opening."

"Come on, Kitty, the car is at the door with Angeline sitting up as if posed for a photographer on the front seat. Why do you take the dog?"

"She attracts attention, and in this teeming town one has to do something unusual to be noticed by the columnists. When you go out, Wendy, tell Propper he will be the only servant on duty. I've let the others have the afternoon off as we are dining out. You ought to appear at the senator's this afternoon, Josh—"

Kitty Crandon's voice diminished into a murmur as she and her husband went down the stairs. Wendy listened.

That's the front door closing, she's gone. Can she cajole and argue herself out of the spot in which "I married Josh for his money" landed her? Maybe. She can be mighty sweet and fascinating when the spirit moves. I won't have much time to devote to the books opening. Better put Father's letter where it can't be read.

She unlocked the one drawer in the desk

that had a key, in which she kept jewelry, canceled checks and account books, and slipped the letter under a band that held others.

All that and the automatic, too, she thought, and picked up the .25. Loaded to the hilt. Thanks be I didn't have to use it that terrifying night. Holding it brings back the blood-chilling horror of that ride. I can see the driver as he gave it to me, hear his low hoarse voice, "Shoot if anyone tries to stop us." Can see the streets with jostling crowds through which we raced, can hear the shouts, the shots, the screams.

There goes the clock. Gal, you'd better stop what a psychiatrist would call your "life habit of introspective imaginings," and get ready to leave the minute Van—

"Help! *Help!*"

What's happened? Who's yelling? Sounds like Prop —

Gripping the automatic she had been about to replace in the drawer she hurtled down the stairs.

XIII

Another yell. Josh, this time. Has something awful happened to Mother?

Her feet felt as if dragging ball and chain as she ran through the hall. On the threshold of the smoking room she looked from white-faced Propper braced against book-shelves to her mother's husband gripping the mantel above the fireplace as if his hold on that alone kept him on his feet.

"What happened? What *happened?*" she demanded hoarsely.

"They're out to g-get me, Wendy. L-look—" Crandon' s mouth in his gray face wobbled out of control. Her eyes followed his shaking finger pointing at a large wooden box on the broad, flat desk. Her mind spun like a top, her heart stopped, for one frantic second she feared she would be sick.

"It's — it's — a nightmare. It can't be real.

It is. It's coming out. What's this thing I'm clutch—"

She leveled the automatic. Fired. One. Two. Three.

That did it. Was that sound of ringing in her head? Two thuds. What fell? Josh! Propper flat on the floor. Horrors! Had she hit them? Glass crashing. Was her brain go—

"Wendy! Wendy, darling! What happened?" Van Tyler's arms were around her. "What are you doing with that gun? Give it to me. My God! Did you shoot those two men on the floor?"

"I — I — d-don't think so."

She shook her head pressed against his shoulder. He snapped the safety on the automatic and slipped it into the pocket of his dark blue coat.

"Don't you *know?* Why did you shoot, Wendy?"

In the safe haven of his arms she pointed to the two prostrate figures.

"I didn't s-shoot them. They fainted. Two he-men. Out c-cold."

"Wendy! Wendy! *Wendy!*"

He shook her gently.

"Stop laughing, darling, stop."

"I — can't. It's s-so funny. I heard them yell. I — I r-ran down — and then I saw —

L-look in the b—" A shudder finished the sentence.

"Sit down." Arm tight about her shoulders he seated her on the red leather-covered sofa. "Stay here until I tell you to move." Her eyes followed him to the desk, watched as he looked down.

"Is — is it d-dead?"

He nodded.

"Van! Van, you're ghastly. D-don't you dare f-faint. I c-can't take any more."

"You won't have to." He swallowed hard. "How the devil did this thing get here, Propper?" he demanded of the man sitting on the floor pressing a shaking right hand to the back of his head.

"I — I don't know, sir." The butler looked up with glazed eyes. "Mr. Crandon thought it was a box of books he expected. I opened it — it had been setting in this warm room quite a while, and then — and then that awful thing—" A shudder finished the sentence. "Mr. Crandon seemed to think it was a reprisal, that an enemy of his had sent it. If you'll give me a hand up — Thank you, sir." On his feet, he pulled down the sleeve of his plum-colored coat to cover an unobtrusive wristwatch, looked down at his employer prone on the hearthrug.

"His eyelids are moving, he's coming to,

sir. I'll get the brandy." The keys he drew from his pocket shook like castanets in action.

"Give me those. Take it easy. You're too groggy to walk, Propper. Which key? Is the brandy in the sideboard?"

"I know where it is. I'll go." Wendy took the tinkling bunch from the butler's shaking fingers. She ran to the door, keeping her eyes averted from the desk as she passed. Van Tyler caught up with her in the dining room.

"You're still shivering, Wendy. Give me the keys. Go back and sit down."

"In the room with that horrible thing? Not a chance. You'd better get the brandy. This is the key. It's the r-right door of the buffet. Be quick — I feel funny. I—"

He caught her before she fell, seated her in a chair and bent her head to her knees, knelt beside her till the color stole back to her face.

"You'll be all right in a minute. You didn't really faint. Sit up. Rest your head against the wall. Keep quiet while I take the brandy to Crandon. Something tells me that Propper will appreciate a wee nippy."

The lightness of his voice helped restore her to normalcy. Eyes closed she waited for what seemed hours for the prickle of returning circulation to pass.

I almost fainted, she admitted to herself. The first time in my life and I've seen some horrible sights — nothing like that, though. How did the box get here. Was Josh right? Is someone "out to get him"? Is that the real reason for his worry, his urge to leave Washington?

"Drink this." Van Tyler held a glass to her lips. "Stop shaking your head. Drink it."

"I'm all right now. I don't need it."

"Do as I say. *Quick.*"

She looked up at his colorless face, met his intense eyes and sipped.

"Ooch! That burned its way down. Lucky you're here. How did you happen to arrive at just the right moment?"

"Take another swallow and I'll tell you. That brings the color to your face."

"We ought to take care of those men in the smoking room. What will we *do* with that — that—"

"If you shudder again I'll carry you upstairs to your room."

"The Big Stick." Light and laughter returned to her eyes. "You ought to be on a throne somewhere. Why waste such dictatorial genius in Congress?"

"Wendy is herself again. Watch your step. No back-sliding. I meant what I said. How did I happen to arrive at just the right moment? Have you forgotten I was due to take you to the studio? As I reached the front door I heard a shot. No one answered my furious ring. After the third shot I smashed a window. I suffered the tortures of the damned getting to that room. There's the bell. Now who wants to get in?"

"It's the back door. The maids are out. Will you open it?" She followed him clutching a corner of his coat.

A red-haired ruddy-faced teamster with a heavy box on his shoulder grinned apologetically.

"I'm Casey. Sorry to trouble you, folks. I left the wrong box here. I'll leave this and take the other that's goin' to the zoo. Some kind of new feed they're tryin' out, I understand."

"This way."

The teamster followed Van Tyler. Wendy followed the teamster to the smoking room where Propper, slumped in a chair, was clutching his head. Joshua Crandon, haggard lines etched deep between his mouth and nose, eyes closed, huddled in a corner of the red leather sofa. Van pointed to the desk.

"There's your feed, Casey."

"Cripes, you've opened it, now I'll have to nail it up again." He set down the heavy case he carried. Flexed his shoulder. Picked up the cover which had been pried off. Looked into the box. For an instant he stood as if petrified. One terrified yell and he slumped to the floor.

"Another red man bites the dust," Wendy declaimed theatrically and went off into a gale of laughter that was fifty percent sobs. Van caught her in his arms.

"I told you to stop that. We'll see if this will do the trick." He pressed his mouth on hers and held it there until she wrenched her face free and pressed it against his sleeve.

"Don't! I *hate* to be kissed."

"Then stop laughing or you'll be kissed again. Thunder, there's the phone. Take care of that guy on the floor, Propper. I'll answer in the hall. Come on, Wendy." He caught her hand.

"I'll come, but you needn't drag me as if I were a prisoner destined for the lockup."

"I want you where I can see you." In the spacious closet he indicated the one chair. "Sit there." He answered a demanding ring.

"Crandon residence — Good lord, it's you, Rolfe — Where are we? — I'm not quite sure myself, but I think we're at Red Terraces — Who, *me* stop kidding? Take it from me — It's darned lucky I can. The audition? Boy, we'd forgotten. It's Rolfe,

Wendy. Wants to know why we're not at the studio."

"Tell him — that — that it's the Case of Casey the Careless Teamster — " She swallowed an hysterical giggle as she met his warning eyes. "Ask him if we can come later?"

He spoke into the receiver.

"Can you give us time later? Uh, uh — Sure, we'll be there, come hell or high water. Okay. Eight sharp." He cradled the phone.

"The studio will be free for an audition at eight. We'll go somewhere for dinner and make it on the minute."

"Should we leave Josh and Propper and — shouldn't we take care of—"

"Go to your room, please, and stay until I call you." He followed her to the foot of the stairs. "Can you get up alone?"

"Of course, don't be foolish. I think I should stay and help—" she hesitated on the second stair.

"Are you going under your own power or will I have to carry you?"

"I'm going, but—" she made a little defiant face at him. "Don't rock the boat, lady." His foot was on the step below hers. "Better go while the going's good."

She went swiftly, breathlessly, remembering his tender, husky, "Wendy, Wendy,

164

Wendy," feeling the pressure of his mouth on hers, trying to erase the memory of his intense gray eyes as they warned her, reminding herself that "rock-ribbed, girl-resistant" bachelors had a perfected technique. At the top of the stairs she turned. He was looking up. She quickly closed her door behind her.

Autocrat. He didn't even ask if she cared to go to dinner. Wise man. He knew she felt as if she must get out of this house. How long would it take to clean up that mess in the smoking room? She'd take a chance that she would have time to dress for dinner. After which she would phone Lucie and ask her to go to Ford's Theater tomorrow.

Later, in a black frock with glistening white top, a white felt sailor with a matching cockade of ostrich tips, pearls at ears and throat, she opened her door in answer to a knock. The look in Van Tyler's eyes was the response she liked to see when she had gone all out to make herself attractive, but he said only, as he held out the automatic:

"Put away this gun. I've taken out the shells. Here they are." From the threshold he watched as she unlocked the desk drawer.

"Ready? Wear these." As she took the cellophane box he added, "Brought them for you to wear at the audition for luck. When I heard those shots I dropped the box like a hot cake." He watched as before the long mirror she pinned on the two exquisite pink camellias.

"Add the last perfect touch, don't they? Give me your coat." He settled the white broadtail jacket over her shoulders with lingering care.

"Come on. Let's go."

There were a few diners, enchanting music, soft rosy lighting, beautiful giant pink chrysanthemums in tall silver vases in the restaurant where an attentive maître d'café seated them.

"Glad to see you back, Monsieur Tyler. Thought you might have left us for the more plushy night spots."

"I've been away. I ordered by phone. See that the dinner moves right along, will you, Jean. We have a date."

"Certainly. Service always moves right along, monsieur." With an indignant sniff Jean hurried to greet newly arrived patrons.

"Something tells me I've hurt his feelings. He was an Irish busboy here in Father's day, now he's gone French. That's a snazzy costume you're wearing — Mrs. — Miss Adair." His laughing correction brought color to her face.

"Invitation to Learning. The frock is the 'afternoon-and-on' type, and sailors are in

166

again. I strive to please."

"You're skating on thin ice when you look up under those sensational lashes, lady. You please, all right. At the moment you are this night spot's Exhibit A."

"Pin the medal on the camellias."

"That's a matter of opinion. I brought you here where there is music but no floor show that we might talk without being distracted. Think you are steady enough to give me a blow-by-blow account of the late disturbance at Red Terraces?"

She told him, told him to the muted accompaniment of strings and harp, that Josh Crandon had invited her to see the opening of the choice Dickensiana, of pelting downstairs with the automatic in her hand when she heard his yell.

"How come you had the gun?"

"I was locking up Father's letter. The .25 was in the same drawer. I had picked it up with the intention of unloading it, but I sat holding the thing, living over the events of the night it was given to me. When I heard the first yell I instinctively gripped it and ran."

"Luckily. That was a nasty customer you shot. Propper got the impression that Crandon thought the contents of the box had been sent by an enemy. Did you hear 'good old Josh' say anything like that?"

"When I dashed into the room he muttered, 'They're out to g-get me, Wendy.'"

She resisted the temptation to tell him of her early morning trip down the terraced path and her find. No. She would try out her hunch that the 13–4 was a date and the rendezvous Ford's Theater. After that she might have a fact, not just a suspicion to confide.

"If Crandon thinks he has enemies he needs protection."

"But the teamster proved that the box was left by mistake, it couldn't have been sent by an enemy."

"That's right, but it doesn't explain your stepfather's suspicion that it was. There's never smoke without some fire."

As they talked broiled grapefruit was succeeded by succulent roast duckling and olive sauce accompanied by potato puffs frothy as whipped cream; green peas of melting delicacy, a delectable salad of white grapes and slivers of fresh pineapple in nests of pale green lettuce; sultana roll entirely surrounded by luscious claret syrup. They had reached the demitasse and mints stage when Wendy said thoughtfully:

"Josh told me something yesterday just before I phoned you, which, tied up with what he stammered this afternoon, has set me wondering. He didn't tell me in confidence. If I pass it on it may help clarify the mystery, and I'm beginning to be creepingly convinced there is a mystery, besides the one in which I appear to be involved."

She told of Joshua Crandon's appeal to her to help persuade his wife to leave Washington, his admission that he was worried, was taking stuff to make him sleep; repeated the conversation she had overheard unintentionally in the library between him and Zaidee Latour; told of his refusal to allow Señor Cardella to be invited to dinner.

"On top of that I've been wondering why your political enemy, Russ Ruggles, is playing round with the South American who, I am sure, still is shadowing me."

"You told me you hadn't seen the guy since that night at the embassy."

"I *haven't.* I just feel it. Must be that extrasensory perception with which, you told me, porters are especially endowed. You're not listening to me."

"I am. I can repeat every word. Glad you remember something I said on the train. My mind was doubling on the job. I was thinking as I listened."

"Might I inquire what you were thinking to cut two sharp lines between your eyes?"

"'God moves in a mysterious way His

wonders to perform.' William Cowper thought up that one, in case you're interested." He rose and held her white coat. One arm in a sleeve she looked up at him.

"Just how does that quotation apply to what I have been telling you?"

"I give you 'the Case of Casey the Careless Teamster.' Come on. Let's go or we'll be late for the audition."

XIV

The Owl and the Pussy-Cat went to
  sea
In a beautiful pea-green boat:
They took some honey, and plenty of
  money
  Wrapped up in a five-pound note.
The Owl looked up to the stars above,
  And sang to a light guitar,
"O lovely Pussy, O Pussy, my love,
  What a beautiful Pussy you are."

The charming voice with a lilt in the high
notes came from the loud-speaker on the
wall of the foyer in the broadcasting station
where Van Tyler was sitting. His eyes stung.
The words conjured the memory of the
hours he and his elder brother had listened
to his mother's tender voice reading Edward
Lear's nonsense verses after they had been
tucked into their beds. Both gone now, he

171

alone of the family to carry on. God help him to do it credit.

> You are,
> You are,
> What a beautiful Pussy you are.

It was the close of the "Let's Sing for Our Supper" audition. It couldn't help being a smash hit. Wendy had played piano accompaniments of her own composing, her pronunciation was as cultured as her diction was clear. Kids would love it and parents ought to offer a little prayer of thanksgiving for the program.

The place was as busy as Union Station. Girls and men, their hands full of papers, hurried past as if life depended on their presence in a certain spot at a certain moment — probably their jobs did. Phones rang. Voices answered. A harried girl announcer demanded chairs for the audience waiting admittance to her studio, an equally harried boy answered, "There ain't no more."

He thought of Wendy, of his terror when he had heard the shots at Red Terraces, of his fear that she was in peril. His love for her so possessed him it seemed incredible that she didn't feel it, didn't respond to—

"Panic invaded the historic home of a well-known sportsman just outside the city this afternoon."

The comments of a popular local reporter coming through the loud-speaker above his head broke into his thoughts.

"A box, supposed to contain a rare set of Dickens, was opened and a contribution ticketed for the zoo — a Golden Cobra — reared its ugly head and spread its hoops. While the two men present passed out in a dead faint, the daughter of the house shot the creature with her own automatic. Page the guy who first dubbed woman the weaker sex. The teamster who mixed the babies up after one look joined the masculine contingent on the floor. At last account the three gallant males were doing as well as could be expected while the charming markswoman was seen gaily dining with a prominent congressman.

"The boys on Capitol Hill agree that the senator talked of to head one of the more important committees now in the spotlight is okay for the job, that he is dependable, liberal on the questions where liberalism is needed, and is a square dealer. Note the word square, not new."

The voice went on but Van no longer listened. His thoughts reverted to the commentator's first announcement. What was back of Josh Crandon's suspicion that the box with its terrifying occupant had been sent to him as a reprisal? Of whom, of what was he afraid? Of Zaidee Latour and her threat of "trouble"? Why had he forbidden his wife to invite Cardella to dinner? Had he known the smooth Señor before his arrival in Washington days ago? The commentator had broadcast the fact that Wendy owned an automatic. Had it been registered with the police as required by law?

"How was it?"

The eager question brought him to his feet.

"Miss Adair, you were a smash hit. You sang as if you were singing to very special children you love."

"I was. Believe it or not, as I sang I saw the Browns' two little blonde girls, Sandra and Eve, part of the time I visualized a small girl-and-boy combination, Linda and Denny, neighbors at home, I wasn't on the air, I pretended I was with them, it helped me get my music across. I love children."

"I'm completely sold on kids myself. Did you land the job?"

"Sure, she landed it," Rolfe Sanborn answered the question as he entered. "She has signed on the dotted line. I waited for the report of our music critic, Miss Adair. He's all for the program, he says, quote, 'Seldom are taste and talent so perfectly blended.'"

"Thanks a million, Mr. Sanborn."

"Don't thank me, you earned the citation. What about the yarn that came over the air? The home of a well-known sportsman, et cetera. Sounded like good old Josh. Are you the charming markswoman, Miss Adair?"

"Modesty forbids me to agree to 'charming,' but, I did shoot—" her voice caught in her throat.

"I'll give you the round-by-round account later, Rolfe," Van Tyler agreed. "I arrived in time to revive the butler—"

"The *butler?* Do you mean that Propper, *Propper,* fainted at sight of—" Surprise cut off Sanborn's voice.

"Let's forget it." Van held the white jacket. "Hop into this and we'll take in a movie, Wendy."

"I'd love the movie, but, I must go home and make sure that Josh has recovered from his scare."

"He isn't there. I phoned Red Terraces before the audition. Propper reported, 'Mr. and Mrs. Crandon are dining with friends.' Period."

"Was Propper back on the beam, fella?"

"Except that his voice had the shakes, he appeared to be. Rolfe, the first cloudy, blustery day, you and I are to take Miss Adair duck hunting."

"It's a date. Tomorrow I'll begin to practice. Keeping up with a crack and charming markswoman will take some doing. Used to a 16-gauge, Miss Adair?"

"No, but I'll try anything once."

"That's the spirit of '76. Remember, one week from today at five-thirty you go on the air. Tell good old Josh, nix on opening a box of books on that day."

"I'll tell him, but a mistake like that wouldn't occur once in a thousand years, if ever again. Thanks for liking my program, Mr. Sanborn. Good night."

Apparently the picture was entertaining, Van heard Wendy's soft laugh, but his thoughts were on Crandon's terrified, "They're out to get me!" Shock could have unsettled his mind for an instant, no, that wasn't the explanation, for he had expressed the same fear twice, first to Propper, then to Wendy. He reviewed his acquaintance with the man. At all times he had seemed fearless and unafraid — fearless? Wait a minute, come to think of it, he never would express an opinion about congressional decisions or the men who made them, would laugh, smack his lips and parry, "Don't ask me. I ain't no politician." Had he reason for not wanting criticism traced back to him? The lights flashed on with the puzzle still unsolved.

"Let's go where there's music and have a snack," he suggested as they left the theater.

"Don't you ever want to go home?"

"Home is where the heart is. I'm at home this minute." She laughed.

"As I remarked earlier in our acquaintance, you are a quick thinker. If you feel snack-minded, come back to Red Terraces, we can tune in on the radio for soft music while we forage for eats."

"The ayes have it. The car is parked two blocks from here. Think you'd better walk that distance? Quite a wind blowing."

"My word, don't treat me as if I were just up from a fit of sickness. This aged woman can manage to toddle that far, Mister."

"No slur upon your youth and beauty intended, Mrs. Van."

"Please, *please* stop reminding me of my crazy outburst on the train."

"Nothing crazy about it. I like it. To return to the aged woman angle, you've had a tough experience. I want to make your life's walk as easy as possible al—"

Lucky you swallowed that always. You're

going too fast. Better watch your step. Walk and not run or you'll lose her, he warned himself.

They had walked a block in a street where branches of mammoth trees waving against golden pools of lights cast fantastic shadows, when she whispered:

"Listen! Someone is following us."

"Nonsense, that secret mission you put through for the Department of State has left you with a scare hangover."

He caught her hand and drew it under his left arm. He had heard the measured tap, tap of feet behind them, had been tempted to turn, then had argued himself out of the suspicion that there was a furtive quality in the sound. It was not yet eleven o'clock. Naturally there would be other persons on the street.

"Maybe it is nonsense, but—" the sudden turn of her head finished the sentence. Her eyes were wide with consternation as they came back to his.

"No one in sight," she declared softly. "It couldn't have been my imagination playing tricks. You heard the footsteps, didn't you?"

"Yes, but why make a mystery of it? With this breeze blowing, whoever it was might have stepped behind a tree to light a cigarette."

Tap. Tap. Tap. The measured sound behind them began again.

"Hear it? It's weird."

He answered her shaky whisper with a nod and tightened his hold on her hand.

"I still think you are having an acute attack of heebie jeebies. There's my convertible about two minutes ahead, shining in the light from across the street."

"It looks safe as a church. Hurry."

As she stepped into the car he looked back. No one in sight. There had been footsteps. Who was putting on a disappearing act and why?

As the silver-gray convertible coupé slid smoothly from the parking place, Wendy settled back against the seat with a sigh of relief.

"Perhaps you were right, perhaps being suspicious of those footsteps was a case of nerves," she admitted, "but, so many strange things have hap—"

"Why did you break the word happened in half? Haven't you told all? Are you holding out on me?"

"No-o. I just seem to be living at a terribly fast, scary pace, that's all."

"That 'fast pace' reminds me, have you registered your automatic with the police?"

"No. Should I?"

"You should. When we get back to Red Terraces, better turn it over to me until you get a permit to keep it."

"I will, pronto. It would be the last straw to have a run-in with the police." She sank lower in the seat and pulled off the white hat.

"I love to feel my hair blow. I adore an open car, and so far what a winter this has been to use one, like spring with the thermometer at seventy degrees. Almost I can detect buds on the perennials in Lucie Brown's garden."

"Do you like Lucie Brown?"

"Very much. I helped her hang out the laundry this morning and we hopped aboard the friendship train. She's having a tough time at present. Husband out of a job and two adorable but superactive children. She didn't complain. Merely stated facts. I can see where I can help by baby-sitting and free her to get away from the house for a change of thought. She has promised to personally conduct me on a sightseeing tour. We — we are to do Ford's Theater tomorrow afternoon. I'm taking Mother's roadster. It's a beauty."

"How about a license? You've been in the U. S. a little over a week."

"You wouldn't be license-minded, would you? First it's a gun to be registered with the police, next a license to drive a car. Must be your legal training that inspires the checkups. The lawyer of Grandmother's estate renewed my driving license each year while I was out of this country. I never knew how soon I might return and need it. Now that is taken care of, to your satisfaction, I hope, have you ever been to the Lincoln Museum?"

"Not for years. It is interesting. The vibration in your voice indicates that you expect to find it breathlessly exciting."

"The breathlessness is just me, the way I take life. Aren't the stars gorgeous? They shine as if hand-burnished.

Sit, Jessica. Look how the floor of heaven
Is thick inlaid with patines of bright gold.

Forgive the lapse into Shakespeare. I'm a pushover for romance under the stars."

"I'll remember that. Pity I haven't my trusty light guitar to twang, but I'll do my best to back up the stars in their romantic appeal. I can sing:

O lovely Wendy, O Wendy my love,
What a beautiful Wendy you are.

Adapted from 'The Owl and the Pussy-Cat' for the occasion," he explained lightly.

"Why haven't I discovered before that you sing divinely? You should be on the radio, not I."

Judging from the coolness of her comment his burst into song had left her unmoved. He couldn't say the same for himself. The passionate fervor of his voice had startled him.

"Haven't sung before for years. Your reference to the stars touched off my voice, as it were, you and the immortal William."

"What do you know about stars? First class in astronomy rise. I've been chattering ever since we started to drown the uncanny echo of those—"

"What do I know about the stars? Not much," he interrupted in an attempt to switch her thoughts from the footsteps. "Let's see, I know that the tail of the Big Bear is the handle of the Dipper, which swings about the Pole clockwise throughout the night. That shred of information makes me realize what infinite fields of knowledge there are above us as yet unexplored, even by the scientists."

"And so many, many things below to be explained. It seems trivial to bring up the problems of one person among the billions on earth, but, in the studio I heard the commentator's reference to the late unpleasantness at Red Terraces, and at intervals since I've been wondering what was back of Joshua Crandon's explosion of fear."

"That question has been getting my almost undivided attention. Today I heard a broadcast by an officer of FBI, it was a warning to watch out for amateur volunteer investigators who offered to trail subversive suspects. He argued that a spot in the vanguard of volunteers in an amateur organization would be meat for a subversive individual. I'm telling you that in case you should feel it a patriotic duty to follow up the Josh Crandon angle. Your interest might be misunderstood. Don't do it. Which request—"

"Order is the word."

"I'm glad you recognize it as such, see that you obey. As I was about to say — which request brings us to Red Terraces."

"Thank heaven."

"I don't care for that deep breath of relief. Have you been so terribly bored?"

"You know I haven't been bored. You'll think I'm in a chronic state of fright when I tell you that I couldn't get the sound of those padding footsteps out of my mind except when you were singing. Your voice pulled up my heart by the roots. Here's the key. No sense calling Propper to the door. He's had a tough day."

The broad hall with its black and white tessellated floor and Persian rugs was brilliantly lighted.

"Mother and Josh haven't returned or the lights would be lower. He smolders if the house isn't ablaze when he comes home." As he lifted the white jacket from her shoulders she whispered:

"Shall I get the automatic now or wait until you are ready to leave?"

He heroically resisted the urge to kiss her upturned face.

"Get it now, before anyone comes."

He paced the hall while he waited for her return. The house was sepulchrally quiet. What was going on within these walls? What was back of Josh Crandon's terrified "Someone's out to get me," of his refusal to have Cardella at dinner? Now what's happened? He sprinted up the stairs to meet Wendy who was running down.

"Van," she whispered. "Van, it's gone."

"What's gone? The automatic?"

She nodded.

"Come down."

In the hall he caught her shoulders.

"Steady, Wendy. Are you sure?"

"Yes. You saw me put it in the drawer. In my excitement over these gorgeous camellias I forgot to lock it. Thank goodness I didn't leave the—"

"Why did you stop as if you were afraid to tell the rest? *What* didn't you leave?"

"These." She touched the pearls at her throat. "The key was in the lock."

"Didn't you tell me that the dog sleeps in your room? Wouldn't she raise the roof if a stranger touched your desk?"

"Yes, yes. Angeline was there." Her breath caught in a sob of excitement. "I couldn't wake her. She'd been drugged."

XV

Seated at the desk in his sunshine-flooded office Rolfe Sanborn frowned thoughtfully at the back of the man in gray.

"The key of the drawer was in the lock? That was making the thief's job easy. Sure the dog had been drugged?" he inquired.

Van Tyler turned from the window, drew a chair opposite his and crossed arms on the desk.

"I went upstairs to check. Angeline, that's the poodle's wacky name, was snoring to beat the band. The dog made no response to Wendy's voice. The appeal in it would have brought me back from the dead."

"So that's the way it is with you?"

"That's the way it is — for keeps." He cleared his voice of huskiness. "I lifted the poodle's eyelids, pupils dilated, felt for the heartbeat, faint. I patted and slapped but Angeline snored on."

"Then what?"

"We decided it would be quicker to rush the dog to the nearest M.D. than to try to get one on the phone. I was halfway downstairs with Angeline in my arms — heard Wendy's excited gasp, turned and said:

" 'The doc will fix her up. Don't worry, Mrs. Van — ' "

"Mrs. *Van?*"

"I call her that sometimes. Remember the story of our marriage she told to throw Russ off the track in the Pullman?"

"I remember. Go on. You were coming down the stairs—"

"Right. Enter the Crandons plus Russ Ruggles in time to hear 'Mrs. Van.' Tableau. The expression of the cat that swallowed the canary had nothing on his smug grin. It called for prompt and vigorous action on my part."

"Take it easy, fella."

"Easy is right, I had to. My arms and hands were full of that darned poodle. Wendy explained what had happened."

"Did she mention the missing automatic?"

"No. She suggested that as dogs weren't drugged as a joke, the three of them better cover the house and check for theft while she and I took Angeline to the doctor."

"What was Mrs. Crandon's reaction to the situation?"

"Cool as the proverbial cucumber. She volunteered the information that when she reached home after a round of teas Angeline, who had been in the car all afternoon, dashed to the pantry for her supper."

"Had the Missus returned before you and Miss Adair left for the studio, via dinner?"

"No. It was five o'clock when you phoned Red Terraces, we waited until I was sure Propper was fit to set Casey, the teamster, and his box on their way. All I cared about was getting Wendy out of the house. She'd had a tough scare."

"You've said it. If she could hit a target after that fright she must be an A-1 shot. Did the three fall in with the checkup suggestion? How did Josh react?"

"Poor guy, showed the effect of the afternoon shock, face gray, eyes drawn, looked as if he had been through a fit of sickness, but he was game. By the way, he told Wendy the other day that he was worried, had been taking stuff to make him sleep. They were starting for the silver safe in the pantry as we drove off with Angeline."

"Any mention made of the afternoon scare?"

"No. I'll bet if Russ had heard of it he

would have dragged it into the spotlight."

"What did the doc say about the dog?"

"Drugged. He administered a shot. Wendy reported over the phone this morning that the poodle was gay as a lark, much gayer and peppy than she herself felt after the last twenty-four hours."

"She wouldn't be on top of the world. She was up all night after the dinner and cards at Red Terraces. She was wandering about the place at approximately four yesterday morning."

"How do you know?"

"Remember I told you not to have her safety on your mind? That I would be responsible for it?"

"I do. Does that mean—"

"That I am standing by that promise, in what way is my business. Someone, a man, also was roaming around the garden at dawn."

"A man! Are you insinuating that Wendy went to the garden to meet—"

"Sit down. I do not insinuate, I make statements. I know that she was on the path between the terraces, hid near the birdbath. The white poodle found her there, lingered a minute and dashed away."

"Then what?"

"She stole back to the house. I don't

know what drew her to the garden — perhaps she had seen a mysterious figure — but I have a hunch she found something — a message, perhaps — and placed it in the drawer with the automatic, someone got wise and went after it — unfortunately for all concerned she forgot to turn the key. The job of finding out what it was I'm handing over to you."

"Thank goodness, I didn't leave the—" Wendy's strained whisper echoed in his memory. Was Rolfe right? Had she found a message? Why hadn't she told him? Is she planning to follow up what she found? She couldn't be so reckless after—

"Was anyone but Propper in the house last evening?"

Sanborn's question threw him off the trail of conjecture.

"I heard you say at the studio that the Crandons were dining out."

"We didn't see anyone. I wonder if what happened after we left the movie could possibly tie in with the mysterious person in the garden."

He told of the now-you-hear-them, now-you-don't footsteps on the shadowy street.

"Wendy is obsessed with the idea that because of the papers she smuggled out of S.A. she's a marked person. I'm beginning to think she may be right, that our Department of State has kept the delivery so hush-hush that the gang after information as to their disposal is hopping around like popcorn in a radar range trying to locate them."

"Could be. Have you thought that the rifled overnight case and the stolen automatic may be missing pieces in the puzzle into which could fit the delivery of the wrong box at Red Terraces?"

"That suspicion is not even debatable. Leaving the zoo box in place of the books was Casey's mistake, nothing else."

"Maybe, but Casey's 'mistake' did reveal — stop me if I'm wrong — that Josh Crandon fears reprisal. Didn't it?"

"It did, Perry Mason."

"Okay, fella, grin, but mull over the suggestion. It may make the grade — in time."

"That grin is only skin deep, chief. I sense an undercurrent at Red Terraces that chills me to the bone." He rose. Walked to the window, returned. Hands gripping the top of a chair, he looked down at the man at the desk.

"It seems unbelievable, but do you detect a trace of Russ Ruggles's Machiavellian tactics behind it?"

"I've had the possibility pricking in my mind. He's mighty thick with the Crandons.

191

Orchids, camellias, gardenias for the Missus — don't get me wrong, she likes admiration expressed in corsages — what woman doesn't — but, that's as far as it goes. She lassoed her Midas. It isn't like Russ to throw money around. Why is he doing it? Memory rings up the answer. You told me Mrs. Crandon was arranging a marriage for her daughter with Ruggles."

"Trying to arrange. She can't put it across. Wendy doesn't like him, she won't go out with him."

"That will put him on his mettle. Anyone can see that you've gone off the deep end about her."

"Is it as apparent as that?"

"Perhaps the word 'anyone' is an exaggeration. Miss Adair's dislike has bruised Russ's ego, already badly dented by the fact that the girl to whom you were engaged married him, then divorced him as soon as you retired from the service. He told me you broke up his marriage."

"That's a cockeyed claim. You know, as do others, that while I was at home, I never spoke to Clare, never even saw her till she came to Washington."

"Sure I know, but that isn't all of his grievance. You beat him at the polls. Is it a wonder — he being what he is — that he is out to get you? Have you read the morning paper?"

"No. I've had a lot to follow up, couldn't settle down to it. I know by your voice you have something up your sleeve. Spring it." Sanborn pushed a clipping from a newspaper across the desk.

"Take a gander at that."

Van picked up the slip. Read the printed words twice.

"Where did you get it?"

"Buried in the middle of the 'As I Hear It' chitchat."

"Not so deeply buried, though, that it won't be read by thousands. Do you think it refers to me?"

"You're the best judge of that. Hand it over. I'll read it aloud. I'll pull out all the emotional stops in my voice, it will be easier for you to decide."

"This may not prove to be the joke you're making of it, chief."

"That's right. Sorry, fella. Listen:

There is a persistent rumor that a certain ranch owner, oilman, wealthy representative from the great Northwest posing as a bachelor was secretly married several weeks ago to the charming daughter of a family socially prominent in our fair city. Why the hush-hush, congressman?

"Now, what do you think?"

" 'From the great Northwest' clinched it. I'm the target, all right. I only hope Wendy doesn't see it. It would be so like her to feel that because of it she ought to say, 'Yes,' when I ask her to marry me. That gem of rhetoric ties it. I won't ask her till the author of the choice bit of chitchat retracts in his column. I've heard that revenge — or what have you — makes some men crazy. Something tells me that our townsman is balancing on the brink of the pit."

"He won't go over. Don't kid yourself. Remember him as a boy? Remember how he'd twist the wrists of the smaller fry till they yelled from pain?"

"I do. He's a congenital hector."

"His attitude toward you isn't all that puzzles me. He's mighty thick with Señor Antonio Cardella."

"A man good old Josh won't have in his house."

"How do you know he won't?"

"Mrs. Crandon told her daughter that when she planned to invite the smooth Señor to dinner — at Ruggles's suggestion — Josh said, 'No,' a mighty 'No.' She couldn't understand it, never before had her husband interfered with her guest list. What do you make of that?"

"It's something to let the deep mind — commonly known as the subconscious — play with. There's one lad we haven't had under the microscope this A.M. What do you know about Steve Graham who dragged Miss Adair into this mix-up by loading her with secret papers to deliver?"

"Nothing but what she told me. They have been friends since they were children. Apparently he had the freedom of the Adair home. He's set to be a career man in diplomacy. Why quiz me? I'll bet you have his dossier from the cradle on."

"Correct, but I'd like to know why he followed her here so quickly."

"Ask him."

"Perhaps she'll tell me. As no two persons see the same event in the same way, I have your version, to make sure I get all the angles of that box episode yesterday, I've sent for her to hear her side of it."

"Sent for her to come here? To this office?"

"Sure. Why not? She'll drop in after lunch, I gathered."

"Expect me after lunch. The lady is entitled to the presence of her lawyer while

195

being third-degreed. In case you've forgotten, chief, I'm a lawyer and hers. If she gets here first, keep her until I come. And for Pete's sake, keep that clipping under cover." He closed the door to the outer office quickly behind him to shut off a possible protest.

Clare Sanborn sprang up from a typewriter desk. A dark green pullover and matching skirt accentuated the gleam of earstuds and necklace that were no more golden than her hair.

"I've been waiting for you, dearie. I sent old Hood off to lunch so we could talk." She was breathlessly eager. "I was afraid you might think I was that way about Steve Graham because I went stepping with him the other evening after dinner at Red Terraces. I'm not. He's a lot of fun, that's all."

"Why the excitement?" He tried for the light touch. "It's nothing in my life if you are that way about him. Go ahead. Have fun. From what I hear he's an all-right guy."

"I don't want to go ahead, dearie." Tears welled, spilled and rolled down her cheeks like glittering diamonds. "Please forgive me, Van. Two months after I married Russ I realized I still loved you. I — I told him that when I begged for a divorce.?

That confession was behind Ruggles's venomous animosity, that and his determination to beat him in the fight for the congressional seat. Doubtless it accounted for the poisonous innuendo in the morning paper. All Clare's ex needed now to clinch the belief that Van Tyler had broken up his marriage was to barge into the present situation. He caught the hands gripping the lapels of his coat and tried to loosen them.

"Clare! Clare! How many times must I tell you—"

"Van! You're breaking my fingers." She tipped back her head in invitation. "You still love me. I feel it. Kiss—"

The door opening. Had his thought of Ruggles materialized him?

"Oh! Excuse—" Wendy Adair's shocked whisper. Wendy Adair on the threshold.

XV

Racing down three long flights of stairs —
— it had been done before in a dream —
pushing open the heavy glass door, almost
knocking over a sailor who was coming in
— dashing, dodging across the traffic-
glutted street — at the risk of life, to say
nothing of such minor casualties as broken bones or fractured skull — to the accompaniment of Did he see me? I must
get away. Darting into a restaurant, drop-
ping into a seat at a table near the window
from which she could watch the revolving
door of the building across the street. Why
fear that Van might follow her? He was
too—

"Were you frightened, Miss, or were you
running away from someone?"

She looked up at the ruddy round face,
met the blue eyes sharp with suspicion of a
headwaiter. Good heavens, perhaps the man

suspected she was a pickpocket being pursued by police.

"I was frightened. I jaywalked — I'm from a small town — saw a traffic officer coming toward me and dashed in here. I wasn't trying to escape a fine, really I wasn't, but publicity."

She glanced around the large room. There were signed crayon sketches on the walls, a television screen behind a long bar, a few men at tables covered with red and white checked cloths, a mixed odor of cooking, beer, and cigarette smoke. For the second time fear of pursuit had landed her in the wrong place. She looked up into the blue eyes still regarding her with suspicious intentness.

"Shouldn't I be here? Aren't women allowed? Must I go?" The smiling appeal did it.

"Sure, Miss, women are allowed. T'ain't a stylish place, but the food is okay. Take it easy. I'll send a waitress for your order."

She opened the menu he handed her before he walked away, but she wasn't seeing the printed lines, she was seeing a girl with head tipped back, a man's hands gripping hers, seeing the lines cut deep between his nose and mouth.

Why did I run? she asked herself. I'm sure

he was too intent on her to see me. Why didn't I make with a laugh and wisecrack, "Sorry to interrupt at this climactic — that's a good word — climactic moment," then follow through with a tolerant, boys-will-be-boys smile and fade gracefully into Rolfe Sanborn's office?

Why didn't I? Because I was stunned by surprise. Question and answer raced through her mind. The night Van Tyler dined at Red Terraces he declared she was not, never would be his Clare. That clinch I barged in on looked like it, like fun it did.

"What's the big idea thumbing your nose at the traffic, Miss Adair?" Rolfe Sanborn's breath came fast. He pulled out a chair beside her. "Publicity stunt for the radio act?"

Still too angry with herself to speak she shook her head. He studied the menu.

"Let's eat. What will you have?"

"Nothing, thank you." The voice she forced through her constricted throat was strained. "I dropped in here when I discovered I was too early to see you. I didn't realize that it was a ninety percent masculine lunching place. I'll do an errand now and return to your office later."

"Sit down, sit down. Let's have our talkathon here. While we eat. Saving of time for both of us. If we do Van Tyler will be set to brain me, as he declared earlier that he intended to be present when I talked with you, but I can take it."

She sat down quickly.

"It will be fun to lunch with you, Mr. Sanborn. Your time-saving suggestion is an inspiration. I have a date to pick up Lucie Brown who has agreed to personally conduct me on a sight-seeing tour, the sooner I get to her house the better. I've just realized that I am practically starving. The menu announces Chicken-Pie Day. I'm a pushover for chicken pie."

Too gay, too ebullient. She'd better calm down or he would suspect that her excited patter was a cover-up, that she had made an ill-timed appearance at his office — he must know that his best friend and his sister were romancing. No use to try to fool the keen eyes behind those bifocals.

"When I invite a lady to lunch with me I expect her undivided attention, Miss Adair. I've inquired twice if you'll have coffee now or later?" The warmth of his smile eased the smart of memory.

"Ask her once, ask her twice
Ask her pretty and ask her nice,

adapted from a square dance call, in case you are interested, maestro."

"Glad to hear laughter in your voice. From the first glance I had at your face when I came in I expected that late or soon you would burst into tears on my shoulder. To return to my question," he poised a pencil above an order pad, "coffee now or later?"

"With my luncheon, please."

He handed the slip to a pink-frocked white-capped waitress a-quiver with thrilled curiosity.

"And, Susie, serve the coffee hot in a pot."

"Sure, Mr. Sanborn, I know how you like it. And will your young lady take cream?"

"Will my young lady take cream?" He chuckled. "You're not committing yourself to being my young lady by answering, Miss Adair."

"I would like cream with the coffee." As the waitress glided away he laughed.

"As you could see, you have provided the food for romance for Susie. She is deeply concerned at my bachelor state."

"Do you never invite a woman to lunch?"

"Not here. My guests choose a more top-drawer locale."

"How did you know I came here? You did know, didn't you? It wasn't coincidental that you arrived a few minutes after I came in, was it?"

"No." He twisted a glass tumbler the exact shade of the red in the tablecloth and set the ice within it tinkling. "I was at the window of my office looking down at the street figuring on a problem when the frantic tooting of automobile horns drew my attention to a girl in — what color is your costume?"

"*Couturiers* have a name for it — blonde."

"In a blonde outfit even to shoulder bag and shoes, who was dodging and darting in front of the hoods of trucks, cars, and taxis. Each time she turned I caught a flash of pink — you're a marked woman with those camellias. You wore them to the studio last evening, didn't you?"

"That's right."

"To continue the saga, I broke my own speed record through the outer office, ignoring my sobbing sister huddled behind a typewriter, ran down the stairs and at the risk of voiding my life insurance policy bucked the traffic and crossed the street." He folded his arms on the table and leaned forward.

"Have you ever thought, Miss Adair, that there are a lot of less messy ways of ending it all than being crushed under wheels — if that was your idea."

"It wasn't, of course it wasn't, equally of course the jaywalking stunt was a crazy impulse. I don't know why I did it. Let's charge it up to brainstorm and get to the reason of the summons to your office. Is it to cancel the radio contract?"

"No. Where did you pick up that fool idea? Susie is bearing down on us. I'll explain later. Why are you taking off that corsage?"

"Too sensational for this hour and place."

The waitress fairly tingling with secret understanding smiled at Wendy.

"Isn't there something else you would like, dear?"

"Thank you, no. Wear these when you go off duty."

Susie hesitantly took the camellias she offered, looked at Rolfe Sanborn.

"I'd love them, shall I take them, sir?"

"Nothing in my life. I didn't give them to her."

"Then I'll wear them. Thank you again. Apple pie à la mode is out of this world today, folks." Tray under her arm, camellias prominently displayed, she hurried away.

He lifted the flaky crust from the small casserole in front of him. Sniffed.

"Delicious aroma. I always look to be sure there is an onion among those present. This time there are two. All's well with the world."

Thank heaven, I was afraid he intended to follow up the subject of the camellias, she thought. Of course he knows that Van Tyler gave them to me. Remembering the close-up in that office I couldn't wear them another minute. His sister was sobbing, was she? Joy affects some women that way. Aloud, she said:

"Now, please explain the command appearance."

"I want your account of the excitement at Red Terraces yesterday."

She crumbled a roll with her fingers and thought — He said excitement — he means the exchange of boxes — shall I tell him of my safari into the garden at dawn — of what I found — no — if I do he may not let me follow my hunch this afternoon—

How about it? Don't stall."

His crisp reminder steeled her resolution to keep the secret for the present.

"I wasn't stalling. I was mentally getting the story into line so that I could tell it quickly. This is what happened."

As she talked the large room filled with men, a few women and blue tobacco smoke. He appeared absorbed in the enjoyment of his luncheon, but he prompted her memory occasionally with a pertinent question, sharp as a whiplash. She concluded with the discovery that the automatic had been taken from the drawer of her desk and a description of the trip to the doctor's with the drugged poodle.

"Quite an experience for you," he observed thoughtfully. "Is that all that happened?"

An edge in his voice brought warm color to her face. Did he suspect there was something more? Let him. She would not tell him what she had seen or found in the garden till she had followed the hunch that "Ford" meant Ford's Theater.

"My word, isn't that enough? Joshua Crandon adores Angeline. I thought he would be terribly upset about her, especially after having been laid low by the mixed-boxes episode, but, apparently he took it in his stride. That poodle has such an air of social superiority I'd think every dog in the neighborhood would gang up against her," she added in the hope of preventing a repetition of his question, "Is that all that happened?"

"I've met women with that same complex. What sort of a person is 'good old Josh' in his home? Don't answer if you'd rather not."

"I'm glad to, for before I came to

Washington I had made up my mind to detest him." She leaned a little forward in her earnestness. "I thought he was the type of man who would make the kind of off-color remarks that set my face a-fire, that he was the sort who would go overboard for younger girls and women."

"And he isn't like that?"

"No. *No.* I would trust Joshua Crandon in any situation. I didn't *intend* to like him. I didn't *want* to like him, he broke up our home. But, I not only like him, I admire him for his patience and — just let it go that I admire him. Pretty weak-minded of me, isn't it?"

"Pretty fair-minded, I'd say. It doesn't excuse him, of course, but he must have had some come-on from the woman in the case. Don't answer. I've kept you talking. Eat your lunch while I check your story as I understand it. Interrupt if I make a misstatement."

It was amazing how quickly and correctly he repeated what she had told him.

"Period. Did I skip anything?"

"That just about does it. Now, if you will excuse me, I'll be on my way to pick up Lucie Brown." He rose and drew out her chair.

"Have you the courage to pass up apple pie à la mode?"

"I have, but with profound regret. It's been fun having lunch with you. Good morning. My mistake, it's afternoon, isn't it?"

In the sunshine under a cloudless Della Robbia blue sky she drew a deep breath of relief.

Had I stayed at that table one more minute, Rolfe Sanborn would have discovered why I dared Fate crossing the street, she told herself. He was leading up to it. When he asked, "Is that all that happened?" I had a curious feeling that in some way he knew I found that message. How could he? Unless—

"At last we meet, Señorita."

Her heart did a double-handspring and settled back with a dull thud. It wasn't a nightmare, it was Cardella twisting an end of his already sufficiently twisted mustache. His dark eyes reflected the hint of triumph in his voice.

"Have I your gracious permission to walk with you to your car, Señorita?"

"Sorry, Señor Cardella, but I am expecting a friend—"

And here he is, she concluded mentally as a workingman with cap tipped at a ribald angle, hands thrust into the pockets of his dark blue jeans, shouldered his way between them.

"Gangway, buddy, gangway!" He laughed tipsily and lurched against Cardella with a suddenness and force that sent the surprised Señor sprawling into the street.

"St—!"

"Scram, Miss," the man's whispered command broke into her startled exclamation. "Get going. Looks like I've started something."

"Get going" was a masterpiece of understatement of the speed with which she moved. From a safe distance she looked back. She had a glimpse of the two men face to face, one gesticulating furiously, the workman patting his victim's shoulder, of a traffic cop running toward them before the crowd closed in.

"Steve!" she said under her breath. "Steve Graham!"

XVII

A distance steeple clock was intoning the hour of three when Wendy stopped her mother's dark green roadster in front of the one-time overseer's cottage on the Red Terraces estate, which was now a charming small house.

"Ready in half a shake!" Lucie Brown called from a second-story window.

Wendy shut off the engine. Experience had taught her that Mrs. Gib's "half a shake" meant anywhere from five to fifteen minutes. All right with her. This was the first moment she had relaxed since she had opened the door of Rolfe Sanborn's outer office. Ooch! Why think of it? Hadn't she been told that Van Tyler was a rock-ribbed bachelor? Only yesterday her mother had warned her not to fall in love with him, had reminded her that Josh had said he was girl-resistant. No use deceiving herself. She had definitely decided on a spinster career when along came a man with tender eyes and a heart-warming laugh and she had fallen at his feet, figuratively speaking.

Forget it. Never, never let him suspect you were the person who opened the door at that critical moment, she cautioned herself, he was too absorbed to see you. Remember, you are to be a leetle more cordial in your manner to him the next time you meet — here's hoping the generous gods will postpone that meeting indefinitely — play his game but play it harder. Why can't I forget it? Why dwell on memories that hurt this gorgeous day?

Gorgeous was the word for it. Incredible as it seemed the November air smelled of spring. Sunlight had turned the brick façade of the small near-Georgian house to rosy-pink, dappled with gold the greens in the window boxes and the few leaves on the swaying vines that framed the white door. In the brilliant atmosphere the bare branches of a towering pecan tree in the background had the effect of a drawing in India ink against the clear turquoise blue of the sky.

Little birds with greenish backs hopped busily among a clump of rhododendrons, two larger ones with red tops and black spots at the neck were pecking at the lawn.

Crouched on the sill of a first-story window, a cat shiny as if modeled of black porcelain, paws folded under its breast, watched their activities with unblinking yellow glare, motionless except for the sinuous undulation of a long, glossy tail. Angeline's antagonist indubitably. From the distance the marks of the recent fight were not discernible. The poodle still carried the scars of conflict.

The sight of the cat flashed her thoughts back to the early morning when the dog had dashed away from the birdbath. She checked incident by incident that followed, winced away from the memory of Van Tyler with a woman's hands tight in his, relived the luncheon with Rolfe Sanborn, dwelt on the workingman who had proved to be Steve Graham.

Her eyes were on the rolling hills of Arlington across the Potomac but she was seeing again the crowded street, feeling the shoving shoulder, hearing the whisper, "Scram, Miss. Get going. Looks like I've started something." What was back of it? Was Steve shadowing Cardella?

The opening of the cottage door set her thoughts scampering like fallen autumn leaves in an October breeze. She pressed the self-starter as red-haired Lucie Brown came out as if catapulted from within.

"Sambo, quit watching those birds," she called, and dashed on along the flagged walk between flower beds which flaunted an amazing amount of color considering the season. She buckled the belt of the short jacket of her brown wool suit with one hand and pulled a green felt sailor down more securely on her flyaway coiffure with the other. The shoulder bag which matched her hat swung and bobbed as she ran.

"Let's go, glamour girl," she panted as she sank into the seat beside Wendy. She leaned forward and called:

"Go away, Sambo. *Stop* watching those birds!" In reply the black cat waved its tail a little faster and settled down more firmly on the window ledge.

"Darn that pest. The children adore him or it would be 'off with his head.'" As the car shot ahead Lucie drew a pair of soiled beige gloves from her bag and pulled them on. "We can't keep a bird or a squirrel on the place."

"Birds and cats seem congenital enemies."

"Likewise some cats and some dogs. Sambo crawled in yesterday morning looking as if he and Joe Louis had been battling and the champ had handed him a left to the eye. It was the lady Angeline. That poodle doesn't pull her punches. I didn't hear the fight. I was dead to the world, but Gib ran into it on his way home. Heavenly day."

Yesterday morning! Wendy's pulses broke into quickstep, a habit they had acquired since that terrifying night of the revolution. Angeline had come home with a bloody nose. Gib Brown had heard the fight, Lucie said. Why was he out again at 4 A.M. after leaving Red Terraces? Had he been one of the two shadows?

"Allah be praised we're out of hearing of the house," Lucie drew a long breath and slumped in the seat. "Our phone has rung like all get-out since dewy morn."

"You are too popular."

"Says you. It wasn't for me. Someone calling Gib. I hope it was about a job."

"Did the person finally contact him?"

"No. Whoever it was wouldn't leave a message. He went to town. It slays me to have him so discouraged. I'm scared he may do something desper—" The word broke on a sharp sob.

"Scared of what, Lucie? Not of another woman. Anyone with half an eye can see that he thinks the sun rises and sets in your shoes."

"Boy, oh boy, I haven't that worry to face. I am frightened, though, something happened this morning — if I don't get it off my chest, I'll crack. I'm going to tell you, Wendy. I can't talk to Mother, she and Gib don't jibe, she can't forgive him for not being spectacularly successful."

"Tell me, Lucie, it may help."

"You'll think I'm disloyal and crazy but here it is. I have a gorgeous diamond and emerald dinner ring Father gave me on my college commencement day. I was class historian. When Gib and I took out theft insurance — which we have had to let lapse — it was valued at four thousand dollars. It's gone."

"Gone! Stolen?"

"I don't know, that's what's driving me nuts. Late last night I was too dead tired to lock and unlock the drawer in which I keep my jewelry. I dropped the ring on top of a letter I had been writing on my desk — I wear it at dinner, it helps boost my morale. While I was dressing this morning the children were fooling with the cat in our room. I ran down to get breakfast, after that I got the adorables ready so that Gib could leave them with their suitcase at Mother's on his way to the bus. After they had gone I started on my own breakfast and in the midst of it remembered the ring. I flew upstairs to put it away. It wasn't there."

"Perhaps Gib saw it on the desk and took care of it."

"He wouldn't do that without telling me."

"Had anyone but the family been in the house?"

"Not between midnight and 9 A.M."

"As you tell it the ring was in plain sight on your desk. Perhaps the children picked it up to see it sparkle and dropped it somewhere."

"They never touch our personal possessions. Gib and I may be criminally indulgent parents — Mother speaking — but we have drilled into their minds respect for another person's property, that's why I can't really believe that Gib—"

"Lucie Brown! You're not telling me you think your husband took that ring?"

"Borrowed it, that's all. We are terribly hard up, hounded by bills. Gib might have taken it to raise money—"

"Pull yourself out of that nightmare and quick. Of course he didn't."

"In my heart I don't really think it — but where is the ring?"

"Why don't you phone Gib and tell him about it?"

"I would if I knew where to reach him. That's the number one comfort of having a husband, Wendy, someone with whom to talk over things, things you can't speak of to anyone else. Telling you has made me realize what a disloyal fool I am. Forget it. God's in His Heaven, Mother has taken the adorables for two days, and I'm off on a party. Heavenly day." She leaned forward to glance in the windshield mirror. "Gosh, my hair looks like a Golliwogg's or a Fuller mop." She rested her head against the back of the seat.

"Boy, I'm tired, my cleaning woman walked out on me. I'll bet I could sleep for a week."

"Try it."

"Says you, a gal whose breakfast is served in her room, who looks this minute in that blonde outfit as if she'd just been unpacked from sheet after sheet of tissue wrapping."

"This gal hasn't always had it easy, Lucie, and I'm not crazy about breakfast served in my room. I'll take over the adorables from two to five every afternoon next week. The day I'm broadcasting I'll return your treasures at four. We'll go to the zoo. They might like the Smithsonian. We'll drive, have picnic tea in Rock Creek Park, so that you may have a quiet house in which to rest. When excited the Brown gals produce a yell that would make an Indian war brave pale with envy. I can hear them at Red Terraces."

"You're telling me. Now they've reached the giggling stage, you should have heard

217

them in our room this morning, whispering and giggling, with the cat spitting and meowing protest. They love their Sambo, but they're terribly rough with him. In spite of that when the three are in the house the cat is at their heels. You're an angel to suggest taking over, but I won't accept the offer now, later perhaps. Already I can feel my nerves and muscles unknotting. It's my own fault. I knew better than to play cards till 2 A.M. at Red Terraces. I had to sit up till twelve last night to catch up with my mending, Gib was having such a good time winning moderately that I hated to break in on his streak of luck. Boy, but the Latour femme cleaned up. I loathe her, what's more I'm afraid of her."

"Afraid?"

"I'm not jealous, if that's what you're thinking. Instinct, common sense, whatever it is warns me she's a tough cookie. She's everlastingly buttering Gib. Why? What's she after? She must know he hasn't any money. Could be she wants him to photograph her for nothing. He's a wizard with a camera when it comes to the woman beautiful — and he has a way of transforming the unbeautiful into glamour girls. Her charm beamed at him was running on all cylinders the evening at Red Terraces. They even took the air on the veranda for a while. I wondered if there was a person among those present whom she was trying to make jealous. Didn't you get on to her?"

"I didn't stay long enough. As the party seemed to be under perfect control without me, I went to my room to write letters."

"Clare Sanborn and Mr. Graham, Rolfe and Van Tyler left early. Van never stays late."

"Look at that flower shop, Lucie! The day is so warm they've banked pots of salmon-pink geraniums outside and along the curb of the sidewalk and giant trees of the same plant at each side of the entrance. I've never seen geraniums trained like that before. The windows are full of feathery white and mauve chrysanthemums. The effect is a knockout. Where were we when I went starry-eyed over the flowers? I remember, you were speaking of Mr. Tyler. You and he are old friends, aren't you?"

"We are, added to that he's been an angel to Gib and me since we came to Washington to live two years ago. He has sent me a ticket for a seat in the visitors' gallery when the section reserved for the public was crowded. Several times I have had lunch with him in the House Restaurant. The children adore him. He's the dream-boy of their lives."

"Strange he hasn't married."

"It would be more strange if he had. The

girl to whom he was engaged married another man while he was overseas, didn't even have the decency to write and break with him first. On top of that his one brother was killed in action, that broke his mother's heart, her husband followed her within a year. That left him alone. I told Gib I believed Van had been hurt so much that his heart is too numb to feel anymore."

Wendy's memory flashed a close-up of his stern face as she had seen it first.

"What became of the girl to whom he was engaged?"

"Divorced the other man, came to Washington two years ago, took a job and has been after Van hell-for-leather ever since. If she gets him there ain't no justice."

"Gets him? She can't get him unless 'Barkis is willin',' can she?"

"Boys and girls of the radio audience, never underestimate the power of a pursuing woman. Clare Sanborn is on the warpath."

Clare? Clare? Wendy's memory put on a recording. "Van! You still love me. I feel it."

"The girls my age went haywire when Van got engaged to her, we agreed she wasn't good enough for our hero. I went into a North American Indian war dance when she ditched him to marry Russ Ruggles."

"Ruggles! *Ruggles!* Is he the man from

whom she is divorced?"

"Sure. You've gone white. Why should that fact knock you into a cocked hat?"

"It shouldn't. I don't know why I was so surprised." She couldn't tell Lucie that in the presence of that same Ruggles she had declared she and Van Tyler were married.

"She isn't the only one," Lucie's voice and giggle was a magic carpet that whisked her back from the dining car of a Pullman.

"There are others making a bid to be Mrs. Vance Tyler. Discounting the fact that he has what it takes in character, intelligence — his friends at home say he'll be governor in a few years — personality and sympathy to make a girl fall for him — men like him too — he owns a fabulous ranch plus oil fields, an historic estate a few miles out from this city, with a man and his wife caretakers — he invited us to dinner there last Thanksgiving — the adorables never will forget that party — and lives in a sharp apartment in one of the spectacular hotels here. He is one of the Washington bachelors — may their tribe increase — who *keep* dinner engagements and *return* hospitality."

"Stop and get your breath, Lucie. Like him, don't you?"

"Like him! I've been crazy about the two Tyler boys since I was a small girl. They were both dark and handsome. We went to the same church. When the family was in town they were always in the pew in front of ours. I didn't have to be bribed or forced to attend divine service, you bet, Van was my special Prince Charming. Neither he nor his brother looked at me, I was a mere kid to them."

"Fortunately for Gib."

"I wonder."

She was silent so long that Wendy looked down at the relaxed figure, at the short red hair blowing, expecting to find her asleep, instead her green eyes flecked with amber were staring at the sky.

"Perhaps if Gib had married a more de-manding woman," she spoke slowly as if cor-relating her thoughts, "he wouldn't have allowed his bursts of temper, which have cost him several wonderful photography jobs, to get the upper hand; perhaps a dif-ferent kind of wife would have kept his nose to the grindstone, inspired him to work hard to make the ambition of his life to be a cameraman in scientific research come true."

She straightened out of her slump, put on her hat and made a distasteful face at her re-flection in the car mirror.

"What's the use imagining? Gib is ten years older than I, but the minute I met him there was no other man in the world for me. He says it was the same with him. It was love at first sight, all right, and the feeling has lasted."

"That is because as you came to know him better he proved to be as fine as you thought him. Love — it's wonderful — but sometimes the spark of attraction goes dead."

"What's happened to make you an unbeliever in love, Wendy Adair? Your voice sounds as if you'd been left waiting at the church."

"I haven't — yet. Aren't the hills beautiful in this light?"

"Yes, and how it illumines the white stones that mark the graves across the river. Turn here for Ford's Theater. I'm still wondering why of all the points of interest you picked the one in downtown Washington as the first stop on our sight-seeing travelogue."

"Sentiment. I suppose you've seen it innumerable times. I hope you won't be bored."

"I'm never bored. Life is too exciting. Even with all my problems I never feel defeated. Left turn here. There's a flower shop that will make you purr. Pink mums banked outside and the windows full of pale violet and purple glads and a tray of waxy gardenias in their midst. Heavenly day."

"You've remarked that twice before. I agree that it is. Lots of traffic, I'd better tear my eyes away from the flower windows and attend to my knitting."

"Ford's is that old brick building ahead. Wendy, be an angel and forget I went haywire about the ring. Makes me sick when I think of my suspicion of Gib. At least, I might have been loyal enough to keep it to myself."

"There are times, Lucie, when one just has to let loose. Talk it over with your husband. Men are grand stabilizers, I know, my father could always straighten out my problems. We've arrived. I'll have to find a place to park."

Now that she was here the bottom dropped out of her courage. Was she crazy to follow her hunch that the message she had found had set this place for an appointment, had she started down a dead-end street? No harm done if — Lucie grabbed her arm.

"Look, Wendy. Am I seeing things, or is that Gibson Gary Brown standing at the door, smoking?"

XVIII

It was Gibson Gary Brown talking animatedly to a tall man in gray who wore a rakishly tipped gray fur-felt hat, whose back was toward the street. She would recognize the tilt of that brim if she saw it in Iran, the thought contracted Wendy's throat. What had happened to vitalize Gib Brown — his long thin face was alight with enthusiasm.

"Well, for crying out loud," Lucie's voice was shrill from surprise. "Gib knew I had this date with you, but why did he come and where did he pick up Van Tyler?"

"You answer that one," Wendy replied with an attempt at lightness while her thoughts raced on.

Is Gib Brown the person at whom the rendezvous message was beamed? Is he here in response? Can't be, the person didn't get it, I did. Perhaps it was he who tucked the envelope into the hand of the bronze nymph

— Lucie said he was out that morning — and not knowing I have it is here expecting to meet the party inside for whom it was intended. I've flattered myself that I am a go-through woman, but this minute I'm as jittery as if I were walking over mined territory — and I mean mined.

"Why are those two men here? Did you know they were coming, Wendy?"

"Pull yourself together, Lucie. Of course I didn't," she protested as she stopped the dark green roadster before the entrance.

"Gib, angel-boy, you're the last man on earth I expected to see," Lucie's voice was gay without a trace of fatigue. Her husband grinned as he opened the car door.

"Were you expecting a first man, Reddy? Lead me to him. Have you been double-crossing me? If you insist upon an explanation, I was in Van Tyler's office when I happened to mention that you and Miss Adair were coming here this afternoon. He suggested we come along and take you girls on a binge after you had paid your respects at this shrine. Hop out, Miss Adair. I'll drive the car to a parking meter. Stay where you are, Lucie."

Wendy ignored Van Tyler's outstretched hand as she stepped to the sidewalk.

"Gib! What's happened? You're on top of

226

the world," she heard Lucie whisper.

"Got a job. Scientists. Van did it," he answered before he drove away.

"Shall we wait outside for them or go in?" Van Tyler asked.

"Let's wait." Would the presence of the two men hinder her search for the person who left the message under the birdbath? It ought to help. As one of a party of four no one would suspect her of an underlying motive for being here. Looking for the writer of that card in this crowd would have hunting for a needle in a haystack licked to a finish.

"Expecting someone?" The tone of the question sent a soft surge of color to her cheeks.

"No. Just interested in the expression of the faces of visitors as they enter, it is reverent, the same look they have when they mount the steps of the Lincoln Memorial and see above them the massive bronze figure gazing out upon the city beyond those marble colonnades."

"I feel when I go up those steps as I feel when entering a church. Is this the beginning of a see-Washington pilgrimage?"

"Yes. I'm stunned with surprise to see you here." Why were Lucie and Gib so long getting back? Was she telling him about the

227

missing ring? Too bad if she confessed her suspicion of him.

"Expectant is the word I would use. Your thoughts seem too well organized for stunned."

"I insist that the word is surprised."

"Not a perceptive person, are you? Could be I've been too subtle in my approach. We'll have to do something about that. Have you forgotten you told me last evening that you and Lucie were coming here today?"

"I told you so many things last evening."

"That's right, too bad you omitted the before-dawn trip to the garden."

For the first time since she had stepped from the car her eyes met his directly.

"How did you know?" she whispered and admitted in the same breath.

"Why didn't you tell me about it? Didn't we agree to be a combat team?"

"Yes — but—"

"Did you think we were lost?" Lucie Brown's gay query interrupted. "We looked for a parking meter near Van's convertible and waited till the occupant backed out. Come on, let's go in. I always feel choky when I come here."

"Choky" proved to be an understatement of Wendy's reaction as she entered a room walled with glass cases filled with faded me-

mentos of Abraham Lincoln. There were letters in his angular script, yellowed photographs, rusty sabres, and crossing the floor a line of painted footprints.

"The footprints show the path taken by Booth as he ran out through the wings of the stage." A blue-uniformed guide explained to the awestruck group hanging on his words.

"I'll be d—" Gib Brown's curtailed whisper shocked Wendy back from the fragment of an historic past she had been visualizing. Her eyes followed his to Zaidee Latour posed in the doorway. Her sable cape was the last word in elegance, a crimson velvet toque did things for her dark hair and gardenia-tinted skin. Huge gold rings glinted at her ears. Her brows met in a suggestion of annoyance as her eyes traveled from face to face.

Wendy held her breath as they reached Gib Brown. Lucie had said she had been "buttering" him. Had he and she planned to meet here? Absurd as it had seemed to her a few moments ago, the suspicion persisted that he was involved in the Ford 13–4 appointment and "Or else" threat.

Wrong again. Zaidee Latour's eyes passed over him, no hint of recognition changed her expression. Whom has she come here to meet?

"Oh!"

"Don't be frightened," Van Tyler must have heard her quick drawn breath as Cardella followed by Russ Ruggles came down the stairs from the floor above. "He isn't interested in you, this time. We'll mix in the crowd going out and make our getaway." He tapped Brown's shoulder.

"Wendy and I are leaving. Coming?"

"You bet." Gib caught his wife's arm and followed to the foyer. Zaidee Latour turned, saw them and exclaimed:

"See who's here!" She nodded to Van Tyler and Lucie. "Gib, I've been trying to contact you all day. I think I've stumbled on a job you'll go all out for. Give me a buzz tomorrow. Fancy meeting you here, Miss Adair. Excuse me if I run away. I must follow that group of schoolchildren. I'm here to get material for a write-up of their impressions." Dashed was the word to describe the speed with which she moved toward the room they had left.

"I feel as if I had been caught up in a twister," Wendy exclaimed as they reached the sidewalk. "I've never heard anyone talk so fast and I've met a few nonstop conversationalists in my time. Is she a report— ?"

"Miss Adair, as I'm alive." The gay hail interrupted her question. "This must be old home week at Ford's Theater. Haven't seen you two since the dinner at Red Terraces. Why did the Browns shoot ahead? They're not mad at me, are they?"

Steve Graham. Steve's eyes warning her that their previous meeting today was not to be the subject of comment. Why is he here? He can't be a piece of the puzzle, can he? Is it possible that he tucked the appointment into the nymph's hand? Maybe he's on the trail of Cardella. How did he manage to escape jail after that fight?

"How are you, Graham?" Van Tyler's cordial greeting broke in on her hectic speculations. "The Browns and I are pledged to show the lady recently arrived from South America the sights of our city. This was the first stop. Now we're off to a movie. Join us?"

"No can do, thanks. I'm on the sightseeing bus myself. I've only two days more here. Sorry I couldn't accept your invitation to lunch at the House Restaurant, it would be mighty interesting. Will you make it breakfast tomorrow morning?"

There was nothing in Van Tyler's expression to suggest it but Wendy had the impression that this was the first time he had heard of the invitation to lunch in the House Restaurant.

"Sorry you can't make it for lunch, but breakfast suits me at my rooms." Van's voice held the perfect note of enthusiasm. "Make it any time between eight and nine. I report at my office at ten." He drew a card from his pocket. "My address and phone number in case anything comes up and you have to cancel."

"I won't cancel. I'll be with you at eight-thirty."

"I'll count on seeing you, Graham. We'll wait for you, Wendy." With a nod Van Tyler joined the Browns.

"That was darn white of him to give me a minute with you, lovely," Steve Graham caught her hand. "Drive to Mount Vernon with me tomorrow afternoon, will you?"

"Call for me at Red Terraces after lunch, Steve. Are you really leaving the country?"

"Don't whisper or we'll be suspected of being conspirators — everybody watches everybody else in this town — and don't ask questions. Run along. Tyler is looking back."

He turned away before she could answer. He isn't here in the interest of historical research, she decided as she hastened to join the Browns and Van Tyler. How had Steve escaped jail after his rough treatment of Cardella? Was it coincidental that Zaidee Latour, the South American and Ruggles had converged at the same spot at the same hour? She glanced at her wristwatch. Ice prickled along her veins. Four o'clock to the minute.

She didn't sense much of the movie, she was wondering if she had lost a trick by leaving Ford's Theater, if she should have remained to watch developments. How could she after the arrival of Van Tyler and Gib Brown?

"Now, we'll go to the Mayflower and dine," Van Tyler announced as they left the movie.

"It's a pity not to go to a plushy place when we girls are dolled up with the sensational gardenia corsages you bought for us, Van, but instead, come back to the house and have bacon and eggs and waffles," Lucie pleaded. "Mother has the adorables, it will be fun for us to stage an impromptu party, won't it, Gib?"

"You bet, out of this world with no small voice chanting upstairs, 'I want a drink of water. Want a drink of water.' Not that I'd be content to live without that small voice," he acknowledged hastily, "but it sure cramps one's entertaining style."

"What do you say, Wendy?" Van Tyler passed the decision to her.

Would it mean driving back to the cottage

in his car while Gib and Lucie went in hers? She didn't want to be alone with him. She might reveal that she had seen him with Clare in Rolfe Sanborn's office. Ever since under a thin film of pride the hurt to her heart had throbbed ceaselessly.

"If it takes so long to decide you can't be titillating with enthusiasm, Wendy Adair."

"Oh, but I am, Lucie. It will be fun. I was working out a plan for the trip back. You came in my car—"

"She will go back in mine, God and Gib willing," Van Tyler declared. "How about it, Gibson Gary?"

"Okay with me, double okay if Miss Adair will take me as a passenger."

"That's all that is needed to make the plan perfect. I rather dreaded driving through this strange city after dark. With you at the wheel I can sit back and enjoy every moment."

And in spite of the nagging ache and the indefinable feeling that she had lost something precious, she did enjoy the drive. Colored neon signs, red, orange, green, blue, shed a fairyland glow on buildings that had been drab and dirty in daylight.

On the broad avenues great arc lights made opaline pools on black pavements, windows glowed; the pyramidal cap of the monument glistened, planes flashed silver wings; the dome of the Capitol gleamed; above it floated the floodlighted Stars and Stripes.

She glanced at the sharp profile of the man at the wheel. A good face, a trustworthy face but not the face of the only man in the world for her. One meeting of eyes and Lucie for Gib, Gib for Lucie. The instantaneous emotional response between a woman and a man was one of the inexplicable mysteries of life.

As they passed the imposing structure with its flanking office buildings which towered over the city, Gib Brown's voice broke in on her reflections on the profound secret of one human being's attraction for another.

"That flag lasts about six weeks, I've been told. Day and night it flies above the Capitol. Wind and weather take a destructive toll."

"You've been better than a guidebook, Mr. Brown. I've learned more in this short drive than in all the time since my arrival."

"Don't be formal, call me Gib. Glad it seemed short. I love the place. I was born here, both of my parents were."

His answers to her many questions gave her a picture of Washington of other days when life was less hectic, more gracious. As they approached the Crandon home he suggested:

"What say we leave this roadster at Red Terraces and walk across the garden to the cottage?"

"It is an inspired idea." Not until the car had been left in the garage did she realize that it might result in Van Tyler's driving her home.

"Lucie and Van have beaten us to it." Gib Brown indicated the silver-gray convertible in the road in front of the cottage. As they entered the house he exclaimed:

"Gosh, doesn't it seem empty without the kids? Old Sambo misses them, too. Here he comes dragging himself down the stairs as if he'd nothing left to live for."

"Gib, you dawdler, we've been back ages. Began to fear you were lost." Lucie tucked her hand under his arm and squeezed it.

"You can't lose me as easily as that, Reddy. Been doing the guide act for Miss Adair. She says I'm good."

Van Tyler's hands on Wendy's shoulders sent a tingle along her veins.

"Better take off this jacket. At what are you staring as if hypnotized?"

"At him!"

Three pairs of eyes followed her finger pointing at the black cat perched on the newel post in the act of daintily restoring its makeup with a glossy paw.

"Do you all see what I see?" Excitement caught at her breath. "Something glittering halfway down on Sambo's tail?"

"My ring!"

With a shriek Lucie made a grab for the cat. The frightened creature jumped to the floor, shot into a small, book-lined room, leaped from the back of a chair to the top of a filing case, hit a box that fell with a crash which loosened the cover. Gib Brown scooped up the scattered contents and dropped them into a desk drawer.

"Gib! We must get that pest down." Lucie was on the verge of tears.

"Gib's busy collecting the ruins. I'll get Sambo." Van Tyler pushed a desk chair in front of the filing cabinet and stepped up into it.

"For the love of Pete, hold this thing steady, girls," he pleaded as the chair, being of the swivel variety, swiveled. "That's better. Scratch me, would you, fella. I've got him. Take your pest, Lucie. Hold him."

She sank to the green leather sofa with the struggling cat in her arms. She was sobbing in her relief.

"Pull it off, Wendy, while I hold Sambo. Now I understand what the adorables were giggling about in my room this morning."

"They put this on for keeps. Stop spitting, Sambo. I'm being as gentle as I can be. It's coming. There!" Wendy triumphantly held up the ring. "Take it, Lucie." The cat sprang to the floor and vanished. On her feet Lucie counted the emeralds and diamonds.

"The stones are all here. That cat has been wandering round since morning with a four-thousand-dollar ring on its tail and I thought — Oh, Gib! Gib, darling!" She flung herself against her husband. "Forgive me, I thought—"

"You thought what?" Gibson Gary Brown tipped up his wife's chin to look into her eyes. "Reddy, you didn't—"

"Here's where you and I fade." Van Tyler caught Wendy's hand and drew her along the hall to the kitchen and closed the door.

"We're outlanders in that situation. What's it all about?"

"As you heard so much, I won't be betraying confidence if I explain." She told of Lucie's concern about the missing ring.

"Gib's face was white when the cat knocked off that box, it was gray when Lucie sobbed, 'Forgive me.' I hope it was from shock, not anger."

"I noticed his eyes when he sensed the meaning of that word, it wasn't anger that darkened them, they looked as if they had been knifed."

"Under the circumstances, the hateful bills and all, it wasn't strange that she should imagine just for a minute that he might have — have borrowed it."

Wendy defended her friend in spite of a conviction that Lucie's doubt of her husband was unbelievable.

"A man has a right to expect his wife or the girl he hopes will be his wife to trust him under any circumstances, Mrs. Van."

"Here we are," Lucie's eyes were red as she entered the kitchen followed by her husband. "Who opened that?" She pointed to a window above the white enamel sink.

"Not guilty," Van declared.

"You must have left it open when you dashed out of the house this afternoon, you were in a terrific hurry," Wendy suggested.

"I'm sure I didn't. Something about the way the dark outside world stares in at me gives me the heebie jeebies. Boy, suppose the children had been alone here and—"

"They weren't. Take it easy, Reddy." Gib patted her shoulder. "You've forgotten to close a window before this. Did I dream it or was a mention made of scrambled eggs and bacon plus waffles?"

XIX

It happened as she had feared. After a delicious supper which had its hilarious moments with Lucie's laughter only a degree above tears and her husband's smile never reaching his eyes, after the dishes had been washed and dried, Van Tyler suggested:

"Better call it an evening, Wendy. I'm taking you home."

The no-appeal note in his voice flashed a close-up with sound effects of a man in gray beside her chair in the Pullman, saying:

"There will be a seat for you at my table."

"It is such a short distance, you needn't have me on your mind. I can dash across the garden in a split second."

"No marathon tonight. Lucie, remember that your family has a date at Arcady for Thanksgiving. Don't be too hard on the adorables — or anyone else — for the ring episode, Gib. Their experiment shows creative imagination."

"Plus remarkable judgment," Wendy attested. "They had forced that diamond and emerald treasure on so hard it took all my strength to pull it off."

She prolonged her departure wondering if she could conceal her hurt during the short drive to Red Terraces; hoping that pride would come to her aid in the romantic tradition of a disillusioned heroine.

"The carriage waits — Your Highness." There was a trace of laughter in Van Tyler's reminder, an understanding glint in the eyes that met hers.

"Sorry I've kept you waiting. It has been a perfect party, Lucie. See you tomorrow. Good night, Gib. You're a grand guide to Washington."

"Is that jacket warm enough?" Van Tyler inquired as he slipped into the seat beside her behind the wheel.

"In this springlike air it would be a sufficient wrap for the midnight ride of Paul Revere."

"Glad to hear that. We're driving down Arcady way."

Arcady. Lucie had said that was the name of his family home.

"It is too late. Mother will think I'm lost."

"It isn't eleven yet. I'll have you back at midnight. No occasion for Mrs. Josh to worry. I phoned Propper to tell her you are with me. I have things to say to you. I'll never have a better chance. I knew by the tinkle of ice in your voice this afternoon that when you opened the door of Sanford's office you jumped to the conclusion that I was lying when I told you Clare means nothing to me and never will."

"You didn't say never had been?"

"No. It wouldn't have been the truth. As you know now, apparently, we were engaged."

Was he waiting for her to deny that she had reached that conclusion?

"Don't apologize. I interrupted a tender interlude. I was embarrassed to tears and vanished pronto. Nothing to me whom you kiss."

"No? I consider that a solid gold mandate to go ahead, kiss whom I please. I told you the truth about Clare. Take it or leave it. Just for the record my interest in a person who doubts my word, who can't trust me, is absolutely nil. Relax. All that is incidental. My real reason for boring you with this drive is that I want a firsthand account of your early morning expedition into the garden at Red Terraces."

"You referred to that before. How do you know I was there? You were about to tell me when the Browns appeared."

"Rolfe told me."

"Rolfe Sanborn! How could he? I didn't mention it when we had luncheon together."

"So that was where you went when you disappeared from the door of his office? He knew. I don't know how. It is important that I have the facts. At least you might trust me with those. There may be more at stake than you can conceive even with your vivid imagination. Go on. Give."

He was right. She was taking an unwarranted responsibility in holding back information about the message she had found. The bottom had fallen out of her plan to follow up the discovery.

"Did the visit to Ford's Theater result from something you saw or heard?" He was making it easy for her to begin.

"From something I found."

He drove slowly while she told of going to the balcony, of hearing low voices, of seeing two shadows; went on with an almost step-by-step account to the moment when she had decided that Ford 13–4 was the place and date of a meeting.

"Smart girl. Was the plastic envelope with the card enclosure stolen when the desk drawer was ransacked?"

"It wasn't there. The little traffic cop who flashes GO! STOP! in my brain — ever have a warning sound off in your mind as clear as a voice speaking — told me not to part with it."

"Where is it now?"

"In a chamois bag to protect possible fingerprints, suspended on a thin gold chain — if you read the papers you've heard of a plunge neckline — that's where it is."

Her lips twitched in sympathy with his spontaneous laugh. One could love a man for that laugh alone. Perhaps it was because for two — almost three years — she had been in an environment where there was little laughter that his meant so much to her.

"Sure, I've heard of it — I'm a reader of assorted advertising. Glad to hear the lilt back in your voice, began to think you regarded me as a sort of ogre. Trust me with the plastic envelope, will you?"

"Oh, brother—"

"A moment's pause for station identification — there is not a tinge of brotherliness in my response to you. Now go on."

"Don't you recognize a colloquialism when you hear one?" Her light voice was a triumph of will over a surge of emotion. "I was about to 'chortle in my joy,' 'Brother, it's yours.' I'll be glad to turn over the responsibility. I haven't been so hot as a private eye. I was brought up on the 'Do it now' principle. Here goes."

She reached under the collar of her jacket and pulled out a thin gold chain, an extra tug brought a small chamois bag. She unfastened the safety pin that held the two together.

"Take it." He took the little bag, warm from her flesh, and slipped it into an inside pocket of his gray coat. "I've felt guilty every minute since I evaded Rolfe Sanborn's questions at luncheon. Now my conscience will stop needling, I hope."

"Watch your step that you don't give it something more important to get busy over — doubting a friend, for instance. How did you work out that 'Ford 13–4' meant today at the Lincoln Museum?"

She told of poring over the guide to Washington.

"I'm not at all sure that my solution had rhyme or reason, that it wasn't merely fuzzy thinking, if real thinking can be fuzzy, but when I saw Gibson Gary Brown standing in the doorway at Ford's Theater—"

"Why the full stop? Where does he fit into your free translation of the hieroglyphics on the card?"

"It was free all right. Forget I spoke of him. It isn't fair that my imaginings—"

"Listen, Wendy. You are suspected of smuggling papers—"

"Papers! The person who rifled my overnight case was after jewels."

"*Jewels!* How do you know?"

"Steve told me. Now that you've heard so much I'd better tell the story from A to Z."

"Jewels! Smuggled!"

"Why the startled pause after smuggled, if there is such a thing as a startled pause. I'm not suspected of transporting anything else, am I?"

"No. *No.* Settle back in the seat again. That 'startled pause' was for dramatic effect. I am trying to impress you with the necessity of reporting to Rolfe and me everything that happens, even events which seem to you to be of trifling importance, not to frighten you."

"I'm not frightened. I was at first. Perhaps my mind is becoming conditioned to fright if my heart isn't. That organ has acquired the habit of zooming to my throat then grounding in my shoes at the least suggestion of excitement."

"I don't like that heart activity."

"Can't say *I'm* crazy about it but nothing can be done to correct it till this mystery is

cleared up. It is getting 'curiouser and curiouser, said Alice.'"

"We'll clear it with a little time and your
complete confidence. Give me the works.
Why were you startled to see Gib Brown at
Ford's? Tell me every thought and suspicion
you've had since you stole down the terrace
path yesterday morning."

"That's a large order."

"You may omit personal matters."

"That's noble of you."

"Quit fencing, Wendy." Then as if to cushion his abrupt cease-fire order, "Rolfe and I
are up against a tough proposition. We need
your help."

"I *want* to help. I'll go all out to help, but
your lordly 'I was a king in Babylon and you
were a Christian slave' manner gets under
my skin, sometimes. After all, I am an individual with ideas."

"You're telling me. As I remarked before,
you are not a very perceptive person. Let's
get back on the beam, it will make easier
going — for me. Why were you startled to
see Gib Brown?"

In a low voice, as if she feared her story
might get on the air, she told of Gib's report of the dog and cat fight just before
dawn; of her own suspicion that he might
have been one of the two shadows, could

have tucked the plastic envelope into the hands of the bronze nymph and that he had gone to Ford's to meet the man or woman for whom the "Or else" threat was intended in ignorance of the fact that she had it.

As she talked the silver-gray convertible slid smoothly through the soft box-scented air along a black road checkered with shadows of tree branches waving across circles of gold flung by arc lights; past ornate iron fences through which were visible façades of red brick Georgian houses; by stretches of dark river. A plane droned overhead. Her eyes followed the lights which paled the stars till they winked out in the velvet indigo of the sky. A few cars cityward bound passed on the lane the other side of the freshly whitened line.

"That's all. There isn't any more," she concluded. "I've turned my memory inside out, I feel as if it had been gone over thoroughly with a vacuum cleaner. I can't figure out Zaidee Latour's presence at Ford's Theater this afternoon. That rigamarole about writing up the children was window dressing, I'll wager. Why was Cardella there with Russ Ruggles in his train?"

"That's an easy one, Cardella — not Ruggles. When you and Latour deplaned she called, 'Good-bye, Mrs. Smith!' Cardella, the man you suspected was trailing you—"

"Knew is the word."

"Knew was trailing you — was there, wasn't he? That farewell call was to identify you for his benefit. Rolfe and I are sure the two are working together. Graham's tip about the stolen jewels adds a splinter of light though no reports have come through that the two have been seen together before today."

"We're not sure they were there to get together. Where and how does Mr. Ruggles fit into the picture — or doesn't he?"

"You've got me there. You told me that good old Josh wouldn't allow Cardella to be invited to dinner. One would think his pal Ruggles would respect his dislike of the man and out of loyalty keep away from him. And that reminds me, if you can possibly avoid it don't meet or speak to Russ."

"That will be difficult unless I pack my bags and depart from Red Terraces. Would it be possible to explain why I'm to wipe him off the slate?"

"Ruggles is Clare Sanborn's divorced husband."

"Lucie told me."

"Lucie's a grand girl, but she could double easily as the town crier. I ask you to keep away from him because Rolfe and I suspect he's up to mischief. He might trap you into admitting you carried the papers, and in that way plunge our embassy into trouble and your friend Graham into danger. Only one answer. Keep out of his way."

She mustn't speak to Ruggles because she might reveal the fact that she had carried secret papers. He and Cardella were pals. She had been right when she had felt that the appearance of the South American in her life meant trouble. Apropos of nothing, merely to change the subject, she admitted thoughtfully:

"I'm curious about Madame Latour. I watched her when she came into the museum this afternoon to see if her eyes would find Gib Brown."

"Why Gib?"

"Lucie said that the evening at Red Terraces she was 'buttering him.' She named his disqualifications for the woman's interest then added that it might be she wanted him to photograph her."

"He's an ace at the job."

"So I've heard. I had a rootless thought when he scooped up those rolls of films."

"What rolls of films?"

"They came out of the box Sambo knocked over with his bejeweled tail. Didn't you see them?"

"No. I was too busy, trying to corral that black devil. I didn't see the films and I didn't open the kitchen window. Who did?"

XX

He drove slowly, his mind occupied with the varied facets of Wendy's experiences and observations, trying to fit them together as if they were colored scraps of a puzzle, as indeed they were; trying to figure out a way to prevent Ruggles from contacting her — suppose he went to Crandon and laid the case before him?

"I've been thinking about that open window," her voice splintered his self-questioning. "We should have gone through the house before we left to find out if there had been theft."

"Lucie probably left it open and forgot. She's a trifle irresponsible."

"Not in the big things. She's a wonderful mother and her husband adores her. I hope he was not terribly hurt by her suspicion."

"Distrust can cut to the quick. Forget them. There is nothing an outsider can do to smooth misunderstanding between husband and wife. It's like fooling with an explosive to try it."

"You speak as if you had had boundless experience in trying to patch up marital quarrels."

"No experience. I speak from observation. We are now passing Arcady," he announced in the tone of a conductor of a seeing-Washington bus.

"Really!" Wendy straightened. "Do you mean there, behind those sensational iron gates?"

"Yes. Those same gates are considered collector's items. My grandfather bought the place — it had an interesting history then — when he came to Washington, the first senator from his state. You can't see the house, it is too far back. A portico at the rear faces the bay. You'll see it from the blind when we pull off the duck party."

"Am I still invited?"

Just a hint of a quiver in the gay question reminded him of the voices of the adorables when aggrieved. He couldn't bear to see a child hurt. The girl beside him wasn't a child, he reminded himself, and sternly resisted the urge to put his arm about her and draw her head to his shoulder.

"Sure, you're invited. Why not?" He managed to pitch his response in precisely the right key.

"You told me that your interest in a person who doubted your word — you meant me — was absolutely nil."

"Did I say all that?" The temptation to take her in his arms was almost irresistible but he had made a compact that he wouldn't tell her he loved her till the news item had been wiped off the slate, he reminded himself again.

"I never allow personal antagonisms to exclude a good shoe from a duck hunt." The remark was a masterpiece of amused indifference. "Almost, if not quite, I would include Russ Ruggles. He's tops with a 16-gauge. Here's where we come about en route for Red Terraces."

As he turned the car she looked back.

"From the little I could see I know that your Arcady — I love the name — is a heavenly spot. How can you bear to have it closed?"

"It isn't closed. Didn't you hear me invite the Browns to help me celebrate Thanksgiving there? I hope to have other—" The rest of the sentence was lost in the throb of a plane directly overhead. The sound dwindled to a distant hum.

"That pilot was flying too low even for

this country with few houses. I hope the prowl car got his number."

"Will there be a prowl car at this time of night?"

"There should be one paid for by the residents. Lots of irreplaceable marketable treasures behind these brick façades. That wacky pilot's stunt interrupted a question that has been pricking at my mind. How do you account for your friend Graham's presence at Ford's this afternoon? Struck me there was something phony about his explanation."

"I can't account for it. It is as inexplicable as his behavior outside the restaurant, where I had luncheon with Mr. Sanborn. As this appears to be 'Tell All Day' I'll give you a thumbnail sketch of what happened."

As he listened to her recital of Steve's collision with Cardella he wondered if that were why Graham had invited himself to breakfast, the apology that he was sorry he couldn't accept the invitation to lunch at the House Restaurant was trumped up, of course, no invitation had been given him to lunch at the House Restaurant.

A sound behind them. Wendy had heard it, her hand closed on his arm.

"That really is all," she concluded gaily. "There isn't any more to my s-story."

"The air is getting crisp. You'll need the coat I have in the backseat. I'll—"

"Don't look for it," a gruff voice ordered. "I have you both covered." A pressure on Van's shoulder emphasized the threat. "Drive on till I tell you to stop. Then I'll take the jewels the girl's carrying round."

Van looked ahead at the long shiny black road. Not a car in sight on either side of the white line. The white line!

"Get going," the order from behind was accompanied by a reminding dig. "And keep going."

"By the red lights?"

"Sure. Who's checking on lights this time of night?"

"Okay! You're the doctor."

He kept his eyes on the windshield mirror hoping to catch a glimpse of the man behind. Apparently he was experienced in backseat holdups, he kept his head out of sight and the gun pressure steady — if it were a gun. When had he climbed into the car? While they were in the cottage, of course. The open window. Probably he had been ransacking the house, had heard Lucie and him arrive and had made a getaway, without stopping to close it behind him.

He looked down at the girl. Her face was white, her eyes seemed enormous as they met his. Of course she hadn't the jewels, but if the heel hiding in the back seat were convinced that she had — he winced away from the possibilities. He must get her safely out of this, if he failed — he wouldn't, he *couldn't* fail.

"Van, you might tell the passenger in the rear that I don't know what he means by jewels." Her voice was cool, undisturbed, there was even a hint of laughter. Good Lord, didn't she understand—

"Keep your mouths shut, both of you. I'll do the talking."

No sound after that but the swish of tires on macadam; a car in the other lane whooshed by. The pressure on his shoulder increased. Since the turn at Arcady he had been aware he was carrying a third passenger. Twice he had heard the sound of hard breathing, tried to convince himself it was his imagination keyed to fever pitch because of his anxiety about Wendy's safety. A car coming. A touch on his arm. Her eyes with a question in them met his in the windshield mirror, her lips formed the word, "Prowl?"

It could be but there was one chance in ten that it was. Why raise her hopes? He shook his head. Came a reminding dig at his shoulder. The backseat rider had ears also.

"Pass that auto comin' an' pass it quick.

Give any kind of signal and—" a pressure finished the sentence.

"You'd better keep out of sight," Van threw over his shoulder. "It's the prowl car."

"Quit tryin' to be funny, there ain't no prowl car this time of night."

"Perhaps there ain't," Van agreed, with a careful adaptation of his English. He met Wendy's eyes in the mirror, not blue now, deep purple with excitement. His lips warned, "Hold on."

He didn't notice her response, he was watching the car cruising toward them at a leisurely pace. He figured the distance. When it was about thirty feet ahead, with a fervent prayer that the brake would hold when he needed it, he swung the convertible across the white line and shot toward the oncoming car.

Screech of brakes. Two officers spilling from the prowl car. Furious red-hot phrases he hadn't heard since he left the service. Fierce light in his face.

"What in he—" Fury choked the voice. "What d'you mean swingin' across into this lane, you—"

Stop swearing, Cap! Pull out the guy in the—"

"There he goes! Catch him, officer!" Wendy shouted, "Catch him! Come back,

Van. Remember, he has a — Come *back!* They have him."

They had. Arms securely linked in his they pushed a fantastic figure forward. They hadn't stopped to pull off the brown paper bag over his head, with holes behind which eyes glittered. Who was under it, Van wondered, as the officers bundled their catch into their car. The man whom he had called Cap, a cop whom he had known for years, approached with a notebook and touched his hat.

"You could a knocked me over with a feather, Mr. Van, when I caught on who was the fella crossin' the white line into outgoin' lane. I've known you an' your folks for years an' I never knew one of you to break a traffic law. I thought for a minute you'd been drinkin' an' believe me it most made me sick. If one of the Tyler boys had gone woozy there wasn't nothing left to believe in."

"It was the only way I could think of for getting rid of our backseat rider, Cap, with his gun at my shoulder."

"Gun? Where is it? He didn't have a gun when we nabbed him."

"Look on the floor. He may have dropped it."

"You've got the right idea, Miss — or is it

259

Mrs.?" The officer held up a black glove and a revolver. "The guy didn't mean to leave fingerprints. He was hiding under the lap robe. I guess you folks had a narrow escape, all right. Take a look at him, Mr. Van, tell us if you ever seen him before. The lady needn't go."

"But the lady wants to," Wendy announced eagerly.

Van caught her hand tight in his as they crossed the short space between the convertible and the prowl car. "Short" was right. Blood sang in his ears. One more foot and there would have been a collision.

The man inside had his arm across his face. A crumpled brown paper bag lay at his feet. The officer poked with his night stick.

"Take it down."

The arm came down. Van caught his breath sharply. Wendy stifled an exclamation of surprise.

"How about it, Mr. Van. Know the guy?"

"No. Never saw him before."

"You, Miss?"

"No."

"Come on, Wendy." As they turned their backs on the prowl car the officer shook his head.

"What was he after? Running away from someone?"

"Looks to me like a holdup. It's getting to be a major industry."

"Those real pearls round your neck, Miss — Mrs.?"

"Yes."

"There it is. The guy's probably been followin' you for days, watching for this chance. We'll beat it. You'll have to appear at the lineup tomorrow morning at ten-thirty. I won't hand you a card for crossin' the white line this time, Mr. Van, though I bet fright shortened my life ten years when I saw your convertible shootin' for us." He touched his cap. "Good night. Good night, Mrs. Van."

They watched the prowl car turn and shoot toward the city, watched till the light was a mere red pinpoint that twinkled out.

"Hop in, Wendy. The Cap has finally decided who you are. We'd better get back on our side of the road." As the car slipped ahead he looked down at her.

"Steady, now?"

"Yes and no. Remember the Cap said that the guy probably had been following me for days watching for a chance to snatch my pearls? Remember the Tap! Tap! of feet behind us last evening? Was he stalking my pearls then?"

"Stop shivering. I don't believe those footsteps had anything to do with us, if they had it wasn't the same man."

"Glory be, that's encouraging to think *two* may be concentrating on me. That isn't all that gives me the chillies. Every few seconds my breath catches and threatens to choke me. I *knew* you would stop before we crashed, I *knew* that nothing could happen with you at the wheel, but — what induced you to cross the white line?"

"Our passenger was in deadly earnest. We couldn't hail the prowl car. I couldn't risk being pitched out and leaving you at his mercy. The only alternative was to have the cops bawl us out for crossing into the other lane. If a bullet went through my shoulder at least you would be safe with them. Amazing how fast one can think when up against danger. I had the car under control — if nothing broke. The memory sets the roots of my hair tingling. Let's forget it. Sure you've never seen our backseat rider before?"

"Sure. When that brown paper bag came off I expected to meet Señor Cardella's nut-brown eyes. I was never more surprised in my life when I saw a stranger. How did the man know I was suspected of carrying jewels?"

"Either he heard you speak of them after we started or is in cahoots with the South American. Darn lucky you kept your voice low when you told of the Ford 13–4 message. Perhaps he was burglarizing on the side at the Browns'. Lucky he didn't run into Sambo with the emerald and diamond ring. I figure that when he heard us stop in front of the house he made his getaway via the kitchen window and jumped into this car for a free ride back to the city. He caught the word 'jewels.' Heard Opportunity calling and decided to hold us up."

"He's getting his free ride. What was he after at the Browns'? Do you think he is the person who stole my automatic and drugged Angeline? I've read in the paper that sometimes a neighborhood is burglarized by the same man."

"Your guess is as good as mine. Suppose we stop wondering. Rest your head against my arm. We won't speak again until we reach Red Terraces."

"That won't stop our thinking."

"That's right. Okay?"

He felt the nod of her head. She was one hundred percent right, silence didn't stop thinking, it speeded it up. Had the man who had threatened them been an independent worker after Wendy's pearls as the Cap had suggested, or was he a part of a vicious group of which Cardella was a member? Whichever way it was, her safety was threatened. Could he persuade her to leave the city? Nix on that idea. Where would she be as safe as here with Rolfe and himself to guard her?

When they reached Red Terraces they exchanged a whispered "Good night." He unlocked the entrance door, watched in the hall as she ran up the stairs, heard her door close. He stood by the convertible, hating to leave her, wishing passionately that he had the right to go up those stairs with her.

"Anything I can do for you, Mr. Tyler?"

Propper's smooth voice. Propper stepping from the shadow of shrubs. Van thought of Wendy's description of the activity of her heart, its zooming and grounding. The butler's appearance had given him what might be described inadequately as a "start."

"Why the devil are you running round the place at this time of night, Propper?" Surprise exploded in indignation. The butler held his wrist to his eyes to inspect the illuminated dial of his watch.

"Not so late, sir. Just twelve. You phoned you would be here at midnight. I always stay up till the family is in, Mr. Tyler. Miss Wendy was the only member out. Good night, sir."

A dismissal, here's your hat and what's your hurry. In spite of exceeding uneasiness induced by the events of the evening Van grinned.

"Nighty-night, Propper."

Good Lord, will I ever get the complications which have been piling one on top of the other since the day Wendy burst into my compartment on the train sorted and pigeon-holed, he thought as he crossed the foyer of the hotel in which he lived.

Music came through the partly open doorway of a brilliantly lighted salon. To an accompaniment of voices and the clink of glasses, the Marine Band was giving with "From the Halls of Montezuma." He would have known the outfit by the virility of the music if he hadn't seen the splash of red jackets. A woman in a floating pale blue frock and a top brass with a startling array of decorations crossed the foyer to the elevator. A man in dinner clothes with smooth blond hair sprang from a chair and approached him.

Graham. What did it mean? Instinctively he glanced at the great gilt clock on the wall. Graham was due for breakfast. Was it already morning? Had he himself blacked out after the excitement of the attempted holdup? Graham sensed his bewilderment and laughed.

"Wrong, Tyler. I haven't come to breakfast." Gravity replaced amusement. "I must talk with you. I didn't dare wait until morning for fear someone would get wise and — stop me."

XXI

"Nice place you have here. I like red tones in a man's room. Rich-looking."

Steve Graham settled back in a deep chair at one side of a fireplace in which logs smoldered and spat showers of flame-colored sparks. His eyes lingered for an instant on the portrait of a lovely dark-haired woman in a white satin evening frock above the mantel, dropped to the three yellow roses in a slender silver vase below it, traveled on to a large window through which was visible an illuminated tower against a patch of indigo star-powdered sky, came back to his host at the telephone table.

"Quiet as the grave here, isn't it?" he said.

"We are on the tenth floor. What'll you have, Graham? I'll order anything you want."

"Nothing, thank you. When my embassy boss tapped me for my present job I cut out alcohol for the duration. Don't let that stop you, though."

"I don't drink. Smoke?" He indicated a Chinese lacquer box on the stand beside Steve Graham's chair.

"If you don't mind I'll stick to my pipe. It isn't too bad for polite society — yet."

"Go ahead. That covered Satsuma dish is full of the sort of matches you pipe-addicts use."

Van dropped into a deep chair opposite and drew a cigarette from his silver case. Above the flame of his lighter he studied the face of his guest. Tonight it showed shrewd and hard-bitten intelligence, when he had seen it before the gravity had been masked by the man's natural spontaneity of spirit. The embassy boss had tapped wisely, he decided.

"What's it all about, Graham? You wouldn't be here at this time of night unless the matter were important. Does it relate to the papers I delivered to the Department of State?"

"In a way. Safe for me to talk here? This room has a Hollywoodish size and luxury that prepares me for the gum-shoe entrance of a gentleman's gentleman."

"The man who takes care of these rooms, my clothes and serves breakfast goes home at night. Shoot the works."

"As you know that Miss Adair brought important papers from South America you must know also of the revolution from which she escaped. Did she tell you of the rumored theft of state jewels?"

"For the first time this evening."

"At the time of that alleged theft ten rolls of microfilmed vital agreements between the U. S. and the government threatened by the revolutionists disappeared from the embassy files."

"Not for the first time, I understand. We know now that that type of theft has been going on for six years. It got a head start during the war and has been discovered only recently. Was Miss Adair's overnight case searched for jewels or films — Films? Films?" he repeated under his breath.

"You've got us there. We can't figure out just where that piece of rifled luggage fits into the plot."

"Who's us?"

"My instructions were to keep that information under secret, heavy wraps at present. You, of all persons, understand that orders are orders."

"I do. I don't understand, though, why you have come to me instead of Rolfe Sanborn? He was my chief during the war.

Every visitor who comes to this city is screened by his department."

"You're telling me. He put me through the third degree — and how. He must have been satisfied or he wouldn't have given me this."

From an inside pocket of his black coat he drew a billfold, from the billfold extracted a small envelope and held it up.

"The safe-conduct I received from him. You look incredulous. If you don't believe me, take a look-see at the card inside duly inscribed with his signature."

"Return it to your pocket. I believe you. If I appeared incredulous it was because I didn't know that you and my chief had met before we dined at Red Terraces."

"Carrying out instructions I made for his office directly from the National Airport when the plane landed. It took time to persuade his watchdog, Hood, who was alone in the outer office, to admit me to the presence, but after I showed him the strawberry mark on my left arm plus a few other items of identification, he came across and let me in." He leaned forward.

"I'll tell you why I came to you. I have been informed you are a man in whom one may put implicit confidence."

"For the love of Pete, does that mean you don't trust Rolfe Sanborn? You're crazy."

"He's okay, but I don't trust his secretary."

"Hood? He would die before he would disclose his chief's business."

"I understand Hood is Sanborn's first assistant. I am speaking of his *secretary*."

"You mean—?" Amazement short-circuited Van Tyler's voice.

"I do. You may remember that I took the lady stepping the other evening. She is charming, in fact her charm has a heady quality. Fortunately I realized that before I answered her query as to why I was in Washington."

"You're not intimating that Clare Sanborn is under Un-American Activities Committee investigation, are you?"

"That isn't what I mean. She's loyal, in her fashion. She chatters, a habit which spells danger in a department like her brother's. To test her I asked her questions about the nature of her work; the business of her brother's clients; who had called on him that day. She answered, sometimes with a lot of revealing detail. If I had an appointment with Sanborn I wouldn't want anyone to know I had been there. Get my point?"

"Yes."

"Last evening she was at a nightclub with Señor Antonio Cardella."

"Cardella! Does her brother know that?"

"Search me. I understand they do not live together, that she has her own apartment, as you probably know."

"It happens that I don't, that I am not interested in her place of residence. Let's leave her and return to Miss Adair. Does she believe that her overnight case was rifled for jewels?"

"I hope so. That was the idea I tried to get across to her. You are the only person to whom the secret of the missing microfilms has been entrusted. The information is definitely hush-hush, you understand. You and I will work alone."

"Be more explicit. What's my part? Begin with your run-in with Cardella when he spoke to Miss Adair in front of the restaurant."

"Did she tell you about that?"

"Yes. Remember, she and I met under extraordinary circumstances on the train from New York. Because she was sure that Cardella was shadowing her I tried to help. I have felt responsible for her safety ever since."

"You sure helped when you delivered those papers. Since my arrival I've been tailing the near-South American. Today I was a workingman with a jag. He was annoying

Wendy. I gave him a shove. Sanborn's card kept me out of jail."

"Are you tailing him solely because of Wendy Adair?"

"No. I'm in this country to unearth those films or the parties who stole them. Cardella is hunting for something he suspects she smuggled from S. A. Microfilms or the papers she brought? Which is he after? That's the catch."

"I assume she told you of the woman who grabbed her overnight case when they started to deplane?"

"Under the mistaken idea that it was hers? Sure. When the dame called 'Good-bye, Mrs. Smith,' she was tipping off Cardella, of course. Wendy doesn't suspect that, though."

Doesn't she? My boy, you've missed a trick, Van thought before he inquired:

"Has she told you that her seatmate was Madame Latour, the glamorous brunette whom you met at dinner at Red Terraces?"

"She didn't tell me, but Madame did, with trimmings. The face of her host put on an excellent imitation of a thundercloud during the recital. Are he and she old pals? Something told me they had been."

"Could be, though I understand she was invited to Red Terraces because she and

Miss Adair had flown from South America in the same plane. Is the news of the theft of the State jewels public property?"

"I have seen no reference to it in the papers." He paused to relight his pipe. "So far as I know it is still undercover stuff. Why?"

Van told of the backseat driver who had emphasized with a gun the fact that he was after the jewels the girl carried. He watched Graham's face. It turned white, went a dull red. He started to rise, dropped back into his chair.

"No. *No.* Gosh, if he had disposed of you and—"

"He *didn't* dispose of me. But — until those jewels are located and turned over to the owners — Wendy Adair is not safe."

Steve Graham lighted and discarded three matches before his pipe would draw. Through the smoke of a cigarette Van observed his unsteady hands.

"Did either you or she recognize the holdup guy when the cops grabbed him, Tyler?"

"No. Later when they had him safely in the prowl car we had a close-up view. Neither of us had seen him before."

"I gather you think he had given the Browns' house the once-over."

"Work it out yourself. An open first-floor

window; a *Hausfrau* who declared it was closed when she left home in the afternoon; a man with a gun hidden in the backseat of a convertible in the road in front of the house."

"Anything missing?"

"The Browns hadn't begun to check when we left. They didn't know a man was hiding in my car. Luckily a four-thousand-dollar emerald and diamond ring was being worn by their black cat at the time."

"A cat? Are you kidding?"

Van explained. The room rang with Graham's laughter. Nervous laughter, as if he had been released suddenly from a tense emotional strain.

"Some kids. Let's get back on the beam. We're a long way off."

Not so far off, a voice in Van's mind declared with a clearness that startled him. "Don't you ever have a warning sound off in your mind clear as a voice speaking?" Wendy had asked, now he could answer "Yes."

"Did you get a look that would enable you to describe the jerk?" Steve Graham had returned to the backseat rider.

"No. When the cop flashed a light in his face he closed his eyes and distorted his mouth. I doubt if I'll be much help at identification at the lineup tomorrow at ten-thirty."

Graham sprang to his feet, pushed up his dark blue sleeve and glanced at his wrist watch.

"One o'clock. It's tomorrow already. Ten-thirty is now today. I'll be there. I'll bet you'll recognize the guy when you see him. Here's hoping that one or the other head of the two projects has picked for a stooge a minor criminal who will squeal. Why are you staring at my sleeve?"

"I'm not. I didn't realize my eyes had focused on that while trying to visualize the man's face. I—"

"Who's knocking at this time in the morning?" Graham's usually bright blue eyes, now black as coals, were on the door to the corridor. "Could be someone who knows us both. I can't afford to be seen here. It will be a giveaway. I've got to finish the job. This is a heck of a situation." Another cautious knock. "Where can I go?" His low voice had dwindled to a whisper.

"Something phony about this." Van Tyler's hushed comment reflected the concern in his eyes. "No one is permitted to come to my rooms until he has phoned from the desk, no one but Rolfe Sanborn and he has a key. Could be a special delivery, though it isn't probable. Shoot into the bedroom, not that door, that's my study. There are back stairs from the service pantry. Escape that way if you have to, but hang around if possible. We've got to get our plans threshed out. Coming. Coming," he answered another cautious tap.

After Graham disappeared he emptied an ashtray of burned matches onto the blinking coals in the fireplace, brushed a few grains of pipe tobacco from the side table, and cautiously opened the door.

"Van! *Dearie!*" Clare Sanborn slipped into the room and backed against the door she had closed behind her. She was panting breathlessly.

This isn't real, it's a nightmare, Van Tyler told himself and rubbed his hand hard across his eyes. It didn't clear away the vision of a golden-haired woman in a floating frock of lime-green lighted by little running rivulets of silver, a stole of ermine slipping from her bare shoulders, staring back at him with frightened eyes.

"Van. Don't look at me as if you were planning to strangle me." She caught her throat in her right hand. "I was at the ball downstairs dancing with Señor Cardella. I saw Russ coming. He and Cardella are hand and glove at present. Something about my ex-husband frightened me. I felt trapped. The number of your apartment flashed in my mind like an answer to prayer. Rolfe and I came to two of your dinner parties here last winter, remember. I flew up flight after flight of stairs and—"

"Now you'll fly down and — quick. I've heard your trumped-up stories before." The voice he had recovered was hoarse. "Out." He caught her shoulder with one hand, seized the knob with the other and yanked open the door.

"So this is where my former wife disappeared to?" Russ Ruggles leaned a shoulder against the doorframe and planted a shoe in glistening patent leather on the threshold. "Still running away from me to—"

"Shucks, Clare," interrupted a voice.

Van stared incredulously at the man in evening dress standing on the threshold of the study. He patted his hand over his mouth to cover a prodigious yawn before he protested:

"When I told you I'd take you home from the party, Sister, I didn't agree to wait in Van's apartment for you to join me till dewy morn. He might like to get a little shut-eye himself. Let's go."

Rolfe Sanborn drew the white ermine stole over his sister's shoulders. For the first time he appeared to notice the smug-smiling man in the doorway.

"For crying out loud, see who's here! Hounding your ex-wife, Russ? Cut it out."

With a mighty shove he pushed his surprised onetime brother-in-law into the hall and drew Clare from the room.

"See you today as arranged, fella," he called over his shoulder before he softly closed the door.

Van slipped the lock. Brushed his hand across his eyes. Nightmare. It must have been nightmare. Nothing like that happens in real life.

Anything can happen, his inner monitor reminded softly, anything at all.

"I guess I pulled a boner when I warned you against Sanborn's secretary," declared a voice behind him. He whirled. Steve Graham was regarding him with hostile eyes. "I heard her voice. I've been waiting in the bedroom with hands over my ears since the moment I heard her say 'Dearie.' She seemed quite at home here. It would be none of my business if you weren't double-crossing—"

"Mention that name and I'll knock you cold." Pent-up rage exploded in the furious threat.

"You darn kid, don't you realize you were

spotted in the foyer, were seen coming here with me? You said you didn't dare wait till morning for fear you might be seen and stopped. Cardella and Ruggles are at a ball downstairs. That little playlet was staged to catch you, not me. What's it all about? That yarn that state jewels were stolen is a lot of hooey, an invention of your own, isn't it?"

"Right. Faked. Red herring drawn across the trail of information I'm after. When you told me Wendy had been in danger because of jewels it scared the daylights out of me."

"That proves the holdup guy got his tip from what she said in the car. Come clean. Your wristwatch is the 'strawberry mark on your left arm' you referred to as identification, isn't it?"

"Yes. Gosh, how did you get on to that?"

"Following up the stolen microfilms is not your real mission here, is it? There is something more important."

"Sure, there's something more important. That's what I came to tell you, but, hang it all, you haven't given me a chance."

"Sorry, Steve, shoot, but, first, I'd like to know why you were stealing through the garden at Red Terraces at four o'clock the morning after you dined there?"

XXII

Wendy abruptly halted her impetuous rush down the stairs at Red Terraces and looked incredulously at the man who had stepped from the drawing room into the hall.

"Mr. Ruggles! Why are you here in the early afternoon? Mother and Josh are attending a luncheon in honor of a returned general at the Shoreham. They're not due back—"

"I didn't come to see them." He rested clasped hands on the newel post. "I came to see you."

He'd be terribly good-looking in a dark romantic way if those little black devils didn't dance in his eyes. The thought sent a chill creeping along her spine.

"Sorry, you'll have to come some other time. I have a date—" she glanced at the watch on her wrist, "I must punch the time clock in just five minutes."

"Five minutes is all I need. I have tickets for Constitution Hall tonight, three of the Met top stars are singing. Dine with me and take in that, will you?"

"I can't. I go on the air at five-thirty. I'm making my debut before a U. S. audience at Mr. Sanborn's station."

"You won't be broadcasting all the evening. I'll pick you up at the studio and—"

"I wouldn't be dressed for such a white-tie and diamond-dog-collar occasion."

"You didn't let me finish my sentence. I'll pick you up, bring you back here to change, before we go to dinner."

"Sorry." Why had she said that? She wasn't. "No can do. I have a dinner date, a don't-dress date, to follow the program."

"I'll bet you crossed your fingers when you told that one. Perhaps I'm wrong, though. Perhaps you are planning to dine with that husband you're keeping under cover."

"Mr. Ruggles, how often must I tell you that was just a story I was telling Vance Tyler? How can I make you believe—"

"That's easy. Go out with me tonight."

"No, I don't break dates."

"Have it your way, but, here's something to think about. I'm not the only person who is onto that marriage. What paper do you read? I'll ask you again — to go out with me — and soon. Perhaps Josh can change your mind. I'll be seeing you."

The door closed with a mighty slam. His exit was a slice of ham acting, if ever she'd seen one, and she had. What had he meant? "What paper do you read?" "Perhaps Josh can change your mind." Had he a hold on Joshua Crandon? Was Russ Ruggles one of the persons "out to get him"? That was a crazy idea. Weren't they friends? No use standing here wondering. She had promised to take the Brown sisters on a tea party. The Russ Ruggles interlude had left her less than five minutes in which to get to the cottage.

Two hours later she smiled at the little blonde girls on the front seat and stopped the dark green roadster.

"Here we are, adorables. Four o'clock. On time to the minute. 'Home is the sailor, home from sea and the hunter home from the hill,'" she orated in her best dramatic manner.

"Why do you say such funny things, Wendy?" The big blue eyes of the six-year-old were fixed on her face in eager questioning.

"Because I'm a funny girl, maybe, sweetness. We had a grand tea party at Rock Creek Park, didn't we, kiddies?"

"Out of this world, darling, that's what Daddy says when he kisses Mummy. What does out of this world mean, Wendy?" The elder child's voice was puzzled. The four-year-old offspring of the house of Brown was absorbed in watching the windshield wipers she had set in motion.

"Something precious, something you admire, perhaps something you love very much."

"The way you love Van, Wendy? Mummy told Daddy she could just feel—"

"Hey, adorables!" The call Lucie sent ahead as she raced along the path disrupted her daughter's revelation. "Say thank you to Wendy, children," she prompted when she reached the car.

What could Lucie "just feel," Wendy wondered indignantly before two pairs of small arms were flung about her neck in a strangling embrace and rosy cheeks were pressed against hers.

"Thank you, Wendy. Thank you," the children chorused before they clambered out of the roadster. The six-year-old turned and called:

"Next time let us hunt in the creek for frogs the way that boy did, will you, Wendy?"

"Will you, Wendy?" the four-year-old parroted.

"Thanks a million, glamour girl. I'm so rested I can move mountains. Come on, children. We mustn't detain Wendy, she has a date."

Lucie threw a kiss before she started for the house holding a child with each hand as they hopped and skipped beside her, their blonde hair blowing, their identical brief aqua skirts switching with each motion of their small bodies.

"Don't forget the broadcast at five-thirty," Wendy called. "I'll be singing to you, lovelies."

"Okay! Okay!" they shouted in response. The cat crouched on the window sill saw them, leaped to the ground and shot around a corner of the house. They caught sight of the disappearing tip of a black tail and with a concerted, ear-splitting yell started in pursuit.

"Poor Sambo," Wendy commiserated as the roadster slid forward. "Life must be just one thing after the other for him."

She thought of the evening she had tugged and tugged to pull the diamond and emerald ring from the cat's tail; of the drive with Van Tyler which followed; visualized the beautiful iron gates at Arcady; shivered at the memory of the man with a gun hidden in the convertible; wondered if Van had

made use of the plastic envelope she had unfastened from the gold chain about her
neck; recalled his voice when he had phoned
the next morning to tell her she need not
appear at the lineup, he could do the job for
both.

That had been days ago. She had neither
seen nor heard from him since. "The way
you love Van, Wendy?" the child's voice
echoed in her memory. What had Lucie
meant by "She could just feel—"

Why dwell on that? Why not? It had the
virtue of resting her mind from the sen-
tences which had been going round and
round like two squirrels in a revolving cage
even while she had played with and told the
children stories. "What paper do you read?"
"Perhaps Josh can change your mind." Each
had contained a threat. Why should Russ
Ruggles threaten her?

Life was growing more and more compli-
cated. For instance, take the trip to Mount
Vernon with Steve. As the car sped along the
curves of the Memorial Highway, he had
been grave, almost taciturn, so unlike his
usual cheery self that had he been anyone
else she would have thought him tense,
alert, on guard.

To her as they went from room to room,
many of them filled with the original fur-

nishings, the house was permeated with the spirit of the great man who had lived there, but Steve had appeared as if his mind were journeying in a distant land. Not until, head bared, he stood before the ivy-draped tomb in the side of a hill that overlooked the Potomac glistening in the sunlight did he appear to sense what he was seeing. Even there, after a few minutes he touched her arm and moved away.

"Why the rush, Steve?" she had asked as he hurried her to the parking place. "I feel as if I had been shot through the house and grounds of our first president in a rocket ship."

"Got an appointment. Didn't know it when I tied up your afternoon with this expedition, lovely. Step on it, will you?"

He had been so absorbed in thought on the way back to Red Terraces she had felt that an observation of hers would be an intrusion. Puzzled, she had watched his Drive-Yourself convertible shoot out of sight. Something was wrong with Steve Graham. Why not? Something terribly wrong was in the air floating about like a gray wraith listening, hovering, waiting.

Had he returned to South America? At Ford's Theater he had said he had but two days more here. Ford's Theater. What a fiasco her dip into the Sherlock Holmes–Perry Mason metier had been. Not an infinitesimal clue had she picked up to help solve the meaning of the message — if it had been a message — tucked into the hand of the bronze nymph. Van Tyler had the envelope with its enclosure. If he had made progress in untangling the mystery wouldn't he have told her?

Definitely no. Hadn't he declared while driving home from the Browns', "Just for the record my interest in a person who doubts my word, who doesn't trust me, is absolutely nil"? She had doubted him. She had not trusted him. Where did that land her? On the rocks — and how. Even after that she had rested her head against his arm, she had to, to pull herself together. The excitement of discovering the backseat rider coming on top of the staggering shock in Josh's smoking room — Darn! The hideous scene had flashed on the screen of her mind again.

She had returned from the morning service yesterday refreshed, ready to start over, sure that the memory of the blood-chilling experience, her apprehension as to the seriousness of Cardella's appearance, were behind her — church always did that for her. As she approached the great Gothic edifice with its flying buttresses, arches and spires which towered above the Potomac she had wondered if she would feel lost and strange inside, of as little account as a chip bobbing on a boundless sea, but the moment she lifted her voice in the music of the opening hymn wings of peace folded about her heart as they did in the little church at home — and how she had needed comfort the year her mother — Back again in the past.

Red Terraces. She glanced at her watch. Plenty of time to make the studio after she picked up the briefcase with her notes and Grandmother Adair's mink stole she had left on the hall table. The windshield mirror reminded her that she was wearing the green suit and beret she had worn the day she met Van Tyler and Russ Ruggles. Ooch! Better stop thinking of that and get started toward town.

She ran up the steps. The door opened.

"Thank you, Prop—" the name split on her tongue. Joshua Crandon, in topcoat, hat in hand, confronted her.

"Wendy—"

"Josh, dear. Don't stop me." She snatched the briefcase and fur stole from the ornate black teakwood table. Picked up a letter and tucked it in her navy blue shoulder bag. "I can just make the studio if—"

"I'm not stopping you. I've been waiting to string along, I've never sat in on a broadcast. Take me, will you?"

"I'd love it. Come on. Would you like to drive?"

"*No.*"

"Period." She slipped behind the wheel and he settled into the seat beside her. "We may meet Mother coming home," she said as the car slid forward.

"At four-fifteen? Your mother hasn't been home at that hour more than a half-dozen times since we came to Washington. She plays cards usually before she starts on the social merry-go-round. I don't see how she keeps the pace."

"She loves it. Added to that her house runs like clockwork. She's executive, plus. The majority of us will find time and strength for what we want to do most in this world, I have observed. Question: will we? I love books. Since I have been here I've managed to read the daily paper, that's all."

"What do you want most, Wendy?"

"I'm giving that question my best constructive thought while I make with my feet on that same social treadmill. I know this, I don't intend to spend my energies on a lot of different projects. I'll select one big interest and give it all there is in me, hew to the line let the chips fall where they may."

"Will it be music?"

"No. I haven't enough voice for that. How was the luncheon for the general? He was one of my top admirations during the war and has been since."

"His speech was a humdinger. He closed by reminding us that the greatest crime a citizen can commit today is to forget what happened during the war, to become indifferent to the frightful suffering and horror of those who took part in it, and the heart-searing effect on those who worked and waited behind the lines. 'Indifference, *indifference* to what your country is doing, your city, your town, is responsible for conditions which you sit at home and deplore and do nothing about.' The curse of indifference was the theme of his talk.

"As you can see, by my account, he made a tremendous impression on one citizen at least. I was so sure of the way this last election would go, I didn't go home to vote. There was a moment of tense silence after he finished before the hall rocked with applause. I wonder if his appeal will result in a mere wave of civic interest or in a steady sea of determination to improve conditions."

She was getting a glimpse of the real man beneath the breezy, shoulder-slapping surface. This was the side of Joshua Crandon that collected rare editions.

"Some will remember and work, some will sink back into inertia. Utopia would be with us if every member of that audience tackled the civic problems in his district with all there is in him. That reminds me, I'd better give my program the once-over. Mind if we don't talk for a few minutes? This will be my introduction to a United States audience — that sounds as if I expected a coast-to-coast coverage, I don't — it's got to be good."

"It is bound to be. I've heard you practicing. Pity that same public can't see you. Don't have the roadster on your mind. I'll park it. You shouldn't drive home alone. What do we have a chauffeur for?"

XXIII

Principally for Mother, Wendy thought in answer to his impatient question. The car sped on over the shining black road. Black silhouettes of boles and branches were etched against the western sky. The slanting sun had flung a Roman scarf across the horizon. The edges of stripes of crimson, rose, pale green, lemon-yellow melted into each other. The river was a curving red-gold ribbon. Violet fused into the blue of the heavens in which one star shone like a brilliant eye peeking through the darkening curtain as if to admire the glory of color below. Shadows deepened into darker shadows.

"The days are shortening fast, too fast," she said, then as the man beside her did not answer she stole a glance at him. His hat was pulled low, his lips were set in a tight line. He was still beside her but his spirit had moved away from her. What threatened his security if not his life? Was he reliving — she must not think of that afternoon. Unpleasant memories were like an invading enemy, she must defend the citadel of her mind against the attack. The answer to that was to concentrate on the program ahead.

She ran over the short talk between the songs to the accompaniment of the muted swish of tires on macadam. Letter-perfect. She had it all by heart.

"Now let's talk," she invited. "How quickly it gets dark."

"Yes, but what a springlike season we have had in the process. All set for the radio debut?" Joshua Crandon inquired sympathetically.

"Everything under control. Will you be going back with me?"

"No, I'm to meet your mother at a party. I made a trade with her, I would appear at the embassy if after it was over she would come back with me and for just once in months spend a quiet evening at Red Terraces."

"Did she agree?"

"Yes. I — I haven't told her about that — what happened in the smoking room the other afternoon, Wendy."

"Neither have I. It was referred to on the

radio that evening. Do you suppose she heard it?"

"She never listens to the radio. I don't like the idea of you driving from the city alone after dark."

Apparently the subject of the mixed-up boxes was closed. Would she ever know the explanation of "They're out to g-get me, Wendy"?

"I don't mind the big, bad dark."

I do, I do, she contradicted herself. Almost I would welcome a hitchhiker for company. Sissy! You're not starting to be afraid at your advanced age, I hope.

"Perhaps you're not going home after the broadcast? Perhaps you have what is technically known as a date?"

"I haven't, though I intimated as much to Mr. Ruggles when he invited me to the top-drawer concert at Constitution Hall tonight, sponsored by the high lights of Washington society. I know he's your best friend, Josh, and it isn't cricket for me, a guest in your house, to criticize him, but I don't like the man and I will not go out with him." She curbed the impulse to ask if his friend had a hold on him, what he had meant by "Perhaps Josh can change your mind."

Why didn't he answer? Was he hurt or angry? She'd better let him know that she didn't intend to accept his hospitality for long.

"I see so little of Mother that I might as well be somewhere else. I'm planning to fare forth on my own soon. New York beckons."

"Wait until after Christmas. I don't look upon you as either my guest or your mother's, you are part of my family. It will be wiser for me not to know of your aversion to Russ at present — before we drop the subject, he is not my best friend."

The last sentence had a let-it-go-at-that ring. He had batted the ball of responsibility of getting rid of Russ Ruggles's attentions back to her. Was it because he was afraid of the man?

They drove on in silence, he absorbed in his thoughts, she in observing the street signs and traffic lights. The evening she had come for the audition, Van Tyler had been at the wheel.

"Here we are. The Hour spelled with a capital H is at hand."

"I'll park the car, then come to the studio for the broadcast, Wendy." He came around and opened the door for her. "When the program is finished wait for a phone call from me that the roadster is at the street door. Nervous?"

"A few butterflies are fanning their wings in my stomach. They will fly away as soon as I am on the air."

"Good girl. I mean that. Adoring your father as you do, you have carried on gallantly in a tough situation. I don't believe I could care more for a daughter of my own than I care for you."

"And I like you very, very much, Josh."

"Mean that?"

He grasped the hand she extended.

"Cross my heart."

"Thank you." He cleared his gruff voice. "I'll wait here till you are inside the building. Happy landings."

Before she stepped within the revolving door she turned and waved. He was standing beside the roadster, raised his hat in response.

"Enter our prima donna," Rolfe Sanborn greeted her as she came into the studio. He handed her a deep red orchid with a knot of matching ribbon. "I opened the box to save time, in case you were held up by traffic. The card that came with it said, 'Good luck. Have fun.' I knew you would want to wear the talisman."

"From whom?" She slipped off her green jacket and fastened the corsage to her pale blue crepe blouse.

"No name. Here's the card and a letter just delivered by hand."

She glanced at the typewritten address before she dropped it and the card into her blue bag.

"Fan mail, doubtless. I'll look at it later. I have a letter from my father I'm keeping to read after the broadcast."

"Keeping it as a sort of reward of merit, I take it. You look like a million. You'll click in video."

"Have a heart. I hear it adds pounds to figures, blacks out eyes, shows up wrinkles in clothing and washes out lipstick."

"We wouldn't let it do that to you. Something tells me the scarf so negligently flung across your shoulders is mink. Sister, you must spend money like water."

"Not my money." She realized he was talking to help her relax. It must be abundantly evident that every muscle was tense, that her heart was beating a muffled tattoo. "My father and his mother paid the bills for this outfit."

"Still want your name kept out of it?"

"Please."

"Okay. Better get settled."

She nodded to the engineer behind one large window; smiled at the transmitter man behind another, each one shook his clasped hands in encouragement, she had met them when she had been here for the audition; said a rather choky "Good evening" to the blond announcer seated at a table from which he would direct the program; tried not to notice the studio audience behind another window; and sat down at the piano.

She spread her notes on the rack; glanced at the formidable boom which dangled a microphone a short distance from her face; watched the long minute hand of the wall clock sprint round and round the white face with amazing speed; swallowed what threatened to be an unswallowable lump in her throat; fixed her eyes on the man at the table. He raised his right hand to the engineer behind the big window. They were on the air.

His introduction for "Let's Sing for Our Supper" was mercifully brief. Miraculously her throat cleared. Her heartbeat subsided to normal. She talked to the accompaniment of music. Then she sang, trying to forget the curious eyes of the studio audience, trying to think only of the unseen listeners. Suppose there weren't any? That thought helped — like fun it did.

The program of short, very short stories and songs planned to interest the younger contingent who, it was assumed, would be

299

waiting for their suppers at this hour, closed with Eugene Field's charming verses set to music of her own composing.

Have you ever heard of the Sugar-Plum
    Tree?
  'Tis a marvel of great renown!
It blooms on the shore of the Lollypop sea
  In the garden of Shut-Eye Town!

As she sang she visualized the two little blonde sisters in their small chairs drawn in front of the radio in the Browns' softly lighted living room, could see their eyes, blue as their frocks, radiant with wonder, black Sambo on the rug at their white-shod feet, glossy tail swishing slowly. Adorables. Her voice took on added tenderness as she crooned.

So come, little child, cuddle closer to me
  In your dainty white nightcap and
      gown,
And I'll rock you away to that Sugar-Plum
    Tree
  In the garden of Shut-Eye Town!

A few words from the announcer, a wave of his hand to the engineer, and the *première* of "Let's Sing for Our Supper" had slipped into the limbo of the past.

As she collected her notes the studio audience crowded round to congratulate her. Its enthusiasm seemed sincere. Rolfe Sanborn rescued her and drew her into a small office where a man at a desk was talking into a telephone. He cradled the receiver and rose.

"Good work, Miss Adair. Your program is a smash hit. Six adoring fans — grownups — have phoned already. Said it was inspired. Perfect for children of all ages. Wanted to know the name of the singer. Do we need to keep it hush-hush any longer?"

"No. It was just a foolish idea of mine to remain incog until I knew I had put it over."

"You've put it over and — just a minute." He answered a ring. "I'll tell her. Miss Adair, your car is at the door. Mr. Sanborn, this message for you came during the broadcast, but I wouldn't break in."

Rolfe Sanborn frowned as he read the slip of paper.

"Will you excuse me, Miss Adair, if I don't go down with you? Awful breach of good manners not to escort our celebrity to her car, but—"

"Joshua Crandon brought the roadster round for me and is waiting, so don't give it a thought, maestro." She stopped on the threshold. "Please file everything nice that is said about the program — adverse criticism, too, I can take it. Good night."

She had the satisfied feeling of a piece of work well done, as the crowded elevator dropped eleven stories without a stop. Two women spoke to her. Innumerable eyes were fixed on her. Her nerves hummed like bees as they had a habit of humming after a broadcast. The solitary drive home would quiet them. Solitary! Ooch!

The green roadster was directly in front of the building. She dashed toward it. Stopped. The man standing like a guard before the door was smoking, the spark of a cigarette glowed and faded. Josh didn't smoke. Who was it? Cardella? Foolish. If Joshua Crandon wouldn't have the South American in the house he certainly wouldn't select him as an escort for his stepdaughter. Ruggles? Josh wouldn't allow him to come after what she had told him. If it were he, she would turn and run, not run, perhaps, but she would get rid of him — The man stepped forward, touched the brim of a dark blue fedora.

"The carriage waits — Your Highness."

XXIV

Why is Van Tyler driving? Wendy wondered. The clock on the instrument board had registered the passing of ten minutes since she stepped into the car, and neither of them had spoken. Several times her lips had parted but she couldn't get her voice off the ground. In the dim light the stern line of his nose, lips and chin gave her a premonitory chill. He was here for a purpose. What?

"How about it? Have you decided I can be trusted to drive your mother's snappy roadster?" he inquired. "I could feel your eyes probing my brain. Trying to figure out how come I'm here, weren't you?"

"Or words to that effect."

"Good old Josh and I worked out the logistics, logistics in this case meaning time. His detail was to escort you to the studio, mine to get you home safely."

"That explains his request to drive in with

me. Subconsciously I've been trying to account for it. Had he heard of the attempted holdup? Of the man with the gun hidden in your car?"

"Not until I told him. He dropped into my office, by request, this morning. I sounded him out before I told him I wanted to be sure he would cooperate. Your program was a hit."

"Did you hear it?"

"Sure, I heard it. I was one of the humans watching the goldfish through the side of the crystal bowl. Did you mind the studio audience?"

"A little at first. After I was well started on the program I forgot it. It isn't necessary for you to take the time to drive me home."

"Am I spoiling sport? Perhaps you expected Graham?"

"You are not spoiling sport and I did not expect Steve. I have neither seen nor heard from him since the afternoon we went to Mount Vernon, the day after the visit to Ford's Theater, nor from you. Have you traced the message on the card in the plastic envelope?"

"You needn't whisper, Wendy. Before we started I made sure we were not carrying a third passenger. Why are you bending forward to see the street? Sit back and let me do the worrying about the heavy traffic."

"I wasn't thinking of traffic. I suddenly noticed we were not following the route I take to Red Terraces."

"That's right. You were silent so long after we left the studio behind us, I waited for an indication that you knew I was among those present before suggesting that we dine somewhere."

"I'm not dressed for a night spot."

"You look all right to me. The orchid gives a dressed-for-dinner touch. From an admirer?"

"My John, of course."

"Had a hunch you left him in S.A."

"*Mister* Tyler, don't tell me you've never heard that flowers may be *cabled*." He threw back his head and laughed.

"Your game and set, Miss Adair. Like smörgasbörds?"

"Love them."

"Okay, here we go. After that—"

"What?"

"I'm going to Red Terraces for an Information Please quiz, to pick up a few clues in our mystery."

"Really, Van?"

"Really, Wendy. There are questions which, if honestly answered, will tie together a number of so far unrelated facts."

"Propper knows a lot, doesn't he?"

"I suspect he does. Will you let it go at that for the present? I told you that much as a bribe to induce you to dine with me."

As if I need an inducement to dine with him. "The way you love Van, Wendy? Mummy told Daddy she could just feel—" The sound track of memory picked up the six-year-old's high-pitched voice. If her feeling for the man beside her was so evident she'd better watch her step.

"How about it? Is the bribe big enough?"

"Other things being roughly equal, it is. I promise to ask no questions and believe it or not that will take self-discipline."

A few minutes later they entered a restaurant where the ceiling was beamed with heavy dark timbers, where paneled walls were bright with Swedish flags. Seated on a floodlighted dais at one end of the long room musicians in gaily colored peasant costumes were trying out woods and strings.

"It's early, we'll almost have the place to ourselves," Van Tyler approved.

"Isn't this exciting?" Wendy exclaimed after a headwaiter of imposing height and dignity had seated her at a table for two. "I love a place out of the beaten track."

"Better take off your jacket." He waved the man away and lifted it from her shoulders. "It's warm here. Want the orchid?"

"Yes. I love it. It was sent to wish me luck."

He waited until she had fastened the corsage to her shoulder before he took the chair opposite.

"Boy, I like you in that light blue blouse. The silver necklace and earrings bring out your lovely color."

"Thanks. You're the type of man who notices and speaks of a woman's clothes, aren't you? You'll be a joy forever to the girl you marry."

"That's my hope and prayer."

"You'll have to brief me on the behavior pattern here," she said quickly to divert his attention from the rush of tears his grave voice sent to her eyes. "I've never been in a place quite like this before."

"First take a plate. You're supposed to eat smörgasbörd in three rounds. On the first trip to the table you take fish only. Second, meats and salads. Third, sweets."

"'And still they gaz'd, and still the wonder grew, that one small head could carry all he knew.' Don't mind my flippancy. My nerves, tied up tight during the broadcast, are beginning to unknot, that's all."

"I'm glad to hear the lilt back in your voice, Wendy. The 'new world' for which you were bound when we met on the train has been blotched with too many dark shadows."

"Do you mean the things that have happened since Steve exclaimed, 'Gosh! It's a revolution'? I don't call them shadows, they were adventures, a trifle scary, I admit. They didn't depress my heart or spirit." She couldn't tell him that real shadows had been anxiety about her mother's marriage plus the memory of the scene she had interrupted in Rolfe Sanborn's office.

"I've loved it here, this wonderful tourist-thronged city, a shrine to the past, an inspiring, throbbing center of the present and a glorious promise to the future. A place to remember, always. I am drenched in history, I've met hosts of VIPs, I've trod the daily social treadmill, lectures, luncheons, teas of all varieties, dinners, receptions. In many ways it has proved to be the gay and happy hunting ground you wished for me that day in the Pullman."

"My crystal ball tells me you will find more to enjoy. There is so much beside what you have been doing and seeing, the Ice Club at the Arena, indoor tennis, golf, fun on the river and always military events and often thrilling debates in the Senate or House."

"That's a dazzling program."

"That isn't half. Wait till the new Congress convenes. If you think I've sold you Washington we'll return to our present locale, I have the etiquette of procedure here on the authority of a Scandinavian friend. I can tell you the English name of many of the concoctions, I won't risk the Swedish. Ready? Let's go. I'll carry your fur stole, not safe to leave it on the chair."

"I've never seen so much to eat displayed at one time in my life. No food shortage here," she whispered as they approached the laden round table.

Lavish platters of potato pancakes, meat balls, jellied eel were flanked by bowls of pickled herring, salvers of fish cakes, plates of beet salad. There were Swedish brown beans, delectable stuffed eggs, cabbage, anchovies, farmer cheese, macaroni. Rye bread and hardtack. Puddings and cookies in approximately fifty-seven varieties and melt-in-your-mouth Danish pastries.

They ate. They talked. Question and answer.

What did he think of the makeup of the new Congress? It was better educated, more liberal, more experienced. Averaged a year older than last. Fewer lawyers. More farmers. More veterans. The bills it would fight.

The concessions it would make. They discussed the increasing interest of women in politics; ERP; the Wright brothers' plane at the Smithsonian and *The Spirit of St. Louis;* the flare-up of subversive activity; opportunity to hear fine music; absence of the theater.

"Delicious eats, conversation on a variety of enthralling subjects, all this to the accompaniment of the music of *Show Boat* played with exceeding skill and charm." Wendy summarized as a waiter filled small cups with steaming, aromatic, dark amber coffee. He set the silver pot on the table, placed the check beside Van Tyler's plate and with a murmured, "Thank you," departed.

"Did you enjoy the smörgasbörd?"

"Do you have to ask? At this moment I feel as if never again would I need food."

"Mind if we sit here while I smoke?"

"Of course not. Excuse me if I glance over a letter from father which is burning a hole in my bag?"

"I thought I smelled smoke. Go to it. You have two," he commented as she produced the envelopes.

"The second is from a fan, I think. As a special privilege you may read it while I scan Father's." She pushed the envelope with the typed address across the table.

"Sure about this? I don't like to open another person's mail."

"I'll open it for you." She ran her finger under the flap and pulled out a slip of paper. "It isn't a letter. It's a clip—"

Van Tyler reached for it.

"Give it to me, please, Wendy." She shook her head.

"Not until I've read it. Apparently you know what it is." She felt his eyes on her as she read.

There is a persistent rumor that a certain ranch owner, oilman, wealthy Representative from the great Northwest posing as a bachelor was secretly married several weeks ago to the charming daughter of a family socially prominent in our fair city. Why the hush-hush, Congressman?

"So, that is what Mr. Ruggles meant when he asked, 'What paper do you read?' Of course he sent it. Nice of him to make sure I didn't miss the gem of innuendo."

"When did you see him?"

"Early this afternoon. He invited me to a concert. When I declined the invitation, he asked that question, then added, 'Perhaps Josh can change your mind.' Have you any idea what he meant by that?"

"We may find out later. Give me the clipping, please."

"No. You had seen it, hadn't you, and have tried to keep me from realizing how I tangled your life with my crazy story to Russ Ruggles that day on the Pullman?" She leaned forward, suggested softly:

"Van, would it help if we pretended it was true? That we were secretly married — just until this blows over?"

"What do you mean, 'pretend'? Pretend to *live* together?"

"Good heavens, no. I mean we could tell Mother and Josh that it happened in South America — when you were there to be best man—"

"You have what is called a creative imagination, haven't you? Must be Grandmother Adair at the controls. You've forgotten Ruggles heard you remind me that the ceremony took place in New York. Nice of you to suggest it, but when I announce my marriage there will be no pretense. It will be real. The ceremony may be performed as quietly as the bride wishes, but it will be proclaimed from the housetops — figuratively speaking. Read your father's letter. Then we'll start for Red Terraces."

"Nice of you to suggest it." The words glowed like a neon sign, a red one, in her memory. Her cheeks burned. Did he think she had asked him to marry her? From this minute on she would devote her life to the destruction of that idea.

She unfolded the pages of her father's letter, tried to concentrate on their contents. She didn't sense much of it. Her mind was running on a double track, one aflame with indignation. Suddenly a name, *Steve Graham,* registered and shocked her into attention. She reread the written words.

"Van," she whispered. "Van, is anyone at the table behind me?"

"No. Nor behind me. What goes? You're white."

"Listen. Father writes:

The man who was president at the time of the Revolution you so fortunately escaped made his getaway from the country. He has accused certain U.S. citizens of procuring arms for his enemies. I have cabled, written Steve Graham to come back. He pays no attention. Use your influence. Tell him he must come and clear himself. He's the man suspected of being the leader.

Forgotten was her determination to devote her life to proving to Van Tyler that she didn't want to marry him, she appealed brokenly:

"Van, it can't be. Steve wouldn't do that. I know he wouldn't."

"Take it easy, Wendy, or you may be overheard. Put the letter into your bag. We'll talk on the way home, this isn't the place. Let's go."

As they drove along the smooth black highway a rain of shooting stars pelted the heavens.

"Something tells me that a planet about the size of this world just exploded. It had a modern fireworks rocket licked to a frazzle. See it, Wendy?" She shook her head.

"No. I wasn't looking up, I was looking inside my mind. I can't think of anything but Steve."

"Do you love him so much?"

Resentment at his rejection of her offer to pretend they were married to help him defeat Ruggles licked up like a dart of flame from a memory that had been smoldering.

"Of course I love him. He — he's my 'John.' It hurts intolerably to know he may be in trouble. What do you think, Van?"

"If you really care for my opinion, I think he's in something of a spot."

"Have you heard the rumors to which Father referred?"

"Yes."

"Don't be so wooden. Can't you feel that I am terribly anxious? What have you heard?"

"Nothing that is sufficiently definite to repeat. And while we are on the subject, you'd better thank your lucky stars that I can be wooden. If you want my opinion—"

"Of course I want it."

"It is that Steve Graham — your John to you — is as straight as they come."

"Thank you, Van, thank you. I could hug you for that—"

"Don't."

"Don't worry, I won't. I felt that way about Steve, and yet—"

"And yet. Oh, ye of little faith! You and Lucie Brown."

There was nothing she could say in response to that. Both she and Lucie had doubted the men they loved, though heaven forbid that Van Tyler suspected she loved him. The only comment he had offered on the impassioned scene she had interrupted had been:

"I knew by the tinkle of ice in your voice this afternoon that when you opened the door of Sanford's office you jumped to the conclusion that I was lying when I told you Clare means nothing to me and never will."

Perhaps she had been unfair but when a little while ago she had proposed — *she* had proposed — that they pretend that the marriage story was true, he had turned down her offer with a peremptory promptness that had made her cheeks burn, that set them aflame now when she remembered it. She put her hand to her face. He turned quickly and looked at her.

"What's the matter? Headache?"

"No. I never had a headache in my life. Isn't this a gorgeous night? That's a rhetorical question. No answer required."

"Yes, but something tells me we'll get our duck hunt within forty-eight hours."

"I'm not weather-wise but I can't see a damp, drizzly day in the near future. See how clearly the park lights are reflected in the Tidal Basin, look at the clear-cut purple shadow under that lone elm. I love the illuminated shaft of the Monument, in fact I love this city."

"Like to live here?"

"I'd love it if I could find something to do into which I could get my teeth."

"I know of a position for which you'd be perfectly suited."

"Radio?"

"No. A full-time job. You'd have to work at it, though."

"Work! I want to work. You don't think I'd be happy sitting round with folded hands, do you?" She sat up very straight. "We'll discuss my qualifications for that position later. We are almost at the door of Red Terraces. What is it all about? What are you planning to do, Van?"

"Can't tell yet. Don't say anything unless you are questioned. Get that?"

"I do. What, *what* do you expect to find out?"

"Who took the automatic from the desk drawer, who drugged Angeline and why, that's all, this trip. Hop out." He caught her arm as she started up the steps.

"Stop shaking. You didn't do it."

"No," the word was a mere whisper. "But I'm terribly afraid I know who did."

XXV

Kitty Crandon and her husband were playing cards at a small square table in the back drawing room which had been shut off from the front with folding screens. Her pastel crepe frock the exact shade of the feathery pink chrysanthemums in bowls on each end of the mantel made a charming bit of color against the dark green setting of walls and furniture. Diamonds on her fingers, in the necklace of moonstones at the base of her white throat, and in the matching bracelet, shot fiery sparks at every movement of her body. Nibbling her left forefinger as she considered the next play, she looked up.

"Wendy, how long have you been standing in the doorway? I thought you were at the concert with Russ. He told me he was taking you to dinner. Did he send you that perfect orchid? He has a delightful habit of saying it with flowers. Mr. Tyler? How *wonderful*. I didn't see you at first. Come in, both of you. Glad to have company. The evening promised to be deadly dull for both of us."

"Speak for yourself, Kitty, not for me." Joshua Crandon was on his feet. "The broadcast was a hit, Wendy."

"Thank you, Josh. Did you hear it, Mother?"

"No, I wasn't interested. You know, Wendy, I do *not* approve of the contract you signed to go on the air."

"You're in a hopeless minority, Kitty, my love. As I descended in a packed elevator, the consensus was, 'What a delightful program.' 'I'd think mothers would sing hymns of praise for it.' 'I wonder if she would take a club engagement, she can talk as well as sing.' You have a career before you if you want one, Wendy."

What a heart-warming person he is, she thought, and she thought of the paragraph in her father's letter she had read in the restaurant:

Don't let a mistaken feeling of loyalty to me keep you from liking Crandon, my dear. I want your mother to be happy with the man she married. The one thing I couldn't bear would be to know she had wrecked her life.

"Now we can have a four-handed game," Kitty Crandon suggested eagerly. "That is, if you care to play, I wouldn't want to bore you, Van. You don't mind if I'm informal and call you 'Van,' do you?"

"I would mind terribly if you weren't. Cards do not bore me. How about you, Wendy? You've had quite a day."

If the proposed game would interfere with his plan to "tie up loose ends," he wouldn't have agreed to it, would he? Before she could answer her mother declared:

"Of course she will play. For heaven's sake, Wendy, run up and change. It just isn't civilized to appear in a suit at home after dinner. We'll wait. You and I will take on the men. We can put a bulldozer out of business when we play together."

Wendy looked quickly at Van Tyler. His nod of approval was almost imperceptible but she caught it.

"I'll be back before you can say 'Jack Robinson,' " she declared.

She was only too thankful for the chance to change. In her room she carefully removed the orchid. Lovely thing. Who had sent it? It might have been Rolfe Sanborn. Van Tyler thought it came from her "John." So much the better. Time for a shower? Why not? What difference would it make if the

320

card game and the revelations to follow were held up for a few minutes?

Ten minutes later before the mirror she fastened the deep red orchid on the soft green tissue frock with embroidered silver disks. Clasped her pearls about her throat. She glanced at the drawer in which she kept letters and valuables. Was she right in her suspicion as to the person who had opened it the night Angeline was drugged? The possibility sent a little shiver along her nerves.

Propper was at the front door as she ran down the stairs.

"Wait. It isn't time," she heard him say before he closed it. If he was startled to see her standing on the lowest step there was no facial evidence of surprise.

"Someone had the wrong number, Miss Wendy," he explained and continued his dignified return to his domain in the back of the house.

"It isn't time," she repeated to herself. Time for what? Was the butler masterminding a conspiracy? How could she warn Van that something was scheduled to happen, to be on guard? Propper was an expert butler but he had roused her suspicion the first moment she saw him.

"Your mother was about to send out a scouting party, Miss Adair." Van Tyler spoke from the threshold of the drawing room. "The evening wanes."

"Sorry. I was all set to make a dashing entrance when the clasp of my pearls began acting up. I wonder if you can make it fasten."

"Let me take a look."

She turned her back. Whispered over her shoulder:

"Pilot to navigator. Propper just warned someone at the door, 'Wait. It isn't time.'"

"It wasn't quite closed, in too much of a hurry, weren't you?" The clasp snapped. "That does it." He pressed his lips to the back of her neck.

"Don't," she whispered.

"But, you told me it was nothing to you whom I kissed. Not reneging, are you? Come on, your mother is getting impatient. Did I hear thunder? I bet it's ushering in a spell of wet weather. All right with me. We'll get our wild fowl hunt."

After an hour's play Joshua Crandon totaled the score. He chuckled.

"Sand in the gear of the bulldozer is indicated."

"Stop crowing, Josh, it wasn't I," his wife protested. "What's the matter with you, Wendy? You kept putting your hand to the back of your neck. Does your head ache?

You played as if you'd never heard of a card before, much less seen one."

Wendy glanced under her lashes at Van Tyler. The glint of laughter in his eyes as they met hers set her cheeks burning. Did he suspect that she couldn't forget his kiss?

"I'm sorry, I—"

"Have a heart, Mrs. Crandon. It must be darn exciting to broadcast an original program."

"Which was preceded by a picnic with two lively kids at Rock Creek Park, wasn't it, Wendy?" Joshua Crandon added his contribution to Van Tyler's defense. "How about another game, Kitty? Your deal."

"No, thank you." His wife disdainfully pushed away the cards he laid on the table. "Not with Wendy in the comatose state indicated by her playing. Angeline, where did you come from? You're not allowed in the drawing room. Call Propper to take her out, Josh."

"Break the rule for this once, Mrs. Crandon," Van Tyler pleaded. "I'm a pushover for dogs, especially white poodles." He whistled softly, "Here, Angie."

Wendy's heart stepped up its beat. It was coming. What would the next few minutes reveal? Was Josh Crandon suspicious that a crucial moment was approaching? He didn't appear to be. His large well-shaped hands were steady as he sorted the two packs of cards. Annoyance at the loss of the game had turned down the corners of her mother's mouth. The poodle raised a beruffed leg, laid a paw on Van Tyler's knee and looked up at him.

"Remember me, don't you, girl? You ought to. I carried you in my arms the night the big, bad burglar put you to sleep."

"That burglar was a myth of Wendy's imagining," Kitty Crandon declared. "Russ, Josh and I went into every room in the house after you and she left with the dog, Van. Nothing missing, nothing even disturbed."

"How do you account for Angeline being drugged, Mother?"

"I don't believe she had been drugged. Probably she had eaten something that disagreed with her. The servants spoil her. They feed her tidbits to bribe her to do her tricks."

"That's queer." Van Tyler brushed his hand over the fuzzy white head. "The doc declared she had been drugged. Too bad, Angie, you can't talk and tell us who gave you the sleeping tablet."

Sleeping tablet? When had Van discovered that?

"Who told you the poodle had been drugged with a sleeping tablet?" Joshua

Crandon fired the question Wendy had been about to ask.

"The doctor. I phoned him the next morning to ask what sort of drug had been used. Wendy and I were so anxious to get the pooch home and settled for the night I didn't think to inquire while we were at the office. Your diagnosis, Mrs. Crandon, doesn't fit in with the other curious happenings." Van Tyler rose and stood back against the mantel with the easy grace and assurance of a born leader. With a sigh which expressed utter boredom the poodle flopped to the floor at his feet.

"What other curious happenings?" Kitty Crandon demanded and clenched a white hand resting on the table into a fist. "What is behind all this? Are you diplomatically leading up to a dramatic denouement? Do you know, Josh?" She turned to her husband seated at her right.

"Haven't the faintest idea to what he is referring, Kitty, my love. Go on, Tyler. Explain 'curious happenings.' What's curious? What's happened? You have something up your sleeve. You've gone too far now to stop."

"I have no intention of stopping until I find out who drugged the poodle before stealing the automatic from the drawer of the desk in Wendy's room. Startling incidents preceded and followed to which kayoeing the poodle may be the key. Did you take it, Josh?"

"I'll be judge, I'll be jury," said cunning
   old Fury.
"I'll try the whole cause, and condemn
   you to death."

The words from *Alice* echoed through Wendy's mind as she looked at the man standing back to the mantel. He was in desperate earnest. The two sharp lines she remembered had cut deep between his brows, his eyes were black with determination. What had he discovered? She had a sudden frightened urge to grab at the garment of Time to hold it back before a shocking disclosure could break. Joshua Crandon was on his feet. One hand rested on the card table as he leaned forward.

"I don't know what you're after, Tyler, but I have sufficient respect for your mind and achievements to realize you haven't started this quiz for fun. I did not take Wendy's automatic — steal was your word, though, wasn't it? I didn't know she had an automatic till she appeared at the door of the smoking room and fired it."

"Fired it! *Fired* it? In your smoking room?" Kitty Crandon caught her husband's arm and shook it. "What, *what* had you done to my daughter, Josh, that she would try to shoot you?"

"Damn it, Kitty, I hadn't done anything to your daughter, she didn't try to shoot me. She fired at — tell her, Tyler. I can't. It makes me sick to think of it." He brushed his hand across his eyes.

It was amazing in how few words Van told of the box which contained an unsolicited, anonymous contribution to the million-dollar reptile house at the zoo — violet ray light division — of the truck driver's mistake, understating the effect on Crandon and Propper. The recital left Kitty Crandon visibly shaken.

"What a horrible thing. How could it happen in this house? Where was Propper—"

"Did you call me, Madam?" The butler spoke from the threshold.

"I did not. Now that you are here I believe you are the person who can explain these mysterious occurrences. I've never liked you, Propper. I've never trusted you. I've suspected you were here to snoop, and—"

"Kitty! Stop—"

"I don't mind, Mr. Crandon. Every person can't like everybody. I have aversions,

327

myself. What is it you want me to explain, Madam?"

"You took the automatic from Miss Adair's desk, you drugged the dog, didn't you?"

"No, Madam."

"But, you know who did, don't you, Propper?"

"Yes, Mr. Tyler."

"Stop this damn 'Yes,' 'No,' pussyfooting," Joshua Crandon roared. "If you know the name of the guilty party, tell it, Propper." Fury and frustration had stained his face a dark and dangerous red. Wendy caught the butler's quick look at Van Tyler.

"Tell him, Propper," he prompted.

"It was Mrs. Crandon, sir."

"Mrs. Crandon! My *wife?*"

"Yes, sir."

Wendy looked from the face of the butler to her mother's. Except for the touch of rouge at the cheek bones it was startlingly colorless.

"Do you believe him, Josh? You would believe him before you would me, you hired him," Kitty Crandon reminded bitterly.

"Propper, put away the card table and take the poodle with you when you go. That will be all."

"Yes, sir."

Joshua Crandon waited until the man had snapped up the four legs of the table, and with it in his hand, had pushed the reluctant dog ahead of him into the hall and closed the door.

"Now, Kitty," he prompted, "I certainly will not believe Propper's story if you tell me his statement is untrue. Did you do it?"

Wendy held her breath. Mother, Mother, don't lie, she pleaded mentally. She couldn't have told when she first suspected that her mother had rifled the desk drawer, perhaps it had been a nebulous impression floating in her subconscious, then what Van said in the car coming home had given it shape and substance and suddenly there it was, a full-grown conviction. Perhaps that was the way great discoveries, great inventions were born, long germination of an idea a person didn't know was in his mind, and then an apple falls from a tree, steam lifts the lid of a kettle, and presto, the idea has become a living, vital force in the world.

"Not if you tell me it isn't true," Josh Crandon's repetition of his vote of confidence broke the spell of silence which had followed, "Did you do it?"

"All right, all right, I did."

Wendy exhaled in a relieved sigh the breath she had held while awaiting her mother's answer. Now, would Van take over? No. He was looking expectantly at Joshua Crandon.

"Why, Kitty?"

"For heaven's sake, don't turn it into melodrama, Josh. I did it because—" Blood suffused her face, receded, leaving it more colorless than before. She lifted her chin and regarded Van Tyler defiantly.

"Because I wanted to read my hus— Jim's letter. Wendy refused to let me see it."

"Did you have to drug the dog, steal the automatic, to get your *husband's* letter?" Joshua Crandon demanded caustically.

"They went to sea in a sieve, they did," the words singsonged through Wendy's mind. She glanced at Van Tyler, standing straight and tall before the fireplace looking at her mother. She had the curious sense that he was watching the rehearsal of a play of which he was stage manager, that he had known every word before it was uttered, knew every word that would follow.

"You won't forgive that 'husband' slip, will you, Josh?"

"That is something you and I will take up later when we are alone, Kitty. Let's get on with the matter under discussion, the stolen automatic, the drugged dog."

"I object to that word 'stolen,'" his wife

330

protested. "I didn't take the gun with the intention of keeping it. Wendy had left a key in the desk drawer where she keeps her jewelry. I suspected the letter was there. It was. I read it, from the first line to the last. Reread it. Why not? Jim had been my husband for over twenty years. He — he believes in — me." Her voice broke. She impatiently brushed fingers glittering with Joshua Crandon's diamonds across wet lashes.

Wendy looked down through tears at her hands clenched in her lap. Was her mother remembering the words in that letter:

If your mother is difficult, Wendy, remember that even three years isn't time enough for a woman who grew up with ideals of honor and justice to make peace with her conscience for having pulled up those same ideals by the roots, because she wanted more "money and real living." If she *loves* the man I have firm faith that eventually she will become the grand person I saw in her when we married.

"Go on, Kitty," Joshua Crandon's stern reminder brought her back to the charming room and her mother standing white and defiant. "You still have to explain your reason for taking the automatic and drugging the dog."

"You're as relentless as a Juggernaut, Josh," his wife accused. "After I read the letter I noticed the pistol. It frightened me. I have a horror of firearms. I suddenly remembered how strange you had been lately, how worried you appeared, and I remembered that you had been taking something to make you sleep and I just went haywire." She brushed fingers across her lashes and shook her head to clear her eyes of tears.

"Good Lord, you weren't afraid of *me,* afraid I would shoot *you,* were you, Kitty?"

"*No,* I didn't think of myself, I thought, suppose Josh finds this and — and uses it — when he is depressed. I'll put it where he can't find it, later, I'll explain to Wendy. People who are usually levelheaded will do a crazy, unaccountable thing when frightened about someone they love, won't they? You see, I really love you, Josh. I didn't marry you for your money."

The only acknowledgement that her admission had touched him was the draining of color from under his bronzed skin. Even his lips were pale.

"As I said before, we'll thresh out our personal problems when we are alone, Kitty. You secreted the automatic for my safety —

how was I to know the gun was in Wendy's desk? You didn't think of that, did you? My worries are not the shooting kind, they are What-ought-I-to-do type. Why drug the dog?"

"I went berserk, that's all. It could happen to anyone in this room, I suppose. I was afraid Wendy would ask about the gun — I didn't intend to have the vicious thing in the house. I figured that if Angeline was drugged you all would think it the work of a burglar — as you did. I gave her one of your sleeping tablets in a piece of candy. Then I ran to my room and locked the gun in my desk. I suppose the omniscient Propper saw me come from Wendy's room, saw it in my hand. I dressed, and you and I went out to dinner. You looked as if you had stared death in the face and I was glad that I had had the sense and courage — it took courage to get rid of that gun. Never before had I taken the property of another person."

"Which is more than I can say. Go on, Kitty."

"That's all there is. I suppose your stooge, Propper—"

"Propper is not my stooge, Kitty. He is here as my bodyguard."

XXVI

"Propper! *Propper* your bodyguard? Of what are you afraid? Josh, Josh, you're not on the FBI subversive list? Not suspected of being a traitor, are you? I couldn't bear it. I just couldn't bear it." His wife clasped her hands about his left arm. He looked down into her pleading eyes.

"Suppose I am, Kitty? Suppose I am dragged through court? You won't have to stay here and see it. You would have plenty of cause for div—"

"Don't say it, Josh, *don't.* Whatever comes to you I'll share. Honest, I'll share. Believe me?"

Mother is on the way to becoming the grand person Father knows she can be, Wendy had time to think before Joshua Crandon patted the hands on his arm.

"I believe you, Kitty. Sit down, my dear. I suspect we have only touched the edge of

Van's real purpose here. What were the 'startling incidents' which preceded and followed the drugging of the poodle, Tyler?"

"Will you help by telling why you need a bodyguard? Why you thought the contents of the box left here by mistake had been sent you as a reprisal?"

"How do you know I did?"

"When Wendy appeared at the door you muttered, 'They're out to get me.' Remember?"

"Did I say that? It's a wonder I stopped there. The sight of that creature would shock a confession from a hardened criminal. Sit down again, Kitty. I am *not* a hardened criminal. I have Propper to thank for keeping me out of a trap that might have made me appear to be one."

"Propper?"

"Propper and that sixth sense which flashes a warning stop light. Six years ago I was playing round with a group of men and women, all for one reason or another 4-F's, whom I had found congenial and interesting. I had plenty of money and a hard-earned leisure. Poor eyesight kept me out of the recent war. I served as a captain of infantry through World War I. Propper was top sergeant in my company. Six years ago—" He paused as if to recall data with which to go on.

Wendy's pulses quickened. Is this where Zaidee Latour gets tangled in the undercurrent? Will I be caught in the dragnet, too? Dragnet. Van Tyler has one side in a firm grip. Who will pull up the other?

"To return to my interesting playmates," Joshua Crandon resumed. "Zaidee Latour was deputized to swear me to secrecy before she explained that they had worked out a get-rich-quick project. I inferred they'd been given an inside tip on stock about to boom. I liked them. I believed in them. I swore. Then she told me that I had been selected to finance the enterprise. Having worked for my money, naturally I asked what it was. She declared that I wasn't to be told then, that I was to take my friends on faith and put up the cash. I refused to be the angel.

"Sometimes I waken in the night and think what an easy mark they thought me. 'Good old Josh.' Unfortunately, not until I had given my solemn oath not to reveal what I had been asked to do did Propper come to me with the story of their plan." He brushed one hand impatiently through his heavy graying hair.

"The world sank deeper and deeper into the bloody conflict. I had already broken with the bunch whom I had discovered were gangsters, top-drawer variety. Each one was rapidly sucked into a war industry. I gave my time and money where it would help, almost forgetting the trap I had escaped. A couple of months ago Zaidee Latour—"

"Josh! I suspected the night she dined here there had been something between you and that woman, though she appeared as if she never had met you before. Was she your—"

"Not what you are thinking, Kitty. For the last two months she has been reminding me by letter and phone that my old friends are in this city — that they need my help — won't I join them again, if not — the 'if not' was an implied threat. That was what was in my mind when I babbled about reprisal, Van. At the second prod I sent for Propper, with whom I have kept in touch through the years. They are afraid of what I know. Maybe are planning another money-making coup, and for their safety want me out of the way forever. I've feared if caught they would lie and swear I had been up to my ears in their subversive deals, which publicity would have given the name of my wife front-page cover-age with emphasis on the distinguished man she had abandoned for me."

"I could have taken it, Josh."

"I know that now, Kitty. I'm not worried about my safety. I have been beset with uncertainty as to what I ought to do. Should I tell the authorities of what was planned and not put through six years ago? Was I wrong to suspect my onetime pals of treason now? The tragedy of war might have purged them of criminal intentions, I argued."

"It hasn't," Van Tyler attested quietly.

"I know that now. Young Graham—"

"Steve! You don't mean that Steve was one of that gang? Six years ago? He couldn't have been."

Van crossed the room and laid his hands gently on her shoulders.

"Take it easy, Wendy."

She tipped back her head and looked up at him.

"How can I help being anxious? Have you forgotten Father's letter? Forgotten that he wrote—"

"Let Josh finish his story. He wants to get it off his mind, don't you, Josh?"

"Off my mind. You're telling me. Now that you know what it's all about, Van, advise me what to do."

"You won't have to do anything. When Russ Ruggles comes here tonight and brings Señor Antonio Cardella—"

"Cardella! After I said 'No,' did you invite

him to this house, Kitty?"

"Don't roar at me, Josh. I know you're worried but I won't *stand* for it. I didn't know the man was coming."

"Sorry, I guess I'm tuned up to crescendo pitch. Is his visit your plan, Van?"

"Rolfe Sanborn is in it with me. We figured that bringing him face to face with you in this house is the best way to apply the thumbscrews. He has been needling you through a third party, hasn't he?"

"And how. You said he is coming with Ruggles. Does Russ know of my connection with that — that bunch?"

"Has he been a snake in the grass while we have practically given him the freedom of this house?" Kitty Crandon demanded shrilly.

"A snake bearing many floral tributes." Her husband's dry reminder sent a wash of color over her pallor.

"You have suspected him, haven't you, Josh?" Van Tyler asked. "Just enough to make you a little afraid of him, he has insidiously suggested that he knew a secret of your past, hasn't he? Information he has siphoned drop by drop from Cardella. They are due any minute now. I suggest that your wife and Wendy go to their rooms—"

"Not I, Van Tyler," Kitty Crandon flared.

"I intend to stay right here with Josh until—"

"Come in," Joshua Crandon answered a soft knock after interrogating Van Tyler with his eyes.

Propper opened the door.

"Mr. Ruggles and Señor Cardella, Madam." He stepped aside to allow the two men to enter, both sleek and smooth in dinner clothes.

Wendy's eyes were on the South American. He twisted an end of his mustache as he stepped into the room. His easy smiling assurance stiffened when he saw Van Tyler, who had resumed his stand before the fireplace. He bowed deeply to Kitty Crandon who clasped her hands behind her back.

"It is indeed a happiness to meet you at last, Señora. I have known your husband *intimately* for many years."

Wendy remembered his sharp, incisive question to the porter, "Why are you standing in front of that door like a cop on guard?" Not much like this suave, Spanish-accented voice. He turned to her.

"I have not seen you, Señorita Adair, since that moment in Ford's Theater when the appointment we had made to meet there went blooey — as it is so amusingly expressed in

340

the States — you were *so* surrounded by admirers."

Wendy snapped shut her lips which amazement had sprung open. "Stop giving an imitation of an idiot," she flouted herself. Icy, stealthy claws of apprehension squeezed her heart. How did he know she had found the message? What was his diabolical object in pretending they had planned a rendezvous? Russ Ruggles stepped nimbly into the breach created by her stunned silence.

"Good old Josh, we didn't expect to find you here." His cordial greeting might have made the grade if he had controlled the dancing devils of triumph in his eyes. "Kitty, you are ravishing in pink. You have a *femme fatale* of Hollywood licked to a fare-thee-well as always. Miss Adair, you told me you had a don't-dress dinner date. You can't call that green confection you are wearing don't-dress and get away with it. Oh, here's Van, for the moment the forgotten man. Now I know what it's all about. This is an announcement party. At last the truth—"

"An announcement party — of sorts, Russ." Van Tyler's cold voice slashed like a keen blade into what was becoming a non-stop hectoring monologue. "We are waiting for Rolfe who has an interesting item to add. And here he is," he added as Sanborn entered. The door closed behind him apparently without benefit of hands.

"Come on in, chief. The water's fine."

Wendy sat forward in her chair. Her eyes flashed to Rolfe Sanborn as he spoke to her mother, came back to resume their watch of Cardella. I've never seen a ferret, she told herself, but his eyes as they dart from face to face are what I imagine a ferret's to be.

If she lived to be a hundred she would never forget this moment, the tense silence seething with emotional undercurrents; her pale mother in her soft pink frock, clasping and unclasping her fingers with their glittering rings, eyes on her husband's face which was but a degree more colorful than hers; he standing with hands thrust into the pockets of his dinner jacket, frowning a little as he regarded Ruggles who had lost some of his swagger, whose eyes were no longer dancing but were narrowed in suspicion as they traveled from the face of Van Tyler to that of Rolfe Sanborn standing shoulder to shoulder in front of the fireplace. The mirror above it gave back her own green and silver figure perched tense and rigid on the edge of the chair. It gave back also a vivid flash of lightning.

Van was right when he prophesied duck weather, she thought irrelevantly.

"What are we up against? A Quaker meeting?" Russ Ruggles broke the silence. "I'll bite. What's the pitch? Mrs. Crandon invited me to come this evening and bring Señor Cardella and—"

"I did—"

"And you came, Russ." Van Tyler interrupted Kitty Crandon's explosive denial. "That was nice of you. What's the pitch? How about that little item I promised you would add to our announcement party, chief?"

"Let's call it a quiz party, fella," Rolfe Sanborn suggested. He drew a notebook from his pocket. "Cardella, we'll give you the first chance at the jackpot. What were you looking for when you searched Miss Adair's overnight case at the Mayflower?"

"I don't understand you, Señor. Is a quiz party a joke party? Is eet an American custom?"

"Cut out the accent, Cardella," Crandon's blunt command tightened the South American's mouth in a cruel line. "They know you're a naturalized American citizen. Have lived in this country ten years. Now that we have that nicely straightened out, go on, Sanborn."

"We know that you searched that bag, that you were looking for papers which, if dis-

343

covered, would land you in prison."

"Break it to them easy, chief. That last statement washed the color from Russ's face."

"Combat team," Wendy thought and had a flashback of Van and herself on the porch of the embassy.

"What are you implying, Tyler?" Ruggles took a menacing step forward.

"Let me handle this, fella. Wait your turn, Russ. Wait your turn, you'll get it." Sanborn consulted his notebook.

"You searched the bag, Cardella. You came to this house on the early morning of the twelfth to threaten to expose Joshua Crandon for financing a criminal scheme you tried to put across six years ago. The fact that he turned you down you seem to have forgotten. You were frightened off by the barking of the dog while you were talking to the butler — the butler in whom you have confided for years believing him to be your man." He pretended to consult his notes.

"You told him you would leave a message under the birdbath for Crandon, that he was to see that his employer got it and carried out the order or else — you closed the interview with this." Sanborn drew his hand across his throat. "Don't waste your breath denying it. One of your pals has squealed."

344

"But, that is such an old trick, for a man of your experience to try to put across, Sanborn." Cardella's shrug and smile were masterpieces of contempt. He had shed his accent. "I'm surprised you think me such a hick as to fall for it."

"Okay, *Señor.* You're a glutton for evidence, aren't you? We have it. One of your tools returned from South America recently with a haul of microfilms, allegedly of vital agreements between this country and the one from which you came originally, which had been *planted* to be delivered to you."

"That's what *you* think," Cardella snarled.

"There are others who believe it."

Rolfe Sanborn is having the time of his life, he's so slow, he's so cool. This must be what Van meant by applying the thumbscrews, Wendy thought.

"The person who brought the films had reason to think the FBI had become suspicious, got cold feet and turned them over to Gibson Gary Brown, the ace photographer, under the pretense they were moving-picture travelogue reels snapped in South America — he was instructed to await orders before developing them. At Ford's Theater, where Josh Crandon did not appear in response to your summons, you were told by your badly scared pal where the films had been parked and sent a thug to the Browns' house to search for them."

If I hitch forward one more inch in this chair I'll be on the floor, Wendy warned herself. Excitement has almost stopped my heart. Zaidee Latour gave the films to Gib. The backseat rider had been through the Browns' house. That much is clear. Were the planted films in the box the black cat knocked over? Gib scooped them up in a tremendous hurry. All this doesn't explain the paragraph in Father's letter that Steve was suspected of financing a revolution. Perhaps that's another matter.

"And now for the climax, a melodrama should always mount to a climax. I tried to write one, I know."

Wendy could have screamed with impatience as Rolfe Sanborn paused to consult his notes. Of course he didn't need them. Could he be waiting for a signal? A distant roll of thunder accentuated the silence. Go on! Go on! she whispered and clenched her hands on her knees.

"You, being a South American, are of course informed as to the conditions in the country of which you are a native."

If Rolfe pauses to clear his throat once more I'll throw my bag at him, Wendy told herself.

"You know, also, that the president who escaped from the recent revolution has accused certain U. S. citizens of providing arms for his enemies. It is known that you and your gang are the guilty parties, that Russ Ruggles put up the cash—"

"That's a lie—"

"I've taken enough." Cardella's hoarse voice broke into Ruggles's furious protest. He whipped a revolver from his coat pocket and backed to the door. "Open it, Ruggles. I'll shoot you or the first person who tries to stop me."

Why doesn't someone do something before he gets away, Wendy thought frantically. She looked around the room at the figures motionless as if conjured to stone by a sorcerer. Joshua Crandon held his wife close in one arm, her eyes were wide with terror. Van Tyler and Rolfe Sanborn still stood shoulder to shoulder, warily watchful, Van's right hand was in the pocket of his coat. The silence inside the room was the silence that precedes the bursting of a cyclone.

"Open that door," Cardella's face was gray, a suggestion of foam beaded his slight mustache. "Take one step forward, any one of you, and—" Ruggles swung open the door.

Came the sound as of a mighty wind

sweeping down the stairs, through the hall. Cardella turned at the moment the black cat, spitting, meowing, dashed between his feet. The white poodle, barking, whining, bigger, stronger, followed in furious pursuit with a force that sent the man crashing to the floor, his revolver spinning across the rug.

Van Tyler drew his hand from his coat pocket and picked up the gun.

"That about does it," he said.

"Not quite, Congressman," Ruggles's eyes burned with hatred. "Not till I have settled for that lie you and Sanborn cooked up to drag me into the arms-supplying deal."

XXVII

"Are we in luck? The last call of the current open season on wild fowl, and a day *especially* designed for us," Van Tyler jubilated as the outboard motorboat cut through the turbulent gun-metal gray water of the bay. "Cloudy, windy, and as the last perfect touch a cold penetrating drizzle. The thunderstorm the other night blew the spell of fine weather off to sea or wherever fine weather goes when it departs. This ought to bring out the birds."

"Penetrating is the word." Rolfe Sanborn pulled the collar of his hunting coat a trifle higher about his ears. "I can take this weather or leave it. Van's a gone guy when it comes to duck hunting, Miss Adair. How are you doing? Warm enough?"

"Warm enough! With two cardigans under this leather jacket, brown corduroy slacks thick as a board and cowhide boots almost to my knees? I'd say my temperature had shot up to one hundred and five degrees plus. There's a fifty-fifty chance I'm so padded I won't be able to lift my arms to aim a gun."

"It will surprise you to find what you'll do when half a dozen wild fowl fly over." He glanced toward the stern where Van Tyler was talking to the man with a flat nose and small near-set eyes in a weather-beaten face, who was steering.

"I wonder why Murphy isn't on the job."

"And who is Murphy? I'm a rookie of rookies at this sport and will have to have every step of this excursion explained," Wendy reminded.

"Murphy is one of the best hunting attendants in the state of Maryland. Van always has him. Wonder what happened this trip? Here we are. Look good to you, Miss Adair?"

She was glad that the scrape of the boat against the blind cut off the necessity of a reply. What appeared to be a large stationary raft, afloat in an interminable expanse of white-capped gray water, had a hardwood floor, a sheltered end with benches, the roof of which was covered with branches of green.

"From the distance, I thought this was a wooded isle. How far from shore are we?"

she inquired as Van held out his hand to assist her from the rocking boat.

"Not quite half a mile. Get under cover while Rolfe and I bring the guns and other paraphernalia. It looks like a bully day."

It might to him. To her it looked like an infinitesimal island of Time entirely surrounded by nothingness. Could be she lacked the true sporting spirit, she admitted, as she watched Van and Rolfe, excited as two boys, direct the hunting attendant whom they called "Joe," how they wanted the decoys set out, and where the boat was to be tied.

"Here we are, nothing to do but wait." Van deposited four guns in canvas covers on the bench and hung the strap of a binocular case on a convenient nail. Rolfe set down a capacious lunch basket and several boxes of shells.

"Coffee and sandwiches," he announced. "Have a cup now to warm you up, Miss Adair?"

"I'm not cold, really I'm not." She pulled the soft brown felt lower on her head. Her long eyelashes, the short dark hair which escaped from under the brim of her hat, were beaded with drizzle. Thanks be for my natural permanent, she thought. "What do we do first?"

"First, second, and last we wait," Rolfe Sanborn chuckled. "How come we didn't draw Murphy, fella?" he inquired of Van Tyler who was tenderly removing a gun from its canvas cover. "Give me the lowdown while the substitute is setting the decoys."

"He sent word this morning he was sick with virus X, that he had provided a better man than he was, Gunga Din. That last is a lyric touch of mine own. Here's your gun, Wendy. This box of shells is yours. We'll make it a short session. Don't want you to overdo at your first whack and hate it ever after. An old-timer told me yesterday that gray mallards, canvasbacks, blackheads and goldeneye whistlers have been appearing in unusual numbers. How's that for luck, chief?"

"Tops. They must read the papers and know there's been mighty little real duck weather this open season. I hear the bay coots are plentiful as usual. To post you on the law, Miss Adair. Allowance is fifteen coots daily, a four-duck bag, one goose and *no* swan."

"Fifteen coots. Four ducks. One goose. I'll try to keep within the limit set by law," she retorted gaily. "Where does the hunting attendant stay while we are bringing down game, Van?"

"In the boat under that pine-covered mooring at the rear of the blind."

"Can you talk while you work over those guns? Have you time to bring me up to date as to what happened after Cardella crashed to the floor? I saw Propper and a stranger literally drag him out, then you two men disappeared. Since that hectic climax I have almost succumbed to a nervous breakdown waiting, hoping for a phone call from one of you, telling me how, and when you discovered that the papers I brought from South America told of the plot to provide arms and ammunition to the revolutionists. You were so preoccupied when you called for me at Red Terraces I didn't dare ask while you drove me to the float. When you accused Cardella you didn't mention the state jewels."

"There weren't any, Wendy. That was an invention of Graham's to cover up his real mission. I couldn't follow his reason for telling the yarn, it was too subtle for me, but that phase is ancient history. Your friend Steve and Propper were coworkers."

"Steve and *Propper?* How did you discover it?"

"I had noticed the butler's wristwatch. The midnight Graham came to my room he flashed one that was identical. I figured it was more than a coincidence and accused him of having been in the garden at Red Terraces in the early morning to contact Propper."

"Steve? Steve in the garden? Was he one of the two shadows I saw?"

"Could be. There were four men slithering in and about that garden when the dawn came up like thunder outer China 'crost the bay. Adapted and adopted to suit the situation."

"Quoting R. Kipling in this place, at this hour. Your spirit must be on the crest of the wave, fella."

"You bet. What paper do you read? Did you see the retraction this morning of that journalistic gem, 'There is a persistent rumor that a certain ranch owner,' et cetera, et cetera? That relieves you of any feeling of responsibility, Mrs. Van, and frees me of a self-imposed pledge."

"Nice of you to suggest it."

The words flared like an electric sign suddenly turned on. Was he jubilant because there would be no possibility that again she would make the absurd proposal that they pretend the marriage was real? What did he mean by a self-imposed pledge?

"Sure I saw that item." Rolfe Sanborn's reply quenched the flame of her rising indignation. "Accusing R. Ruggles of having financed the supply of arms to the revolutionists was a little thing of my own. It packed a wallop, but when I saw his eyes as he threatened you, fella, I was scared. I had him in my office yesterday bright and early. Advised him that an *immediate* retraction of that bit of secret-marriage gossip would prevent the suspicion being publicized that he had been involved in the arms deal."

"Was he really?"

"If he had been, Miss Adair, I wouldn't have suppressed the truth for any reason. He palled with Cardella because he suspected you were afraid of him. From him he picked up bits of innuendo he was sure would bother Josh. He's a born hector. He hinted that the ex-South American had intimated you were implicated in a subversive plot."

"*I* subversive! That word sets this blind spinning."

"Ruggles knew you weren't, but he stored for future use the information — garnered from the same source — that you smuggled secret papers into Washington. If that cat-dog twister hadn't swept in just as it did he would have sprung it in the hope of saving himself."

"The cat and dog twister — in retrospect — was the funniest thing I ever saw."

Wendy's voice rippled with laughter. "I didn't appreciate the humor at the moment, but when I reached the safe haven of my room I remembered Propper's prophecy, 'That dog and cat sure hate each other. Sometime they'll make serious trouble for somebody.' He was right. I visualized Cardella's crash and laughed till I cried."

Van Tyler looked up from the gun he was loading. The color in her cheeks deepened.

"I was not in the least hysterical." She answered his quizzical eyes. "I am not the emotional type. It was pure laughter."

"I see you haven't forgotten the penalty if you let hysterics get you. Hasn't Propper explained the cat-pursued-by-dog incident? The night Gib Brown and Zaidee Latour dined at Red Terraces she turned over the stolen microfilms to him when they strolled on the veranda, ostensibly to admire the stars. She had brought them with her in the hope that she could persuade good old Josh to help her."

Through Wendy's memory echoed Joshua Crandon's adamantine, "I'm still through."

"She made such a point of secrecy that Gib hid them in the box border, forgot them when he and Lucie started for home, remembered later and went back to retrieve them. He saw Steve Graham gumshoeing among the trees, decided something was brewing and hung around to watch the fun. Later, he saw Cardella contact Propper on the terrace. He saw you, Wendy, steal down to the birdbath. Reported what he had seen to Rolfe the next morning. Correct, chief?"

"Right. I didn't suspect that the films were other than moving-picture travelogues till Gib printed a couple of them. That did it. The night of the dramatic showdown he was waiting at Red Terraces to confront Cardella. Propper thinks the black cat followed him into the house, ran up the stairs to your room where Angeline was bedded. You know the rest."

"Is everything under control now?"

"Yes. Cardella et al, are in jail, awaiting an appearance before the grand jury. Zaidee Latour is bonded to appear as witness. Graham enplaned for South America yesterday."

"Steve! Gone? Without seeing me? I can't believe it."

"He flew in answer to a second cable from your father, Wendy. Left a message with me for you which I will deliver later."

"All set, Mr. Tyler," the man in the boat called as it slid along the side of the blind.

"Okay now for watchful waiting." Van

Tyler adjusted the binoculars and began to scan the thick overhead.

It was such still waiting. A trifle spooky, Wendy thought. No sound but the drip, drip of moisture from the rim of the shelter roof to the wooden floor; the swish of the boat against the raft as it rose and fell with the choppy sea; nothing to see but gray water and the dim outline of shore.

"Here they come! Four of them. You first, Wendy, alone. You're used to a gun, if not this gauge. Go ahead as you see it. If you don't get the hang this time I'll show you later. Might mix you up now. Move quietly."

She stripped off her coat. Took the gun he handed her.

"Four of them," she whispered. "Tell me when."

"They're circling to land. When they're halfway — Now!"

Her gun barked. A bird fell.

"Nice shot." Van patted her shoulder. "There goes Joe to pick it up."

They watched the man in the boat retrieve the duck, return to the blind. He brought the battered bird to Wendy. Offered it by the legs.

"Good work, Miss. It's a gray mallard. Awful good eatin'," he approved and departed for the covered mooring.

She looked at the bloody feathers, at the dangling head of the bird she held by its tiny feet which but a few moments before had been so gloriously alive. This wasn't like clay-pigeon shooting.

"I'm glad I made good for the honor of the company," she declared with an attempt at gaiety. "What shall I do with it?"

"I'll take it." Van Tyler tucked the duck out of sight. "Better get back into your coat. It may be a long wait. How about a cup of hot coffee for our crack shot, chief?"

They talked in low voices as if the wind might carry the news of watchful waiters to wild fowl in the offing. Talked of people in the news, politics, the airlift, problems facing the incoming Congress. The two men ignored the subject of the revelations at Red Terraces as if already they must make way for more recent discoveries and events. Van Tyler lowered the binoculars through which he had been scanning the bay.

"Here they come! Six! Heading this way. Get ready. Quiet. We'll all shoot this time. Wait till they begin to circle, Wendy. Now!"

Three shots rang out. Three birds fell.

"One of them has my name on it," Rolfe Sanborn exclaimed as they watched Joe retrieve the birds. "Hi, where's the guy going?

He's walking out on us. He's heading up the bay."

"He *can't* be." Van Tyler's color faded a degree. "He is. He fired twice into the air. "That didn't scare him. No good to shoot him. Then he'd never come back. Don't worry, Wendy, we'll get you to shore."

"I'm not worried." On a blind one half mile from shore, no boat, a choppy sea, strangely enough she wasn't. "Just one more bead to add to my string of adventures, another stirring event to tell my grandchildren."

"Glad you see it that way." Van Tyler's voice was grim. "On that cheery note let's have a cup of coffee. After that we'll fire every five minutes. Martha or Mac Fenton at Arcady, or a neighbor, may hear and suspect someone is in trouble. Lucie Brown is due at the house at four to have tea with you, Wendy."

"Tea at four? At Arcady in these clothes? Van, you're mad to think of it."

"Keep perfectly calm, Miss Adair. You won't be taking tea at four o'clock at Arcady in those clothes or any others," Rolfe Sanborn declared. "You fire the next two shots, fella."

SOS signals were repeated at five-minute intervals, two at a time. Once came the sound of a motor horn on the shore road and they fired twice and again twice in quick succession. No response.

"Look!" Van was on his feet, binoculars at his eyes. "See what's coming. Six of them! No use to shoot. We couldn't pick them up, it would be murder."

"They're circling. I'll be darned if they're not coming down. *Canvasbacks.*" Rolfe Sanborn groaned the word. "I'll bet they saw Joe streaking for home. See them flutter among the decoys and ride the waves. The cuties are thumbing their noses at us. There they go."

Five minutes later, he reminded:

"The shells won't last forever, Van. You'd think someone in one of those places on shore would suspect that something had gone haywire. Where'd you say you picked up that Joe?"

"Didn't pick him up. Murph sent him, that is, the guy said Murph sent him. Did you by any chance mention this expedition to Ruggles when he was in your office yesterday listening to your ultimatum, 'Retract that secret-marriage gossip, or else'? The situation suggests his signature tune."

"Of course I didn't tell him. I didn't tell—"

Van waited till the shots he fired ceased reverberating.

"Thought of something that brought you to a full stop, didn't you, chief?" he inquired.

"It suddenly occurred to me that Clare was taking dictation when I talked with you on the phone about the time and date for this expedition — and approved your suggestion that we have tea at Arcady after we left the blind. She wouldn't—"

"Oh, yes, she would. I have been informed on good authority that your secretary chatters, chief. I believe that Russ maneuvered this situation — what he expected to gain from it is hidden deep in his twisted mind. In some way he switched Murph for Joe. Remember his threat to me following the climax at Red Terraces?"

"Sure, but I can't believe that Clare would intentionally—"

"I didn't say intentionally. We have only six shells left. Help me wrench the bench loose. I'll float ashore on it. The water is too cold to swim the distance burdened with these clothes. One of the houses beneath those chimneys must have a boat. No use trying for Arcady, it's across the bay."

"No, Van, no," Wendy protested. "I don't mind waiting here for rescue, really. I'm not in the least frightened. It's a huge adventure."

"Glad you're taking it that way, but I'm

going while I can see the shore. It's really raining now. Visibility will be nil before long."

"Let me go, fella."

"No. I had plenty of experience during the war floating past an enemy post on the underside of a log." He flung off his heavy coat.

"Grab hold of the bench, chief. Heave! That started it a little. Boy, but this was nailed down to stay. Thunder, it creaks as if we were tearing apart the whole shelter. That last yank did it. Here it comes. Hoist that end."

Together they lowered the cracked and splintered board into the water beside the pine-covered mooring.

"Hold it while I pull off these boots."

"Van, please don't—" A splash cut off her passionate protest.

"Okay!" The ghostly hail floated back. "I'll be seeing—"

Rolfe Sanborn and she stood side by side barely breathing till the sound of paddling hands faded and died away. Mist twisted in weird spirals. Wind moaned and whistled round the corners of the shelter. Rain beat on the floor.

"We shouldn't have let him go, Rolfe."

"*Let* him go after he had made up his

mind? Lady, you don't know him. Come back under the shelter. He'll make it."

Under cover of the roof he told of many of Van Tyler's achievements during the war; of his popularity in his home state; of his devotion to his family; of his accomplishments the first term in Congress. She listened with one ear, the other strained to catch the sound of oars, of a voice.

"As I reminded you once before, Miss Adair, when I am at my conversational best trying to entertain a lady—"

"I'm sorry, really I am, but, I feel so responsible. He wouldn't have gone if I hadn't been here, you and he would have just smoked and waited. I am terribly anxious."

"Sure, you are. So am I, if you want the truth. Look! See that reddish streak on the western horizon? It's clearing. He'll get through. The minute we hear a boat we'll flash the electric torch. I don't dare use it until we're sure. Can't afford to waste the light. All we have to do now is wait."

"All we have to do now is wait," Rolfe Sanborn had said. WAIT. Never before in her life had she known what breathless expectancy, what dread, what dragging moments the four-letter word could hold.

It seemed as if aeons passed as they walked the floor of the limited space for exercise. The rain ceased. The air turned icy. Every few minutes they stopped to listen. Renewed their measured pacing. She lived over the days since she had dashed into the Pullman compartment, not so many of them, she realized to her surprise. So much had happened the time seemed like months in retrospect. Darkness closed in. She refused coffee. There wasn't much left. Van might need it terribly when he came.

"Listen! Voices? Don't you hear the dip of oars? Excelsior! He made it."

Light enveloped the blind. A voice shouted:

"Courage, Wendy! We're coming."

As if I were the one who needed courage, she thought, and called back gaily:

"Reception committee waiting — Your Highness."

After that she moved as in a dream. Van in dripping clothes and Rolfe Sanborn collected the guns, the basket, the one bird. The man in the boat whom Van had routed out from the first house he hailed landed them at the Arcady float. Up through the box-scented garden. Into the house. The black-silk frocked housekeeper, round, rosy, blue-eyed, gray-haired, greeted them in the great central hall with its blazing fire.

"What happened, Mr. Van? It got so late

365

Mrs. Brown couldn't wait. She had to go home to give the children their supper. Your office has been trying to get you. You are to call back no matter how late. Someone left a present—"

"Stop and get your breath, Martha. Take Miss Adair upstairs to Mother's room so she can pull off one of those cardigans before she has hot coffee. Come on, Rolfe. We'll meet you in the living room, Wendy."

"Sakes alive, Mr. Van is dripping. What happened, Miss?" the flustered woman inquired as she showed Wendy into a huge room with splashy colorful chintz and choice rosewood furniture.

Wendy gave an expurgated account before the housekeeper bustled off. It was a relief to pull off the dark cardigan. The white one under it looked fairly respectable. Her slacks were wet, so were her boots. Side-stepping coffee was indicated.

When later she left the room with her leather coat and surplus cardigan over her arm, Van Tyler met her. He caught her hand in his and they went down the broad stairs together.

"Did Martha look after you, Wendy?"

"She waited on me as if I were a baby. This is a beautiful house, Van," she said as they reached the threshold of the great living room with its ivory walls. "What an adorable curved window with the porcelain birds and flowers. Those carved shutters are price-less."

"Glad you like it, glad to have you see it before I give it away, offer it to—" He stopped abruptly.

Her eyes followed his. In the middle of the carved mantel above the fireplace stood a large three-dimensional photograph in color of a blonde woman in green and silver.

"Offer it to her?" Wendy suggested quickly. "Beautiful, isn't she? Looks as if she were parting her lips to say a fervent, 'Thank you.' I really can't stop for coffee."

"If that's the way you feel about it—" Van Tyler spoke to the man coming down the stairs.

"Drive Miss Adair to Red Terraces, will you, chief? I've got to get in touch with my office — and quick."

XXVIII

"Stop twisting, adorable. I'll never get your hair brushed if you don't," Wendy Adair protested. "You can't go to Arcady unless it is satiny smooth. You'd hate to be left alone here with black Sambo with his yellow bow, wouldn't you? See how he's slicking his coat while he suns in the window?"

The big blue eyes of the six-year-old widened. She shook her head.

"You don't understand, Wendy." She emphasized her words with a gesture of her slim little hand. "Mummy and Daddy wouldn't leave me behind on Thanksgiving Day no matter what I did."

"Something tells me you're right, precious." She gave another gentle stroke to the fair hair with its sheen of gold. "There you are. Fit to visit the queen. Here come Sister and Mummy."

The younger child flung her arms around

her. She snuggled her lips into the soft
neck.

"Um-*m-m*. You smell sweet."

"She ought," Lucie Brown attested. "She
just emptied the dram of choice perfume
over her small self Mother gave me for my
birthday. I don't know what I would have
done without your help to get the children
dressed, Wendy. This has been just one of
those mornings. Run down and put on your
hats and coats, kiddies. Watch for
Grandmama. 'Whoo-hoo' when she comes."
The little girls pelted from the room with
the black cat at their heels.

"It has been fun helping," Wendy declared. "I've never seen anything so ravish-
ingly lovely as the adorables in their
rose-pink frocks."

"Which you gave them. Gib said I
shouldn't have allowed you to buy those exquisite dresses."

"Gibson Gary Brown may be an ace photographer, but what does he know about
clothes? I had the time of my life selecting
them."

"You're a wonderful friend and neighbor,
glamour girl." Lucie pirouetted for approval.
"Like me in this?"

"I do. It's snappy and most becoming. Just
the shade of green — the new lime, isn't it

369

— to emphasize the lovely red-gold of your hair."

"You're the comfort of my life, Wendy. When I asked Gib, he said, 'Is it new? You always look out of this world to me, Reddy.' As if that told me anything about the dress."

"It ought to tell you heaps. How are you getting to Arcady?"

"Mother is stopping for us, Van included her in the dinner invitation. Now that Gib has such a grand job we've had our old car put in commission, but she wouldn't drive between those sensational gates in *that*." Before the mirror she carefully restored the color to a smooched lip. Perched on the arm of a wing chair Wendy watched her.

"Heard the news?" Lucie grinned at her face reflected in the mirror. "About Clare?"

Wendy's heart did a double wing-over-wing and came right side up. Had Van presented his onetime fiancée with Arcady?

"No. What happened?"

"She's been *fired*."

"Fired? From her job? By her brother?"

"Uhuh. Gib was in Rolfe Sanborn's office yesterday and heard the whole thing. He said Rolfe was boiling mad, too mad to care who heard him. Gib told me, made me promise not to tell, but you're safe. I've got to tell someone, it's too good to keep. It seems the day before the duck hunt she told Ruggles that Van and Rolfe were taking you at noon, practically the last minute of the open season, to the blind, that you were to return to Arcady for tea. I can imagine how he needled the information out of her — and the heel bribed the guy who substituted for Murphy to leave you stranded."

"Why take it out on me?"

"It wasn't you. He hates Van. Rolfe hailed Russ to the office the morning he fired Clare. He was fighting mad. Told him that if he didn't get out of the city, pronto, what he had done would be broadcast over his station — that would settle him with his Club. Duck hunting is a tribal rite in this state. Russ flew to France today. Newspaper assignment."

"Where is Clare going?"

"Home on the Range," Lucie chanted. "Rolfe has given her a week in which to pack up. I hope she'll stay there. She was darn snooty the afternoon I waited and waited for you to come. Being marooned on a blind for hours must have been a grisly experience, I would have been green with seasickness. I'll bet, though, you looked as if you'd slid down to Arcady on a fleecy cloud in model sports clothes."

"You should have seen me. My hair

371

dripped. My nose shone like a beacon. My lipstick was invisible. My slacks were damp. In short I was what is known as a 'sight.' Fortunately my departure followed close on my arrival. Where did you see the beauteous Clare that afternoon?"

"At Arcady. She brought a stunning three-dimensional photograph in colors — aren't they wonderful — of herself and put it on the living-room mantel. She waited and waited. She knew you three were coming back there for tea. I sat her out. At long last she left, mad as a hatter, mumbling something about an engagement. Apparently you didn't have time to really see that sensational house. It will be beautiful today. Flowers everywhere. Family silver. Exquisite linen, crystal, glass and food fit for the gods. Van has an immense amount of sentiment about holidays. I wish you were going with us. You're perfect in that thin aqua wool."

"I couldn't go. Mother has planned a celebration at Red Terraces. Whom do you think are to be the guests? Four ranch neighbors of Joshua Crandon's — not top-drawer — two couples who are in Washington to see the sights. She has gone all out to make it a memorable day for them."

"Boy, that won't keep you from our

Senator's waltz party with square dancing on the side, this evening, will it? He's giving it at the Pan American Building. You promised you'd go with Gib and me as our guest. Mother is taking the adorables home for the night so Gib and I can go with easy minds — she really is a dear — One reason we had the car put in order was that we might take you. You do so much for us."

"Pause for station identification, Lucie. Of course I'm going. I'm wearing the *pièce de résistance* of my French, via South America, wardrobe. I've kept it for a grand occasion. It drifts. It floats. It sparkles. It enhances my natural charm to the nth degree." She wrinkled her nose at Lucie's reflection in the mirror. "I don't like to talk about myself, but—"

"Says you. What color?"

"Ravishing soft yellow. Long pale lilac gloves, matching satin sandals and bag. It cries out for a flat bunch of violets. Couldn't get them. Car stopping. Hear those 'Whoo-hoos'?" She ran to the window.

"Is it Mother? Won't do to keep her waiting. Is Gib there? He promised to be an angel to her today."

"He's tucking the adorables into the car. What have they in those little white boxes?"

"A carnation for Van's lapel. He'll be

slightly over-flowered, but they have to do everything alike. Where the heck—"

"For what are you scrambling on the top of the dresser? Can I help?"

"Looking for my emerald and diamond ring. Remember the night I thought I'd lost it? I have it. Coming, Gib! *Coming!* Come on, Wendy, so he can lock the door after us. Bye-bye. Don't forget. We'll call for you tonight."

"Remember the night?"

Lucie's words were match to gunpowder. They set off a trail of memories. Perched on the broad stone wall of the veranda at Red Terraces, Wendy relived the days since she had arrived in Washington. Not much that was exciting had happened since taciturn Rolfe Sanborn drove her home from Arcady night before last, just the usual social treadmill. The pile of fan mail which had been forwarded had been heartwarming. If the writers were to be believed, the program was a smash hit.

Not a word from Vance Tyler. He could have phoned to ask if she had taken cold from the drenching on the blind. Why would he? She didn't rate it. She had been outrageously snippy when she had seen Clare Sanborn smiling from the mantel. Such a beautiful Clare, exquisite, *soignée* in her perfect frock. She had felt like a tramp in comparison.

She sprang to her feet. Sitting here brooding over her sins of omission and commission as if they were insuperable hurdles wasn't getting her anywhere this perfect day all blue and gold, green and russet. The sharp tang in the air set her blood tingling. She glanced at her watch. Glory be, she had been sitting here mulling over past mistakes when she should have been dressing for the early afternoon dinner. Her tailored carnation-red crepe would add cheer to the party.

As she went up the stairs she thought of the pleased incredulity of Josh Crandon's face when his wife had proposed making a Thanksgiving Day for his ranch neighbors.

"It would be wonderful, Kitty," he said. "I'm keen to show them my beautiful wife and daughter."

I wonder, she thought, if Father's faith in Mother expressed in the letter she read could have worked the change in her? She has been almost tender with Josh since the night Cardella was here. Not saccharine, plenty peppy, but just a good companion. Perhaps those two didn't go to sea in a sieve, perhaps Time will forge their marriage into a sturdy, seagoing boat. I hope and pray it will.

After the departure of the dinner guests she sank into a deep chair in the back drawing room. They had stayed on for a supper snack before they fared forth with Josh to see the floodlighted Memorial, Monument and Capitol. She had sung for them, played cards with them, tuned in a television program, had put on a record and waltzed with the men to the music of "The Beautiful Blue Danube."

"Have they really gone, Propper?" Kitty Crandon demanded as the butler stopped at the door. She kicked off her high-heeled, silver-gray suede pumps that matched to a tint her simple crepe frock.

"Yes, Madam."

"Bring me a cup of strong tea. I can't remember when I have felt so completely exhausted."

"It was a fine affair, what you could almost call brilliant, Madam. Mr. Crandon had reason to be proud of his home and family. Tea for you, Miss Wendy?"

"No, Propper. I feel now as if I never wanted to see anything to eat again."

"Very good, Miss. I will bring your tea at once, Madam."

"Do you think Josh was pleased, Wendy?" Kitty Crandon asked when they were alone.

"Pleased, Mother? He was puffed with

pride. I wager he went off with his pals partly to hear their praise of you. He's the sort who will tell you the nice things said about you, isn't he? So many people won't. Going out this evening?"

"*Out!* After this day? As soon as I have tea I'm going to my room, get into something comfortable and park in the chaise longue with a book. You'd better do the same."

"Who, *me?* I'm going to Senator Whosis's ball."

"With whom?"

"Gib and Lucie Brown."

"No man especially for you? Wendy, *Wendy,* I'm terribly afraid you don't encourage men."

Don't I? If you only knew I proposed to Van Tyler that we pretend to be married, you wouldn't think I didn't encourage men, she thought.

"Give me time, Mother. I haven't been in Washington very long. Already I've met a number of attractive bachelors who, believe it or not, have appeared to find me interesting. Courage, Kitty Crandon, some day you may be surprised to find yourself a grandmother." She touched the top of her mother's head with her lips. "You've been a trouper today."

"Because it is the first time since I

married him I have thought of Josh's pleasure before my own, Wendy." She brushed her hand across her eyes. "We're going to his ranch for a few months after Christmas. Don't think I have suddenly turned angelic, I haven't. One can't change a habit of years overnight, but I intend to work at it. I have thought a lot of what you said about reciprocity. I've realized lately what a terrible thing I did to your father, to you, to myself. No matter how much I lie awake at night and regret it I can't undo that, but, I can try to justify Jim's faith in me. I am determined that my marriage to Josh shall not fail."

"It won't fail, Mother."

"Thank you for your belief in me, Wendy. You did some trouping yourself, this afternoon. If you're going out you'd better get a little rest before you dress."

"I will. I am but a degree less exhausted than you are, Mother. I feel as if I could sleep around the clock."

She had been so dead to the world it took a moment to realize where she was when the knock roused her. She glanced at the clock with its glittering pendulum and sprang to her feet. She should have been dressing for the party half an hour ago.

"Come in.

Propper entered with a box.

"Flowers for you, Miss Wendy."

"For me? Who left them?"

"A florist's boy, Miss."

"Thank you, Propper. Mr. and Mrs. Brown will call for me later. They'll wait for me in the car. It has been a busy day for you, too, hasn't it?" Did she dare refer to his connection with the denouement the other evening? "We've had some exciting times here lately."

"Yes, Miss Wendy. I'll let you know when Mr. and Mrs. Brown arrive, Miss."

That seems to be that, I'd like to know a little more about you, Mr. Propper, she thought as she opened the box. Violets, exquisite double purple violets, in a flat bunch to wear at her waist. Why had Lucie done it? They must have cost a small fortune at this season. Next time she would know better than to mention flowers.

They do add the perfect touch, she decided as later she stood before the mirror in the pale yellow frock. Its bouffant skirt, layer over layer of sheer net, sparkled as if sprinkled with diamonds. She tried the flowers at the shoulder of the satin bodice with its tiny cap sleeves of net. N-o-o. Better at the waist. She appraised the effect of her costume. Her pearls were perfect. The pale lilac of satin

pumps, bag and long suede gloves comple-
mented the shade of yellow which accentuated the darkness of her hair and eyes.
Not too bad. She opened the door in response to a knock.

"The car is here, Miss Wendy," Propper
announced. "A beautiful new, green, deluxe
coupe. I know cars. It is an expensive model.
Those nice young people were very extrava-
gant to buy an automobile like that, Miss."

He looks positively worried. I'll wager he
has the first cent he earned working its copper head off for him in a savings bank, she
thought.

"Perhaps they didn't buy it, Propper.
Perhaps Mrs. Brown's mother gave it to her.
I've heard she is a wealthy woman. Tell them
I'll be right down." She caught up her white
fox cape.

Propper accompanied her down the steps,
and opened the car door. From the seat beside her husband at the wheel Lucie called:

"Get in back, Wendy, then you'll have
plenty of room for that bouffant skirt. Don't
look so shocked at our magnificence. We
haven't robbed a bank. When I told Van we
had lost courage about tucking a glamour
girl into our ancient and honorable he suggested we take this. Something to write
home about, what? All set? Let's go, Gib."

"A happy evening to you, Miss Wendy." Propper's voice rolled with the resonance of a benediction. He closed the door and stepped back as the car started.

"That man is mysterious, just plain mysterious," Lucie declared. "Know anything about his past, Gib?"

"Nope."

"I suspect he's other than he pretends to be, that he's one of Rolfe Sanborn's agents. How's that for a guess, Gibson Gary Brown?"

"One guess is as good as another."

"Meaning—"

"That I have no opinion about the matter."

"Mad at me, aren't you, Gib? He's furious, Wendy, because I told you Clare had been fired. I didn't tell all. I could have added that Van packed up the picture Russ Ruggles's ex left at Arcady and returned it to Rolfe's office with a message that it must have been intended for him and was sent to Arcady by mistake."

"You should add now that you promised not to repeat what I told you in strict confidence."

"I won't do it again, honest I won't, Gib."

"You bet you won't, Reddy." He rumpled her short hair as if to take the sting from his emphatic retort. "You'll never have another chance. Even forty plus is not too advanced an age at which to learn to keep one's mouth shut. The party we're bound for will top all the parties you've attended in Washington, Wendy."

Gib was right, she thought, as later she descended the marble stairway among women trailing the most gorgeous gowns, blazing with the most sensational jewels she had ever seen, men in uniform, men wearing the orders of foreign countries, men in the plain black and white of evening clothes.

"There's Van at the foot of the stairs waiting for us," Lucie exclaimed. Heads turned to look at her in her white frock.

"I watched you coming down," Van Tyler greeted her. "It does drift and float and sparkle, as Lucie said it would."

She couldn't answer. The relief, the unutterable relief to know he had forgiven her for those few snippy moments in the hall at Arcady. He had returned Clare's beautiful photograph. She should have trusted him enough to know he would. Her spirit unfolded shimmering wings.

"Isn't this exciting?" she said.

"Meeting me?"

"I meant the party, Congressman Tyler. Where are Gib and Lucie? I thought they were right behind me."

"They have abandoned you on my doorstep, turned you over to me as per previous agreement. Shall we dance? Rumba? Waltz? Do-se-do?"

"Waltz — first."

"How beautiful," she whispered as they crossed the floodlighted patio massed with orchids and exotic blossoms. The muted strains of a distant organ drifted from the house. The gay rhythmic music of a band floated through an open window above.

They waltzed, they rumbaed. Her mother would be pleased, she thought, could she see the interesting men who asked her to dance. Van relinquished her with a laughing protest — he knew them all — but remained in the same spot waiting for her.

"Each time you are returned to me you have a fresh scalp hanging at your belt," he accused.

"That isn't all. I have dates in my mental engagement book."

"Don't make too many. You may have to break them." They sat at a small table in the Aztec garden and ate ices and cakes, drank coffee. Lights sparkled around the blue-lined pool, among towering palms and acacia trees, brought out the brilliant colors of tulips which had been set in pots in the borders. A wandering guitarist stopped at their table, played a melting melody and moved on.

"It is fairyland! I have never seen anything quite so beautiful!" Wendy declared breathlessly.

"Want to dance again, or are you ready to go home?"

"I've had a terrific day. Home sounds good to me. I'm sure Gib and Lucie will be ready."

"I'm taking you back. Didn't you know that?"

She hadn't known but she had hoped. That's the way it is with me, she thought, and something tells me it is the way it will be always.

"I had the top put up to protect your elegance," he said as he started the convertible.

"How did you know I would be 'elegant'?"

"Lucie told me."

"*Lucie*. She would. I wonder — I wonder if also she told you I said I needed violets to perfect my costume? If you sent the beautiful orchid to wish me good luck the day of the broadcast."

"Could be. I never did believe *much* in your 'John.'"

"I'll say thank—"

"Not now. I have something for you when we reach Red Terraces. I'll collect thanks then — I hope. I was glad when you pulled off those long gloves. They made you seem so — so unapproachable."

They drove on in silence, companionable silence, she reassured herself. Lights from approaching cars flashed into theirs and disappeared. An echelon of planes thundered overhead, their silver wings glinting against a golden field of stars. From the open window of a brick house divided by a white picket fence from the sidewalk drifted men's voices singing "The Wild Blue Yonder."

"Airmen home for Thanksgiving."

His voice shattered the spell of silence it had seemed impossible for her to break. The word Thanksgiving provided a conversational topic which she grasped with the desperation of a swimmer going down for the third time.

"Did you have a nice holiday party?"

"Grand. When the company manners of the adorables wore off it turned into a riot. How was yours?"

"Strenuous but successful. Propper was a tower of strength. We couldn't have put it across without him. Mother told me that she and Josh are planning to spend three months at his ranch after Christmas. I wonder if they will take Propper as butler."

"I doubt it. You going along?"

"Going along." As if it didn't matter to him if she went miles and miles away. So what? It probably didn't.

"No, I shall trek to New York."

"Big place, New York."

That ended the conversation. When they reached Red Terraces, Propper opened the door.

"I'm coming in," Van said. "You needn't wait up, Propper. Miss Adair will lock me out." He lifted Wendy's white cape.

"Yes, sir." The first glint of a smile that Wendy had ever seen there lighted the butler's face. He took Van's coat. "I think I can safely leave the locking up in her hands. Good night, and good luck, sir. Good night, Miss Wendy. There is a cosy fire in the drawing room."

"Don't back away to the fire in that gauzy frock. Want to give me heart failure?" Van caught her hands and drew her toward him. "You know why I came in, don't you?" Finger under her chin he raised it till he could see her eyes. "Keep up those sensational black lashes. Answer."

"Sometimes I have thought—"

"You have? Bright girl. Now I want a showdown. Do you know what Steve

Graham told me before he left in such a hurry? That he was stepping out without seeing you again because he knew you loved me."

"Steve has a fiction writer's imagination."

"Don't fence. Why won't you say you love me?"

"You haven't said you love me."

"I've been trying to get the idea across since that first evening at the embassy." He caught her in his arms. "Wendy, *Wendy*. I love you."

"You haven't said yet you'll marry me," he reminded a few moments later. "That is the full-time job I suggested."

"There are more ways than one of saying 'Yes.' I thought when I kissed you like *that* —" She tipped back her head against his shoulder. "Van, Van, will you always love me?"

Arms urgent, tender, held her close. He looked down at her as if considering.

"Always? I don't know," he said slowly. "I only know that to me you are the most interesting, companionable, gallant, lovely girl or woman I ever met, that I respect you, admire you, *like* you besides loving you with all my heart and mind and soul. I want you for my wife as I never wanted anything before in my life. If that isn't a foundation for enduring love, I don't know what would be."

"It is, Van. It is," she whispered. "That is the way I love you."

"Which admission calls for a slight expression of appreciation." He kissed her. "Know why I was late at the ball? I was talking with your father."

"Father? Father is in South America."

"*Miss* Adair, you surprise me. Haven't you heard that there is a telephone service to South America? I told him, after introducing myself, that if I could persuade you to go we'd drop down on him from the air for a little visit before Congress convenes."

"Van. Do you mean that?"

"Will you go as Mrs. Vance Tyler?"

"Go! Try to stop me."

"Wendy, you are a darling. We'll seal that promise with this — for now. Hold out your left hand." He slipped a ring on the third finger. "I told you I preferred a solitaire for an engagement ring. Hope you agree."

"Agree. It is beautiful. I've never seen such a brilliant, huge diamond. I *love* it. Now may I say, thank you?"

"You may. This way." He kissed her tenderly, straightened and released her. "I think that had better close the betrothal ceremonies for this evening."

"Only *one* kiss? *Scrooge.*"

His eyes widened in amazement. His laugh was young and gay and reckless.

"Scrooge. *Me? * Daring me, are you? Come here."

"Van. Van, stop! Please — I never will again. Look! *Look!* In the doorway."

The white poodle squatting on the threshold blinked jet-black eyes, spread her mouth in an elfin grin, barked. Van laughed, the laugh Wendy loved.

"You and Propper, Angeline, the demon chaperones. I bet he sent you. I'm going. Be a good scout. Give me a break. Turn your back while I kiss my girl good night again, will you, Angie?"